FIRE FORGED

BOOK 9 OF THE GIFTING

Fire Forged

The Gifting Series #9

Britt's a fighter and the self-appointed protector of her mom after her father died. No matter what or how, no one gets the best of her. She's strong, self-reliant, and bold with no filter between brain and mouth. So when she accidentally-on purpose pepper-sprays an alien, things can only go from bad to worse. Hell no is she apologizing when she's clearly not in the wrong. She'll just have to stay out of his way on their small spaceship. Easy, right?

Nerx has spent a lifetime in strict control of his emotions, calculating every scenario. His life and grumpy outlook begins to change when he adopts Lily, a human girl. As a father with his daughter's future in mind, he must complete a royal mission to Earth before he retires as supreme commander. A trip planetside ends in blindness, and worse, the woman who attacked him has no remorse. He wants nothing to do with her and plans to avoid her during the trip to Etteria.

Until she triggers the mating bond.

Now he has to somehow convince this shrew to take a chance on him and his daughter. Except, she's not what he expects. She's fierce but sweet, entertaining, and sassy. And the most disobedient woman he knows.

Also by Sevannah Storm

Sol Survivor

***

Plump Playwright Series

Plump Jane

Seducing Amelia

Loving Finley

Keeping Tessa

Kissing Navy

***

COMING SOON

Inkoded

The Justisaar

Dark Survivor

Prologue

NERX BARELY CHEWED THE bite of kreso steak he shoved into his mouth. The succulent meat, as delicious as it was, served a purpose for the activities they'd planned for the day. He was trying to finish his morning meal before his brother, Kyerx, woke up. The magnus sun skimmed the horizon, casting its great rays across the silver landscape. was about to rise.

"You still eating, *damu*?" Kyerx beamed from the doorway.

Nerx grimaced, slowed his paced, and chewed. He should've known better than to out-awaken his older blood-bond.

Kyerx leaned his shoulder against the frame. In his armor, a dagger and a blaster strapped to his thighs, he cut a strong figure in his military garb.

"Expecting trouble?" Nerx gestured to the weapons. He wore his military pants and a padded vest. When they reached the Pools of Berrann, he'd strip faster than his brother would.

"I had food prepared for you, Kyerx," Father said, entering the room. "All your favorites." He gestured to the stuffed pack on a counter.

Kyerx straightened. "My thanks for your consideration."

"Guard Kyerx," Father snapped, tossing Nerx a glare on the way out.

Kyerx thumped Nerx on the back. "You will see. Once I am gone, he will show you favor."

Nerx snorted. "You are perfect, and even though we both bear Father's likeness, you did not kill Mother from the womb." He downed his giyua juice, using the tart flavor to remind him that not all sour things in life were bad. "It is also no secret he hoped I would be a female."

"A foolish hope when females are rare." Kyerx hoisted the pack onto his back. "Come, let us not tarry. The shuttle awaits."

"It is good Father knows not our destination. The southern sparring fields?" Nerx pushed out of his seat to trail his brother. "I do not know how you can deceive so when it is dishonorable."

"With Father, some things are best not mentioned. I lie for his health."

Nerx arched a brow at that silliness. He chose not to dwell on the reasons behind his father's hatred. He could understand grief, but still, Mother hadn't been Father's Dar Eth. Nerx's heart panged. Had Mother been more than a female, had she triggered the Ethera in Father, he and Kyerx would never have known him after she died. The loss of her and the bond the Ethera created would have taken Father too, orphaning Kyerx and Nerx.

Some days, when Father tormented Nerx more than usual, he'd wished him dead. And other days, with the way Father adored Kyerx, he'd longed for Kyerx's death too. Now on the cusp of malehood, Nerx preferred to shove such bitterness aside. Soon, he too would leave for Gikaet and begin his training. He'd never see Father again.

"Nerx, my blood-bond, are you ready to disembark or would you prefer to waste your day dreaming like a *damu*?"

Nerx snapped out of his thoughts then punched Kyerx in the gut, but getting no reaction for his efforts.

"One more day of your personality is all I can endure," Nerx said, then ruined the scathing remark with a grin. "You will miss me."

"Of course." With a smirk, Kyerx stepped into the *kuta*, dropped the pack on the grated floor, then assumed the pilot's seat.

The rectangular shuttle was geared for mining with the console using the least amount of space. Miners and blocks of Fuyra stone would fill the compartment on normal days. Not even a rehydrator or replicator was fitted. Father prided himself on his efficiency and the mines' increased productivity.

Nerx caught a hanging strap as Kyerx powered up the *kuta*. It rose then shot north under his smooth handling.

"They say there are no pools on Gikaet," Kyerx said.

"That cannot be true." Nerx stared out the open door as the stark landscape of Fuyra zipped past. "Gika need water to survive." Pops of deep red trees added color to the silver-white mountains and lakes. Blinding sunlight brightened the orange-tinted clouds feathered across the gray sky. He'd heard that Etteria had a pink sky with red oceans and deep gray soil. Perhaps one day he would see it for himself.

"Perhaps they have underground sources?" He tossed Nerx a grin, drawing him back to the moment.

He huffed. "Do not search for one alone, and warn the males in your unit if you do fine one. Not all Etterians can swim."

"Such a pessimist," Kyerx called. "If I had known you would be this grumpy, I would have left you at home."

Nerx gritted his teeth, just imagining what Father would have to say about not backing up his blood-bond. It took the better part of an hour to reach Berrann Falls. The clear river snaked toward a dark scar where a pale mist hovered, a rainbow arcing over it. They landed on the rocks beside the falls. Already the thundering of water forced him to lower his hearing sensitivity. He leaped out of the *kuta* onto the gray rock slick with water and yellow moss. He tightened his grip on the pack while he waited for Kyerx to join him.

Nerx drew in a deep breath. The air tasted sweeter and cooler. The falls were forbidden to them, no doubt because Mother died here. Kyerx had brought Nerx the day Father had made his hatred known. This place had become their secret, and they only traveled this far from home when their father inspected the farthest mines. He was certain to be gone all day.

Maloidian steel strips had been embedded in the rock wall, forming stairs into the crevice. Having almost slipped last time, Nerx ventured down with one hand on the side. Already the minus sun had joined the magnus sun to warm them.

The spray from the waterfall cooled his skin. Without omeika, the water was clear and not red. Also, no carnivorous fish meant it was safe to swim. One palm-sized fish could devour a male in seconds. He'd never tasted an omeika. They were purported to mimic the consumer's favorite meal, and for this, were Etteria's greatest export.

Breaking onto the pool's sandy bank, Nerx took a moment to gaze at the bright sliver of pink sky through which the water tumbled. He lowered the pack onto a patch of soft moss.

"Nerx!"

Nerx whipped around, searching for Kyerx. Used to pranks, he half-expected a surprise attack. But Kyerx wasn't behind him nor was he on the bank beside him. He swept his gaze up and froze.

Without thought, he bolted to where Kyerx dangled off the edge midway along the cliff. His legs swayed wild as he bore his weight by his fingertips. Nerx sprawled across the steel strips and caught Kyerx's forearm.

"Give me your other hand," he roared.

"I cannot reach," Kyerx gritted, pain hardening his features even as his eyes widened.

Nerx leaned over the edge to where Kyerx's arm hung limp, blood dripping to the ground below. "What the Maker did you do?"

"Now is not the time—" Kyerx yelped when his grip slipped.

If it wasn't for Nerx's hold, Kyerx would have fallen. "I have you, my blood-bond."

"You cannot pull me up, *damu*. The steel will shred me."

Nerx clenched his jaw, studied the sharp edges, then the long path down. Already, Kyerx's weight burned Nerx's arm and shoulder. "I am going to shift you one step at a time."

Kyerx nodded.

The way down was longer than up but less risky. Should Nerx's grip fail, at least the distance Kyerx might fall would be shorter.

Nerx stood with care, hoping to counter Kyerx's weight threatening to drag him off the ledge. He straddled two steps, using his thighs for maximum stability. His knees trembled when he made the first move. He teetered and threw out a hand to find his balance.

"You are a heavy bastard," he muttered through his gritted teeth.

Another shift down a rung had Kyerx swinging too close to the sharp metal, missing it by a hair. The descent was slow going, with Nerx's arm, shoulder, and back on fire. Throwing caution to the wind, he clasped Kyerx's forearm with both hands. It brought him a small measure of relief.

"Thirty to go," Kyerx said.

"That is not helpful." The pain returned, growing excruciating and absorbing all of Nerx's attention. He wanted it to end, for him to die if it meant the agony dissipated. He dared not think about it.

After three more shuffles, his breathing became ragged. His heart pounded in his ears, drowning out the falls and Kyerx's faint and labored breaths. His skin had taken on an ashen hue.

"Speak to me," Nerx said. "I need the distraction." He inched to the next sheet of metal. Every muscle in his body had tightened to snapping point.

"I glanced down to find where you had gone and misjudged the next step. My ankle caught in the gap and toppled me." Kyerx offered a tight smile. "Foolish me."

Nerx glared at him. "I see no humor in this. How do I hide this from Father? He will know the moment we use the med-E.D."

"Let me deal with Father."

"When he will blame me regardless?" Nerx snapped and swung Kyerx along a strip, then another.

He could release him now and perhaps the fall would break only a leg. He peered at the gray rocks below. No, he couldn't risk it.

A pop in his right shoulder snatched his breath. He bit his lip to silence a moan. A wave of blinding pain blurred his vision. His fingers slipped, the strength in his muscles gone. He fumbled but caught Kyerx's wrist. With his dislocated arm useless, all of Kyerx's weight pulled on Nerx's good shoulder. It was a matter of time before he dislocated that one too.

"Release me," Kyerx commanded in a thready voice.

"A few more," Nerx muttered. He shook so hard, he swung Kyerx outward. "How about I lift you so you can grip onto something? I need to pop my shoulder back in."

"Do it," Kyerx said.

With a roar, Nerx yanked up with all his strength until Kyerx's palm passed the metal's edge.

"Got it."

Nerx released him to slam his shoulder against the rock wall. He bit his tongue to swallow the cry then, while swinging his slightly numb arm, he turned to Kyerx.

Who was gone.

"No," he screamed and peered over.

Below on the yellow-mossed bank lay Kyerx, his leg at an odd angle. Blood dribbled from his mouth.

Nerx raced down and kneeled beside him, running his hands over his body. "Why, Kyerx? We were almost clear." He snatched his med-gun out of his pocket, but the device beeped. Tapping it didn't change its reading.

"I thought…" Kyerx spluttered, blood droplets beading his lips and chin. "It did not look far."

Nerx touched and held his fingers to his Optical Data Implant, or O.D.I., embedded in his wrist. "Emergency. Emergency. Track co-ordinates for immediate evacuation. Send a medic."

"Acknowledged. Estimated arrival thirty minutes," the male intoned.

"No, sooner. Send a scimitar. Inform Ambassador Tarx." Nerx grimaced. "Kyerx is…dying." His face cooled as he stared at Kyerx's dulled eyes. Again he tapped his O.D.I. "Father, it is Nerx. Kyerx fell."

"Where are you?" Father demanded.

He sucked in a sharp breath before blurting, "Berrann Falls."

"Alodon's balls!" The comm ended.

Nerx splayed his bloodied fingers over Kyerx's chest, increasing his hearing sensitivity to listen to his dwindling heartbeat. "Hurry, Father."

Darkness expanded in his chest, urging him to cry out, to roar at the universe. He raised his gaze to the sky and sent a prayer to the Maker who'd been absent for all of his life. This time was no different.

Chapter One

Soulless, adrift, eking out a life as oneself.
Endless nights, eternal cold, uncountable stars leading one astray.
No joy, no laughter, to feel is to fail.
Fake glare, fake anger, to feel is to derail.
None know what one hides.
The constant fear, what one must abide.
The temptation to release, to be free
Is a barrage on one's control or one's psyche.
How to find meaning is a conundrum.
To fight, to kill is as dooming
As to love, to thrill in the dull hum of existence.

Nerx huffed at his words. Well, that said it all about his state of mind. He scanned the holographic poem on his O.D.I. then archived it. No one would read it other than himself. He ran his fingers along his brow, checking for the telltale lines of his perpetual glower.

His males hurried past him, carrying panels, beds, and tools, all to aid the arrival of human *damu*. Etterian life had altered after Prince Enyl found his Dar Eth among human women. The species from Earth was weak, emotional, lacking control, and often petty.

Still, the women smelled amazing, the softness in their curves and expressions. No, for him, he wanted a Dar Eth who was harder in character, didn't fear him, and made him laugh. The latter would need to break through the control he'd mastered since he was a *damu*. The void each Etterian carried had begun to expand within him far sooner than anyone he knew and with reason.

He shoved aside the fleeting memory of Kyerx's face.

The darkness that day had engulfed his soul had been the void. Father had ignored him when he'd asked about it, but Medic Skyl had answered his questions in private. So he wore his scowl to deter the sharing of laughter, joy, anger, anything that could cost him his soul.

"Hello," a small voice whipped Nerx's gaze down.

He frowned at the miniature human female staring at him with her huge blue eyes. She was so thin, and she clutched something filthy in her tiny hand. It looked like dirty brown fur from a kreso and appeared to be missing an eye.

What summoned a pang of compassion were the circular scars on her arms. At the abuse she must have suffered, he scowled at the anger exploding in his chest.

"Hello, *minus susa*." He softened his tone, not wanting to frighten her.

"Are you the captain?" she demanded, her gaze fixed, determined despite the tremble in her shoulders.

"Captain?" Nerx repeated the word, disliking the bitter taste of it.

"Uncle Kanzo says this is a large ship, and a ship has to have a captain." At her announcement, she gave him a firm nod.

Nerx exhaled an exaggerated sigh. He didn't have the time nor the inclination to explain the Etterian rankings to an uneducated human female *damu*.

"Yes, I am the...captain." He cringed at the lie. Since he was the acting 'captain,' he wasn't speaking an untruth. Then against his better judgment, he continued, "I am called a sub-commander."

She studied him for a moment, then raised one dirt-smeared hand.

"Up," she said. Nerx stared at her little fingers then glanced around, in search of someone to remove her from his presence.

Since Etteria had adopted abandoned *damu* from Earth, Nerx had expected to meet their caregiver first. He'd spent the last hour overseeing the restructuring of an officer's quarters for their use. Yet, the female was nowhere to be seen, with only this demanding *damu*.

"Up," she said again.

Only then did he recognize the emotion in her eyes—fear.

Something within him shifted, and he found himself lifting her. She was so small and light that he could hold her against his chest with one arm, which he did, just under her backside. She snuggled against him to rest her head above his collarbone.

The swirling warmth in his chest registered... *Trust.* The level of faith she had in him, a stranger, was awe-inspiring. She expected him not to drop her but also to keep her safe.

While holding her, he instructed his males as they remodeled a few officer's quarters to suit the needs of the human offspring. He kept his jaw on the crown of her head to ensure she was secure. Each time he brushed his chin across her hair, her sweet scent rose. Her presence offered comfort he hadn't known he needed. Her breathing became calmer. Her hand slumped. She must have fallen asleep. Yet nothing drove him to put her down, to locate someone to see to her needs. She'd chosen him, not anyone else.

"It's a good thing Lily only naps for about an hour." A human woman smiled at him. He blinked at her exquisite purple eyes.

The *damu* was called Lily? He liked it.

"I'm Olivia..."

He gestured to the modified area. "Please take a moment and assess if this will suit your needs?" He activated the door and waited for her to enter the main room.

A bed rested against the left wall, large enough for an Etterian male. On the other side, there were a few comfys adjusted to a lower height to accommodate the offspring, and more display vids were added to the walls. "The replicators and rehydrators have restricted access, as do the security panels on all doors. The waste receptacles have been lowered. The cleansing rooms now stock smaller wraps. The beds within the bedrooms have been lowered, as well. A male will be on guard as an additional precaution; though the males selected will need to be vetted by you."

"This is wonderful, Nerx. Your males have such a calming effect on the children. I appreciate their willingness to 'guard' them for me." She flashed him a smile.

Nerx grumbled at not being properly addressed by his rank, but he couldn't expect her to follow protocol when she didn't know it.

"Your quarters is across the passage with ladies Ruby, Neve, and Saira will sharing as requested. Theirs is alongside yours for convenience."

"Is there closet space, Nerx?" Lady Olivia asked when she entered the first bedroom. He touched a metallic panel. It opened to reveal shelves and hooks. They too had been lowered for easier access. "I'm happy and grateful. Thank you for going to all this effort." She glanced up at him and smirked. "Need me to take her from you?"

He tightened his hold around Lily, a surge of protectiveness catching him off guard. "May I keep her for now?" he asked.

"Yes, though she may pee on you," Olivia said but a twitch at her lips revealed her teasing.

He grunted. Not many dared to be so casual with him; only his closest battle-bonds risked it.

"She used to when she first came to me. She had fresh wounds, was scared, and the slightest noise would cause her to wet herself." Olivia offered a sad smile then chuckled. "Relax, Nerx, I'm just kidding. She'll let you know when she needs to go."

"Who harmed her?" he growled.

"Her father, so the fact she trusts you and Kanzo is a miracle in itself." Saying no more, Olivia left him to wander through her temporary home.

Nerx rubbed Lily's back. If he had the father's whereabouts, the battleship would make one illegal stop. And start a war with Earth in the process? He scowled at that thought. Perhaps just a *kuta* trip to the surface might be better received.

He went about his duties, ignoring the stares from his males, keeping his voice to a whisper, though just as fierce lest anyone questioned his authority. He stood on the upper platform of the bay, watching his males perform their tasks. When the pilot called out a warning and the shield flickered into place, Nerx slipped into a service closet and shut the door. There he waited for a few minutes until the bay doors shut—the thump easily discernible with his enhanced hearing.

He'd just closed the service panel behind him when a female approached, her steps shorter than his males's.

"Do you want me to take Lily?" Kanzo's Dar Eth, Ava, asked, striding from the direction of the *kuta*.

Again, he tightened his hold around Lily. "I have been given permission to keep her with me for now."

Ava grinned at him and shrugged. "Don't tell the other children, but she's my favorite."

"Trust Lily to find the biggest and baddest alien and make him her champion," a human *damu*, halfway to fully grown, chuckled at the sight of Lily fast asleep.

Bad? He gritted his teeth. "That is an untruth."

"Neve means that Lily found the strongest and fiercest Etterian male to protect her." Ava patted his forearm. The urge to snatch it away pummeled him, but doing so would disturb Lily.

"Then it is a truth." He shared a tight smile as per protocol in these...odd situations. The grimace flittering across Lady Ava's delicate features said he'd failed to appear friendly.

"Here, eat this." She pressed something against his lips.

He tried to jerk back, but she insisted. At the aroma of chocolate, he opened his mouth then scowled at her while he sucked on the sweet human treat.

"I do not need this," he grumbled.

Ava ignored him and shoved the remaining re-wrapped chocolate bar in his back pocket. He slid away, not appreciating her touching him. Did these women not understand personal space?

"Give some to Lily when she wakes up," she called, gathered a few bags, then ushered Neve down the passage.

Nerx finished the chocolate she'd shoved into his mouth, and as the sugar hit his veins, he allowed his shoulders to sag an inch. Only then did he admit he'd needed it. Though he preferred not to consume too much of it, for it dulled the line between control and happiness.

Lily shifted, her breathing altering as she climbed from the depths of slumber.

"Captain?" she whispered.

"My name is Nerx."

She leaned back, almost falling off but gave no indication she noticed her precarious position. Again, his chest swirled with heat. Trust. On the battlegrounds of Aluna, he'd shared such a bond with his battle-bonds. Yet he had never experienced it this quickly or intensely. He prodded his void, finding it hadn't grown. How odd. *'To feel is to fail'* was the Etterian mantra all warriors carried with them.

She cupped his face, pressing to his cheek the ear of the brown thing she carried. "Nerxie? I need to pee."

He glanced at his surroundings, checking to ensure no one was near, then smiled at her. "Come." When he entered their new quarters, she wiggled.

"I can walk."

He lowered her without hesitation, but she grabbed his hand, holding on tight. Adjusting his stride to cater for her little steps, he ushered her to the cleansing room. The door slid open as they approached.

She hurried ahead then faced him. "Please...don't leave me."

"I will be here, *minus susa*," he said, pointing to his feet.

She stared at his boots, met his gaze, then nodded. The door closed, granting her privacy. She broke into birdsong, her voice high and adorable.

Nerx grinned. Her company was not as taxing as conversing with the women.

The birdsong stopped, water ran, then the door opened with her patting her palms on her dirty pants. She slipped her hand into his and smiled at him. His world tilted on its axis. If the Maker shone His light on him, then he'd have a daughter just like Lily.

Chapter Two

NERX BLINKED AT HIS O.D.I. then roared, "Yes."

He broke into a sprint along the passages toward the old barracks that housed the human *damu*. He veered around anyone in his path and leaped over the pedestrian gate. Was he grinning like a mad male? He was. Never had he known this much happiness. He chuckled while dodging noisy children, his gaze searching for Lady Olivia.

"Nerxie," Lily squealed and barreled toward him.

Her cheeks had fattened and now glowed. Her eyes sparkled, and barely a bit of dirty clung to her shocking pink skirt.

He caught her and tossed her into the air. She laughed, then giggled, crying for him to throw her higher. Instead, he hugged her to him, keeping her safe within his arms.

"I see you got my message?" Lady Olivia arched a brow despite the smile she wore.

"Truth?" He held his breath. His heart thumped, almost deafening him.

"Lily chose you," Lady Olivia said. "And King Xeus vouched for you. That's good enough in my book."

"Are you my daddy now?" Lily asked, cupping his face.

"Yes, *minus susa*." He beamed, uncaring who saw him. "And you are my daughter."

This! This was what he'd been searching for, a purpose, some meaning to his life.

"May I take her now?" He focused on Lady Olivia, not bothering to hide his hope.

She laughed. "Of course. She's all packed." She hitched her thumb at the bright-pink bag sitting on the floor.

"Come, let us go. We have so much to do today, like choose a bedroom, fill your closets with toys and garments." He lowered a wiggling Lily to the ground.

She bolted like a Gika out of its burrow. Although, little Lily couldn't compare to that species—she wasn't eight-legged with razor sharp pincers and acidic saliva.

Still, she had the speed and agility of one.

Lady Olivia fake-scolded, "Spoiling her already?"

He jerked back to glance at her. "How so?"

"As orphans, they're not used to lots of anything and the best of everything."

"She will have two bedrooms: one here in my quarters on Issneen and another on whatever battleship I serve."

Lady Olivia gazed at the garden, her attention on the other *damu*. "Well, she'll be loved, cared for, and happy."

Lily lugged her bag over.

Nerx scooped her off the ground, snatching her bag with his other hand. Her cheeks were a brilliant pink like their oceans, and her blue eyes sparkled.

"Thank you," he said, daring a glance at Lady Olivia. A lump formed at the back of his throat and moisture stung his eyes. He hadn't cried since...

He pinched his lips and left.

Lily twisted to better see where they were going. She didn't say anything, but her grip and release of his forearm revealed her nervousness.

On impulse, he veered left, taking her to the food hall. What was he thinking? That she would fit in his quarters? The single room in the barracks wasn't big enough for two. He would have to requisition something larger.

Wincing at having to message Adviser Kanzo over this, he rolled his shoulders back in determination. Kanzo would expect to be the first point of contact, especially since he'd brought the *damu* to Etteria.

"What do you feel like, Lily?" Nerx asked when he halted in front of the rehydrator. The kitchen staff had mastered a few Earthian...human meals, but he doubted they could cater to a child.

"A strawberry milkshake and a...hotdog?" She peeked at him as if she asked for too much.

"Just one?" he teased around another lump in his throat. Anger stiffened his body. Her presence didn't impact the void's expansion, still he couldn't afford to relax his guard.

She beamed, squeezing his forearms as she leaned over to better see the foods. "Pizza?"

He laughed. "If you want."

He hadn't been hungry, but when the pizza, hotdog, and milkshake materialized, he realized she'd share. A deep well of compassion ran through Lily, something he adored about her. Since meeting her aboard the battleship *Kushin*, she'd been by his side whenever they were in the same location.

Days into their return journey to Etteria, she'd asked for an O.D.I. which they didn't implant in *damu* until their tenth birthyear. He'd taken a step back to assess why she wanted one. 'To talk to you, Captain,' was what she'd said. So he'd moved his quarters closer to hers. Within days, she'd learned the route to there and the comm. Somehow, she'd sneaked past their security. He'd set up a playing area for her and any *damu* she dragged with. It had become a common enough occurrence that he'd fired off quick messages to Lady Olivia; 'She is with me.' He hadn't wanted the woman to panic like the first time Lily snuck out.

Kanzo's response was immediate—an officer's quarters assigned to Nerx. He'd declined such when he'd been promoted to sub-commander, having not needed more space. He was, first and foremost, a warrior, regardless of his rank. Now, with Lily as his daughter, she'd appreciate having her own room.

"Do you...like living here, Lily?" he asked as she slumped over her milkshake.

She shoved it at him then bit into her hotdog. "I'm not scared of Uncle Kanzo anymore." She raised her gaze at the many males in the hall.

"Are you scared of me?"

She shook her head, her mouth full. "You my daddy," she said around mashed pizza. Darkness flicked across her eyes. "Not like Bad Daddy."

"Yes." He gritted his teeth. The next time he was on Earth, he had a personal task to attend to.

He glanced at the circular scars on Lily's arms. The med-E.D. would remove those, but doing so without her permission wasn't the Etterian way. Still, he'd have a medic check her. All the *damu* had undergone medical examinations upon arrival in Issneen. As her father, he wanted to be certain all was well with his...daughter.

"Ready?" he asked Lily, who'd taken a bite of every remaining slice of pizza and now bounced and fidgeted in her seat.

"Ah-ha," she said, snatched up her bag and danced around the table to slip her hand in his. "Up?"

He lifted and carried her to their new home. As soon as he stepped into their quarters, he lowered her to her feet. Comfys sat center stage, beyond that against the far wall were the rehydrator and replicator embedded a Fuyra stone counter. To the right was the door to his bedroom.

"What do you think? Where do you want your bedroom? Maybe your own cleansing room?"

She blinked at him, confusion in her blank gaze.

"Where you wash yourself."

"Bathroom?" she asked.

So simple and easier on the tongue. "Yes," he said.

"I can have my own bathroom? And bedroom? Just for me?" she whispered.

"Of course. I am too big to share my bed with you. What if I roll over and squash you?" He was being silly. With Lily, she brought out that long-forgotten side of him. Deep in his soul, he believed Kyerx would have approved of him adopting Lily.

He veered right of the entrance to an empty corner. "How about here?" He pointed to his door across the room. Large windows streamed light in. "My bedroom and *bath*room are there."

She squealed and threw her arms around his legs for a hug then danced through the space.

Soon, males were entering and leaving as they built the bulkheads for two rooms. In and out they came to fit her bathroom, making sure it was at her height. Thankfully, Etterians designed modular spaces to allow for easy customizations. That wasn't something he had to worry about for now. While this was happening, he took her to the magnus replicator to choose her bed. Pillows, linen, toys, garments, and a rug were ordered then delivered to their new...home. He let her order whatever she wanted. Anything she later decided she didn't want could be re-sludged.

What made this all worthwhile was her wide eyes, flushed cheeks, and excitement. She squealed, danced, and hugged the legs of any male who helped. He'd never seen his males so happy and gentle, moving around Lily with care. Their honorable reactions swelled his chest. What truly hit him hard was the way they gazed at him...with respect. Which he was used to as a supreme commander; this time, it meant more...somehow.

Lily's eyes drooped, and when he picked her up, she curled against him and drifted off. He contacted Medic Aldur and asked him to come round in the evening.

"LILY, *ENSA*, PLEASE LET Aldur look at your scars. He will heal them for you." Nerx gathered her tiny body in his arms.

"Will Uncle Aldur make them go away?" she asked, her blue eyes huge in her adorable face.

"Yes, he makes all scars vanish," Nerx said.

A little furrow formed on her brow, and she wriggled off his lap to hold his hand. She ran her fingers over the scar that ran from his wrist to his elbow. With her tongue sticking out, she concentrated on being as gentle as possible.

Nerx rolled his lips to hide a smile, even as his heart swelled at her care.

"He missed one," she said.

The scar had ceased to hurt him physically. Yet, as per his request, it remained as a reminder. He'd received it the day Kyerx died, the day Nerx had failed his blood-bond. When he'd dislocated his shoulder and nearly dropped Kyerx, in grabbing for his wrist, Nerx had scraped his arm across the metal step's sharp edge. He hadn't noticed the wound until Father arrived with a medic.

"This is for me to remember my brother," Nerx whispered. "He died many years ago."

Her brow twitched, and she tugged up the left sleeve of her pink garment she called 'peejays.'

Aldur's breath hitched at the sight of four circular scars on her forearm.

"Daddy wanted me to remember him," she said then peered at Nerx. "Did he die too?" She pulled up her other sleeve, showing three more scars. "They don't hurt anymore. Does yours?" She faced Aldur. "Angel says scars can be deep inside. Do you take away those too?"

"Heal it, Aldur," Nerx commanded in Etterian.

Aldur stepped back and lowered his med-gun. "Do you want me to heal Nerx's scar, Lily?" he asked the *damu* instead.

"Nah, it's for his brother." She twisted to brush her fingers over the jagged edges. "This one is a deep, like mine. It still hurts, right?" She touched his chest.

Nerx found himself nodding at her, admitting to the pain he kept inside.

"May I heal your scars?" Aldur asked her.

She tugged off her tunic, revealing her damaged body.

"Pretty please, and leave one to remember Bad Daddy." She held out her arms and waited while Aldur scanned her with his med-gun.

"Hungry?" Nerx asked to distract her for she'd started to swing her backside and fidget. Any moment now, he expected her to break into birdsong.

"Pizza?" She froze, her eyes wide and hopeful.

He'd spent three nights in the barracks in Issneen for Lily to become used to him. She'd adapted quicker than anticipated, choosing to eat with him, sleep in a bed in his room, and let him care for her as a parent. Her unwavering acceptance had put Oliva's mind at ease.

Now they would leave soon for Earth.

Queen Macera needed a female doctor for her...twins.

Nerx's chest warmed, and he rubbed it. King Xeus had found his Dar Eth, the Ethera triggered. It meant that even the elders may find their soulmates, as the human women called it. Hope had swept across Etterians throughout the galaxies.

"They're gone," Lily squealed, whipping up her discarded garment to bolt for the rehydrator. "Pizza for me, pizza for you," she sang, bouncing on the spot in some sort of dance.

"Peejays on first." Nerx laughed as he bounded to her to pick her up. Together, they leaned over the list of pizzas available.

"Uncle Aldur, you want pizza?" she asked, peering over Nerx's shoulder.

Aldur hesitated, casting Nerx a glance. "I—"

"You are welcome to stay for dinner, Medic Aldur," Nerx said, gesturing to a comfy. "Any preference?"

"Lily can choose for me," he said as he sank into a comfy.

"Oh, risky," Nerx said and held her over the menu to make a selection. He'd changed each meal to display as images. "She is in a banana phase."

"Banana?" Aldur's eyelids fluttered as his O.D.I. explained the word. "A versatile fruit."

When a pizza appeared on the rehydrator's glass surface, Lily slapped her palms together in what she called 'clapping.' She wiggled for Nerx to lower her, then under the weight of the plated pizza, she hurried to slide it on the table in front of Aldur. Then she waited, rocking on her toes with her hands clasped behind her back. A smile teased her mouth but didn't fully form.

When Aldur had yet to take a bite, worry darkened her eyes. "You not hungry?"

"Oh, I am," he hurried to say. "I thought I should wait for you to have your pizza too. Or will you share with me?"

She darted around, unhooked a triangle, then offered it to Aldur. When he took it, she tore off a slice for herself. Again, she watched until Aldur took a bite.

Nerx laughed at Aldur's confusion. "Banana is an acquired taste. Try this." He slid a pizza onto the table. "It has four meats and two cheeses."

As Aldur ate, Nerx scooped Lily into his arms and settled her beside Aldur. She scooted forward on the comfy to take another slice.

"I do like this one," Aldur said after he'd eaten half of the pizza.

"Nerxie, me thirsty," she said and held up greasy hands. "Up."

"Stay. Strawberry?" he asked and hurried to the rehydrator.

'Watch what you feed her. Children will live off junk food if you let them,' Lady Olivia had said. But Nerx figured a kreso knew to eat grass, therefore a human *damu* or child would know what was good for them too. Balancing a small pink milkshake and two cherry sodas, he returned to the table.

He handed the milkshake to Lily and popped the can for Aldur. With Aldur and Lily beaming at him, he tore off a slice and bit into it.

After dinner, Aldur excused himself. Nerx helped her clean up and wash her hands, ready for bedtime. Lady Olivia had been adamant about a child needing sleep, so early to bed he ushered Lily. She asked him questions about leaving tomorrow, and whether she could have a new toy; easy enough for him to answer.

With a kiss to her temple, he dimmed the lighting in her room and rose.

"Do you miss him?" she asked, her voice slurred.

He drew in a ragged breath. "I do."

"I don't miss Daddy." She rolled over. "Night, Nerxie. Love you."

He didn't move for a while, his heart pounding in his ears. This was what Etterians missed, giving up their children to a training regime and not raising them. If, Maker willing, he found his Dar Eth, he'd love her and their *damu* with every ounce of his being.

No way would he be anything like his father.

Chapter Three

Earth

The Domed City of Covenworth

Stay Alive Survivor Store

2252 years, September

SLIMY KEV'S SMIRK MADE Britta's skin crawl. It took everything in her not to smack his smug face. Instead, she glared at the backs of her departing colleagues. Damn if they hadn't found something else to attend to that night—a sick mom, an AA meeting, dinner with the in-laws. Beside her, Kev pressed in a little too close, having just demanded she stay behind for stock taking. As the franchisee's son, he acted as if he owned the survival shop...and her.

"If you touch me," she gritted out, "I'm breaking something."

He raised his hands as if to surrender.

She snorted, spun on a polished boot heel, and stormed into the back storeroom. Something brushed her ass, but the sensation was so slight, she half-imagined it. She snuck a glance at Kev whose cheeks had taken on a ruddiness.

Clearing out clogged sewage drains was preferable to this. Except for the stinking like shit part of the job.

Mom had begged her to stop working there, to resume her studies. But no, Britt, with a bachelor's degree in zoology, worked at Stay Alive survival store, instead. Versus some newly colonized dwarf planet, the shop offered her no excitement, and only boredom. Oh, to be the person to discover bacteria on some faraway moon. She sighed. A woman could dream, right?

She scanned the stuffed shelves, everything in its place. "Didn't we do this two weeks ago?"

"Daddy wants it redone," he said.

'Daddy,' she mouthed. "Right."

If the boss wanted to know where some of his stock went, like snacks and ammunition, he needed to look no further than his spoilt and irresponsible son. She'd taken to recording his 'purchases' and had advised her fellow shop assistants to do the same, lest they be accused of theft. She wouldn't put it past Slimy Kev to get them all fired.

What the shit didn't know was that two days ago, during a dull afternoon, she'd done her own stock take. She pulled out the updated register and started on the closest shelf. She'd be on her way home within the hour.

"But..." Kev spluttered when she moved from shelf to shelf as if she strolled through the aisles. "Aren't you going to check the boxes?"

"When they're sealed?" She arched both brows at him, using her tone to imply he was being an idiot.

"Are they?"

She huffed and bent over the first box to double check. Again, that fleeting sensation skimmed over her ass. She snapped up to scowl at Kev, who ran a finger along a box label that read, 'Camo Caps: Green.'

That was it. She'd warned him, and still, he hadn't listened. What she wanted to give him was a whooping. To do that, she needed him within arm's length. Argh. She swallowed past the bile in her throat, drew in a slow breath, and prepared herself for a little seduction.

"I'm glad you asked me to work late," she crooned, lowering her voice to a huskiness she hoped sounded sexy.

She slid the register onto a box, flicked open the top button of her camel-colored shirt, then fluffed her ponytail, all while giving him a 'sensual' look. She'd have to test it in a mirror when she got home. For all she knew, she came across as insane.

"You are?" he squeaked. Sweat dewed on his forehead.

"Is it hot in here?" She fanned herself and thrust out her chest to best show off her cleavage.

Like a horny teenager, his gaze dipped.

"I've been hoping to get you alone, Kevvy." She dragged out the 'vee' of his name.

Sashaying around him, she snapped the door shut, then cast a glance at the security cam directed at the ceiling. All at Stay Alive knew, the storeroom was a safe zone for kissy-kissy and thieving. So what she did to him would go unnoticed. Lucky for her.

"I like a man who knows what he wants and goes after it." Leaning in, she whispered into his ear, "Have I found such a man?"

He nodded.

"What *do* you want, Kevvy?" She ran her fingertip along his smooth-as-a-baby's-bum jawline.

"You."

Well, she couldn't say she wasn't a little impressed he had the balls to admit that. Still, sexual harassment wasn't the way to 'woo' any woman.

"What would you do with or to me?"

He swallowed so hard his Adam's apple bobbed. When he grabbed her ass, she squeaked, having not expected him to move that fast. Worse, he tried to kiss her, smashing his wet lips across hers.

Bile rose to choke her. All her damn fault for messing with him. She caught his middle finger on one hand and bent them back.

He squealed and froze, his body tight as she threatened to break his digit. "What.... What are you doing?"

"I warned you, Kev."

He offered her a slimy smile, even if it trembled his lips. When he reached for her, she didn't hesitate.

At the snap, he screamed. He leaped back to cradle his hand to his chest while giving her a wounded expression.

"Stock take's over." She fixed her shirt and checked that it was still tucked into her camo cargo pants. "Get your shit together and never...as in ever, pull this stunt again."

"I'm telling Daddy," he called after her.

She faced him. "Sure, tell him how you touch me inappropriately. Better yet, tell E.F.A. They do look kindly upon harassers."

He paled, proving him more of an idiot than she'd initially thought. Earth Armed Forces didn't bother with cases or men like him. Not that she was about to educate him of that fact.

As she strolled to the front of the shop, she relished the elation adding a bounce to her step. She was so getting fired for this.

Chuckling, she closed the front door on Kev's mottled face. *So worth it.*

Her day didn't get better. After sliding into her leather jacket, she tapped on the helmet then tried to start her bike. It stuttered and died. No fucking way was she going into the shop to wait for her mom. Hell, no, she wouldn't even let Mom know about this...set back.

She raised her gaze to the cloudy sky obscuring the moon. *Dammit.* Solar panels meant she needed sunlight, and the day had been dismal. Nor had she checked the back-up battery's capacity in a while. *Idiot.* She unzipped her jacket, flicked open the visor of her helmet so she could breathe, then began the slow trek home, pushing her bike along the side of the road.

She muttered at being late when it would worry her mom. The sun had set ages ago, and she was so hungry, she could eat roadkill. A starving and pissed-off Britt made for one hangry woman. Her solarcycle may not have the biggest engine capacity, but it was beautiful and a gift from her late father. She cherished it.

Despite the chill, pushing the bike made her perspire. Every now and then, a breeze would slip inside her leather jacket and summon a shiver. She cursed Kev and the damned survival shop. Her ass twinged as if he'd left bruises. Pity she only broke his fingers when she'd wanted to do so much more to him. She should've kneed him in the balls and head-butted him, as well. Just because she was a dirty scrapper didn't necessarily make her a good one.

Working at Stay Alive gave her access to guns, ammunition, tasers, and self-defense canisters like tear gas or pepper spray. She grunted as she crested the top of a hill. The weight of a taser rested in her right jacket pocket, comforting her. She'd formulated a plan if thugs bothered her on the walk home. Taser then the pepper spray in her left pocket.

She parked her bike in her neighbor's driveway, planning on fetching it tomorrow. For now, she'd cross to her mother's house through the narrow gate between both backyards. It cut off at least half a mile from her journey. That sounded so good as exhausted as she was.

Tomorrow, she'd have to quit or be fired for breaking poor Kev's finger. She chuckled at having broken his middle one. *Perfect.*

When she stepped into her yard, a tall shadow lurked a few feet in front of her. She froze, shallowing her breath. *Who's that?* By his height and width, she had to assume the intruder was a 'he.' Regardless of his gender, he was visible enough for her to grasp that he watched her mother's house with startling dedication.

She squared her shoulders and raised her chin, hoping her voice didn't reveal her fear. "Hi, can I help you?" she asked, as if dealing with a suspicious customer was an everyday thing.

She wished she'd taken off her helmet. The raised visor narrowed her peripherals. Now wasn't the time to remove it, though. Thankfully, when the solarcycle hadn't started, she'd just unclipped the chinstrap.

She strolled toward him, hoping to get in close enough to use her aforementioned taser and spray. It was risky, being within his reach. He could harm her before she managed to yank the items out of her pockets. Her leather gloves didn't make nimble movements easier. Another regret that she hadn't taken the time to stuff those into her back pockets.

"Greetings," he rumbled in a voice that raised the hairs on the back of her neck.

It was so deep, her nipples hardened. *What the hell?* She shivered, blindsided by a hot explosion of lust.

"Lovely night, isn't it?" She sidled closer; surprised he was letting her.

As she neared him, his incredible height loomed, and the sheer breadth of his chest forced her to shift her head to take it all in. The clouds cleared, revealing a little of his form in the waning moonlight. The silver rays highlighted his stance; wide spread legs with his hands clasped behind him. A military uniform adorned his impressive physique, and she almost relaxed, thinking him law enforcement. Since she worked at a survival shop and they sold similar outfits, her relief was short lived.

"Leave," he muttered, his voice surly.

Leave?

She glared at him, not that he could see her in the dark. He was standing in her mother's yard, spying. He should be the one to go or at least explain his presence. *Dammit, perverts abound.* She ran her gaze up him, doubting she could break any bone in his body or even get her knee high enough to hit his groin.

"I live here. You leave." That wasn't her wisest response, but she was floored by his audacity.

She 'turned' as if to walk away, gripped the edge trim, whipped off the helmet, and swung it into his stomach. He *ooffed* and fell onto one knee. When he began to rise, she dropped the helmet at his feet to fumble for the taser and spray canister. Adrenaline rushed through her, shaking her fingers. Unfortunately, spray happened before tase.

He roared like a lion, his eyes on fire. She winced when the sound penetrated the sleepy neighborhood. Throwing down both items next to his prone body, she bolted, sprinting across the yard at full speed. Thankfully, she'd mowed it last week which meant navigating the grass was easier.

"Mom, call E.A.F. I just decked a man in our backyard...and tasered him." She burst into the house, slamming the back door behind her.

As she entered the lounge through the dining room, she ground to a halt, her sneakers screeching on the hardwood floor. Her mother was somewhere within burly arms. A rather large man, dressed like the idiot she'd assaulted, knelt beside Mom, engulfing her in a hug.

Yikes. Perhaps she'd been too hasty with the helmet? *Fuck it.* After the day she'd had... "Mom?"

Her mom mumbled something to the man pinning her. Scarier than her calm in this weird scenario was the way he held her, as if she was the most precious thing to him.

Another roar from the backyard made Britt jump. "Shit. He's awake."

"Be calm, human female. Nerx will not harm you," Mom's hugger said.

Nerx? What kind of name is that? Swedish?

"Like hell I will not. Alodon's balls, she sprayed some burning shit into my eyes, Aldur. I can barely see," Nerx growled as he stumbled through the kitchen.

Shit. In the light, he was as tall as she'd guessed, maybe six-foot-six, and so huge, his muscles had muscles. Judging by the balance of his arms to his chest to his bulky thighs, these weren't gym-generated muscles, but the kind honed from hours of physical labor.

Did Scotsmen look like this? Swinging a claymore would do this to their bodies. His skin was bronze, like the metal, and it shimmered in the light. She smirked, thinking he was glittered to the max. No man could be called a girl when he looked like that. If he'd stop rubbing his face, she'd be able to see his features.

Peeking through his thick digits was his square jaw and pursed lips, too wide to be classically handsome. Still, he was sexy anyway. *Nerx.* Her eyes widened in recognition.

He was Etterian? Why hadn't the bastard said something? She *might* not have attacked him.

The man holding her mother stood up, lifting her with him. He was so gentle while he ensured she had her balance, it made Britt's heart leap. Maybe this Aldur had an agenda? He sure promised more, something Britt had been praying for her mom. He crossed the room to halt before Nerx, eye to eye. His physique was as masculine. Perhaps it was genetics?

"It looks irritated." Aldur tapped on a device he'd pulled from one of his hidden pockets.

"It stings," Nerx grumbled, rubbing his eyes with his thick fingers.

"My med-gun is malfunctioning." Aldur shook the device. "Did you bring yours?"

When no response was forthcoming, Aldur scanned Nerx's face with holographic lights on his forearm. Britt gaped at that bit of alien tech. "It is not serious, Nerx. Return to the ship. I will heal you there."

"I will not leave you," he said, clenching his jaw.

Aldur tutted. "You cannot see anyway."

"Good point." Nerx tapped his wrist. "Matir, Sena, to me." He leveled his distant gaze at Britt. "Let us hope I never meet you again."

At his threat, the emotions roiling through her made her breathless, uncertain, and nervous. Now that he'd lowered his hands, she had a full view of his face. It was broader at the jaw than his forehead. His nose was tall and hero-like, angular. His pursed lips had relaxed. They were still wide but were enticingly uneven. Dark blue downturned eyes under arched eyebrows, black as sin, completed a striking man. *Wow.*

This... He... She got the sense he would take what he wanted. Nothing like Kev.

She shook herself, trying to snap her womanly bits into some semblance of order. Furious with herself for finding this Neanderthal attractive, she fell back on her defense mechanism... Sarcasm.

"Why? Scared of little ol' me?" she teased, unable to stop herself. "I can floor you again, Tarzan."

Mm, yummy. He could be Tarzan if he freed that long braid she glimpsed, the tail end of it brushing his heels. Even though she had an overactive imagination, she couldn't quite picture him in a loin cloth. Still, she'd spend nights trying to.

"Britta." One word from her mom, and shame settled on Britt's shoulders.

She hadn't always been like this, just sometimes things got out of control. To say she was irritated at all hours was an understatement. Her last shrink had said her anger stemmed from the death of her father. She never wanted to think about that or unravel why.

"I'm sorry," she mumbled.

Nerx harrumphed. "I will accept your apology when my vision is restored."

Two men stomped in, both in military black with long braids to their heels like she'd seen in the digi-mags. Four Etterians in her lounge defied logic, and they dominated the space, almost sapping the air out of the room. Although, that might be all her. As she devoured the sheer beauty standing before her, gone was her steady heartbeat.

Matir and Sena studied her, curiosity in their open perusal and arched brows. Glances at Aldur snagged their focus more. They gasped and grumbled, tossing grins at each other, as if they communicated on another level she wasn't party to.

"Guard, and watch out for the younger female." With that, Nerx lifted his wrist to his mouth. "Edon, one to port."

"His fault for spying," she muttered, whipping their gazes back to her.

As Nerx phased out, her mom jumped back, squeaking.

Britt grinned. She'd seen illegal sci-fi movies, unlike her mother, so Nerx teleporting just looked believable.

"Mom? What the hell's going on?" She gestured to Aldur whose gaze rested on her mother's face with an unexpected warmth.

Mom splayed her fingers onto his firm pec. "Aldur was just about to explain."

He shifted closer to her, almost reverently. Britt's eyebrow shot up. She rolled her lips inward to smother a smile.

"I am on a mission for my queen..."

She snorted. *Yup, sure, a noble quest for my liege.* He didn't glance Britta's way and continued as if she hadn't made a sound. She gathered her irritation, curled her fingers into fists, and bit her tongue. Ignoring someone was the height of rudeness.

"Lady Macera is the Dar Eth to King Xeus. She is a human female and is...pregnant, she calls it, with twins." He ran his hand over his black hair slicked to his scalp. "She asked me to travel to Earth to find an OB-GYN, who had pediatric experience. My king wants this person to be a female."

"I am no longer a doctor," Mom whispered, her cheeks paling.

"This is acceptable, Lady Dahlia. You will not abandon your patients to travel to Etteria. It is just you and your daughter, I am correct?"

Mom frowned despite Aldur pulling her closer. "Yes, but I don't practice anymore."

"It is our first Etterian and human birthing. I would value your expertise, even if you do not assist."

"What do you think, Britt?" Mom glanced at her.

Britt grinned. "I'd love to go." At last, she'd get to see the stars, fly past planets she might have had a hand at exploring. Had things not gone wrong in her well-planned life.

Mom gaped. "You would?"

"I don't like working at Stay Alive anyway, and you do need to find a purpose..." She'd tell her mother later that she probably didn't have a job anymore anyway.

"Can we come back?" Mom peered at Aldur.

Britt gritted her teeth. Come back? Why would she want to? This world was horrible, having taken her father and her mother's love for life. She couldn't wait to leave. Anywhere else had to be better than here.

"If you wish, or you can choose to remain on Etteria," Aldur said, running a hand from Mom's wrist to her elbow.

Britt started for the stairs.

"Britta?" Mom called, "where are you going?"

"To pack, Mom. Where else?" She shook her head, what to take shooting through her mind.

"I guess we're coming with you," Mom said.

Aldur grumbled something. Britta didn't care to eavesdrop. She was leaving this place, and the only sad part was her solarcycle alone and abandoned on her neighbor's driveway.

Chapter Four

"WHAT HAPPENED, SUPREME COMMANDER?" Pilot Edon asked the moment Nerx appeared in the scimitar *Surata's* comm.

"I do not want to talk about it," Nerx snapped, pressing the heels of his palms into his eyes while willing them to heal. "How is Lily?" He raised his chin as if he could see but didn't dare try. Not until Aldur was on board.

"She is well, Supreme Commander. Data Officer Ziot is still with her...drinking no tea out of tiny cups." The strangeness in Edon's voice almost made Nerx smile.

He too had attended many a 'tea party.' "Has she asked for me?"

"Once." Edon tapped a button on the console.

"More tea, Uncle Ziot?" Lily's sweet voice filled the comm.

"Please, Lady Lily."

At Ziot's reply, warmth saturated Nerx's chest at his male's willingness to spend time with his Lily. He had wonderful males, and they deserved to find happiness either by adopting a child or finding their Dar Eths.

Striding to medical took longer than usual when he trailed his palm along the bulkheads. He pulled himself onto the med-E.D. bed, suspecting Aldur would command him to lie down when he arrived.

Rubbing his eyes, Nerx prayed the elder medic hurried up. For a successful mission, Aldur would have to convince the OB-GYN to abandon Earth for Etteria. Alodon's balls, did she have to have such an irritating daughter and could they leave her behind?

Their meeting churned in his mind. He replayed everything he'd said. What had driven her to attack him? She'd demanded he leave, that she lived there. Perhaps he should have introduced himself?

No, her reaction was too volatile for the situation. He'd behaved above board as expected of an Etterian warrior. Anger swept through him, more potent than he'd experienced in a long while. His reaction was illogical. It had to be tied to whatever she'd sprayed in his eyes. Perhaps she'd poisoned him?

Fear, dark and seductive, slithered into his bones. If something happened to him, what of Lily? Who would care for her? He needed to be more cautious.

A wayward thought stiffened every muscle. Working on Fuyra would secure her future. That meant returning home, facing his father, and dealing with his grief.

Staying on Etteria was a no. He didn't know what he'd do with his time. Perhaps he could serve on the Global Council. He grimaced. Politics and untruths grated on him, and he was sure to find both on the G.C. Nor could he serve as an ambassador to Earth, not when he longed to find Lily's father and torture the male.

No, the options he had were Fuyra and remaining as a supreme commander. Would he forbid Lily to visit Berrann Falls? Everything within him roared yes, but doing so would compel her to venture there as he and Kyerx had. For the first time, he understood his father's instructions. They'd been for their safety.

Nerx would construct proper steps with a railing for added stability as his father should have done. And he'd take Lily there often, teach her how to swim. He'd also install sensors, sec vids, and a compartment holding med-guns and other necessities. He'd know the moment she went there alone.

Tension eased from between his shoulders at the path that lay before him. Returning wouldn't be easy, yet he'd do it...for Lily. Once they reached Issneen, he would inform Adviser Kanzo and King Xeus of his decision. Having their support would go a long way with his father.

The burning in his eyes lessoned, though he suspected that was his imagination. What was taking Aldur so long? He rolled onto his side, letting his mind wander.

Blue.

A world so soft and pretty held such wealth.

Yet thorns infested it.

He rubbed his stomach, still smarting from the helmet she hit him with. She'd stunned him next, as if setting his eyes on fire hadn't been enough. The spark had tickled. Had she used a blaster stun, he might have been in worse condition.

No warrior should visit unaware of its hidden dangers.

Not from the exotic animals,
But the volatility of its females.

No, women. A religious text said that the Maker created man first then drew the woman from the man's rib. Possible for a creator, still, it explained the 'wo' part of woman. But women were in no way like men. And men weren't like Etterian males.

He tutted. His thoughts circled and didn't settle.

"This is the common," Aldur said. "Housing medical, sparring facilities, and the rehydrator."

Nerx stiffened, sprawled onto his back, and wished he could see. He wanted to face the woman called Britt when she apologized for her unprovoked attack. Would she be as soft as the other women he knew? Or would her outer appearance reveal a violent nature? A hard human? Did such a thing exist?

"What is a rehydrator?"

Nerx squeezed his eyes shut at that voice—its huskiness rippled over his senses like fire to tinder. *Britt.*

"We order food from it," said Aldur. "I will demonstrate when you are hungry."

"Which is now," she said.

"Britt." Her mother's tone was in warning.

"What?" Britt whined, "I'm starving. And you know how hangry I get."

Hangry? Nerx frowned, not willing to bring attention to himself by speaking the word for his O.D.I. to instruct him.

Aldur said, "Lady Dahlia, I can—"

"Not now, Britt," Lady Dahlia snapped. "It takes forty days to die of starvation."

"And three days from thirst. Yeah, so you've said...many times." Britt harumphed. A crackling followed then a snort. "A mint? Why didn't I think of that? We can save the world's starving masses with buttloads of peppermints."

"Give it back then," Lady Dahlia huffed. "You're behaving like a child."

"Fine, if you must know, I broke Kev's finger."

Aldur gasped.

Britt's admission made Nerx nod. Yes, this woman would do such a horrid thing.

"What?" her mother hissed. "Why?"

"He...uh," Britt cleared her throat, "touched my ass."

Fire burned through Nerx, an anger as potent as earlier. He formed fists and clenched them to his thighs, trying to calm the urge to port to Earth and beat the man named Kev.

"Well, serves him right," Lady Dahlia gritted out.

"I probably lost my job. He'll run to his daddy and tell him I did it for funsies." Britt chuckled. "And it was fun. The idiot."

"And you're telling me this now...here," her mother whispered, no doubt not knowing all Etterians could hear her.

"Like I've had a chance with you stuck in Aldur's arms. No offense, Aldur."

"None taken," Aldur said, amusement saturating his voice.

"Mom, do you think my solarcycle will still be there if we come back?"

"If?" Lady Dahlia's voice spiked. "And where did you leave it?"

"Next door. It wouldn't start... I had to push it home."

"Oh, Britt, you had such a shitty day."

"Yeah, then I attacked an Etterian. I'm so sorry, Mom. I thought he was a stalker."

Why did she apologize to her mother and not to him? "Medic Aldur, will this take long?" Nerx demanded, clipping each word.

"Nerx?" Britt whispered as she drew closer.

Aldur proceeded to scan Nerx with a med-gun—its beeps comforting.

"I do not wish to speak to you, female," Nerx said. "My eyes still burn." Though the sting was fading fast. A good sign.

"I just wanted to apologize," she said. "If you're going to be a baby about this..."

"You dare call me a *damu*?" he roared, sitting up to swing his face to 'look' at her, even when he squeezed his eyes shut.

"I've apologized, twice now. Maybe you should apologize to me, after all you were in the shadows, staring at my mother's house. I did give you an opportunity to explain why you were spying."

"Spying?" His breath caught. "I should apologize?" he boomed.

"If you're sorry, and I'm sorry—" she began on a teasing note that flooded him with anger and...a heat that settled in his core.

"I am *not* sorry, female."

"Neither am I." She chuckled in that raspy way of hers. "Apologizing should be sincere, don't you think?"

"Maker," he grumbled. "This woman's audacity astounds me."

She cupped his jaw, brushing her thumb over his lips. His world titled at her soft touch. His heart leaped and galloped. He jerked away from her, though it took all his control to do so. He'd wanted to nuzzle her palm, to savor the silkiness of her skin. Madness.

"You stay away from me, and I'll do the same. Deal?"

Ice exploded outward, cooling his anger. It had a similar tinge as sadness, but why her leaving him alone would summon such an emotion he wasn't about to figure out. Time away from her to regain his control would be wise.

"Agreed," he said then lay down to try and calm his erratic heartbeat.

She brought out the most powerful emotions he'd felt since Kyerx died. Which worried him. He may be a 'grumpy' male, but he never lost his control. Why did this one woman affect him so? He shuddered. He relived her gentle touch on his jaw, his now tingling lips, as if she'd seared or marked him.

Her soft footfalls faded, then she said, "Show me how this thing works, Sena, please."

"As you wish, Lady Britta," Sena said, then started explaining the rehydrator's functions.

"Alodon's balls," Aldur grumbled as he waved the med-gun over Nerx's eyes, first cooling then lessening the stinging. "I have never seen you react like this. What are you so angry about? Is there anything she did that could justify such a reaction from you?"

"No," Nerx answered hoarsely. "Her reasons for the attack were sound. Perhaps because she blinded me or is truly unrepentant?"

"You can open your eyes," Aldur said. "She used what they call pepper spray. It is meant to incapacitate and not blind."

Nerx blinked his eyes open and moaned in gratitude for his restored vision. They were a little gritty but otherwise good. "Thank you, Aldur," he said.

"Edon is escorting them to their quarters. I suggest you take the time to calm yourself."

Wait, are Aldur's eyes ice blue?

Darkness engulfed Nerx's chest at the thought of Britta being Aldur's. Though his reaction made no sense. Any woman triggering the Ethera, no matter who, was precious to Etteria.

He jumped off the bed and grabbed the medic's shoulders, holding him still. "Your Dar Eth—"

"Is Lady Dahlia." Aldur beamed.

Joy hit Nerx, expanding his chest. "The Maker has blessed you, my old battle-bond." He gripped Aldur's forearm for a warrior-to-warrior clasp, hoping to convey how happy he was for the elder male.

"Yes, He has. I did not expect this, not for one as old as I." He sliced a glance at the common's doorway, no doubt keen to see his Dar Eth.

Nerx released him. "I need to check on Lily."

Aldur bolted, abandoning Nerx.

Sena and Matir sat at the trestle table, kreso before them.

"Edon, set course for Issneen," Nerx spoke into his O.D.I. as he marched to his quarters.

For the women, he'd assigned the officer quarters to them and had three quarters in the barracks converted into his and Lily's. In their small common—the middle room between the two, he found Lily serving Ziot tea. The poor male had colors painted across his eyelids, cheeks, and lips. A strange thing hung around his neck in a rainbow of feathers, and his fingernails were a bright red. Yet, he beamed at Lily, tipping his little finger up as he 'sipped' his tea.

"Thank you, Data Officer Ziot," Nerx said by way of greeting.

"Nerxie," Lily squealed, leaped to her feet then threw herself into his arms.

"*Minus susa*," he said, hugging her tight. "Did you have a wonderful time with Uncle Ziot?"

She nodded, tossing a sweet smile at the male.

Ziot rose to his feet and shook Lily's little hand. "Tea was...awesome?" He arched a brow, as if he was hesitant in using that descriptor.

"You have permission to cleanse, Ziot," Nerx said as he carried Lily to the rehydrator. "Hungry?" he asked the moment the door shut behind Ziot.

"Ice cream." Lily pressed her palms together, her eyes wide with hope.

"For you, anything." Nerx chuckled and placed an order for strawberry ice cream.

As Lily devoured her meal, he pushed his to the side, his appetite absent. His mind roiled, and yet it seemed to return to the same point...Britta. He struggled to understand why he couldn't strip her from his thoughts. He was no longer angry with her, and there would be no more talk of apologies, thank the Maker. Her apology hadn't sat well with him; it had felt wrong, somehow. Her sincerity-insincerity was hard to discern. She vacillated between the two, responding with a sense of humor that was out of place and vexing.

And entertaining. He never knew what to expect from her.

Regardless, he need only endure for the duration of this trip. When they reached Etteria, he would no longer have to deal with her.

Chapter Five

"Okay, spill. What the hell's going on?" Britt faced her mom the moment the door closed behind Edon.

Mom blushed, spun on a heel, then entered a room, it's door swishing open. She came out a moment later. "Bathroom." Striding past Britt, she disappeared into the other room through an archway. The smallish ship meant there was one cabin for her and Mom to share.

"Mom," Britt whined, stomping her foot for added affect. "Why's Aldur all over you?"

"No idea. He said he'll explain everything later." Mom peeked through the doorway, tossing Britt a shrug. "Kinda like his hugs. That man is…" Wearing a silly grin, Mom waved her hand at her flushed face. "Buff. Not to mention his gorgeous blue eyes. Despite knowing it's impossible, I swear my shriveled ovaries applauded."

Britt rolled her eyes. "Next you'll say he's built like a brick shithouse."

"Language," Mom muttered and resumed unpacking, though where she planned on putting her clothes, Britt didn't know.

The only thing recognizable was the bed and two ledges acting as bedside tables. She frowned. Had she missed the tour?

She shook her head, needing to focus. "I've been begging you to return to the dating game for ages, but this is…sudden. He's hugging you like you two have been getting it on."

Mom freaking laughed.

Britt huffed, grabbed her bag, then dumped it on the bed. She bit her lip, waiting, expecting Mom to say something. Instead, she stroked the top right corner of a panel, and pop went its door, revealing a hidden compartment. When the silence continued, Britt jumped in front of her to grasp her shoulders. "Mom."

"I don't know," Mom snapped. "He said later."

"So what now? Do we even know how far away their planet is?"

Mom nudged Britt out of the way to reach the closet. "You were all gung-ho to come, so no, we didn't exactly ask any of the pertinent questions."

"Right. My fault, I guess." Britt slumped onto the bed that was large enough to cater for two adult Etterians.

"I'm not complaining. Now that we're on our way, I'm getting excited." Mom grinned then snapped the closet shut with a touch. Seamless metal panels clicked.

"Everything's so...clinical." Britt gestured to the metal walls, floors, and ceiling with its hidden lighting.

"Makes sense for a warrior species." Mom shrugged and waltzed out of the room.

"Warrior? Yeah, that's what the news was saying." Britt snatched her unopened bag and shoved it into another closet. She skipped after her mom to find her browsing the rehydrator. "I need a little vacay. So however long this trip is, I'm going to sleep in, read, eat exotic foods, and maybe find a new sport or hobby."

"You do that," Mom said, cradling a mug of herbal tea she'd ordered. "I need to brush up on my medical knowledge and any new breakthroughs we've made since... Well, you know."

Britt sat opposite her then leaped to her feet with a squeak. "Did that thing just move?"

Mom pursed her lips to hide a grin, failed, then chuckled. "Yup, it does that to match the shape and size of your backside."

"Right," Britt huffed and tried sitting again. Surreal was beyond how it felt when the chair cupped her ass with an almost loving touch. "Why didn't you react?" She narrowed her eyes at her mom.

"Aldur warned me." She shrugged.

"About a chair, but not about the time it takes to reach his home?" Britt rolled her eyes. "Mom, you're hopeless."

"Ask him yourself, or better yet, speak to Nerx. He *is* the commanding officer."

Britt's heartbeat scattered at the memory of stroking his jaw. *Damn, that man is gorgeous.* "I've got much groveling to do. All he had to do was tell me why he was watching our home, but no, an alien commander doesn't need to explain himself." She pouted at her whining. One sentence from him would have steered the encounter in a whole different direction. Now she had to play nice or probably apologize again and be sincere about it.

She folded her arms across her chest and glowered. He could damn well hold his breath. The blame lay with them both, and if the arrogant ass didn't see that, then that wasn't her fault. Nor was it her job to show him the error of his ways.

There was plenty of eye candy, even on board this ship. Though to be fair, Sena and Matir didn't spark such a violent response in her as Nerx did. They were too sweet, and she ate such men for breakfast. She wanted a man with a little fire who could handle her more...volatile personality. Most ran for the hills.

But Nerx? Nope, no way. He could suck it.

"Well, better start on those medical journals." Mom placed her empty mug on the table. "What are you going to do first on your 'vacay?'"

"I brought my tablet. I want to find a spot on this...thing." She swept a hand at the ceiling, indicating the ship. "Somewhere I can be alone to read or journal."

"Maybe it has a place where you can see the stars," Mom said, leaping to her feet to disappear into their bedroom. She returned with their tablets in hand and a shawl.

"Want me to ask if we can up the heat a little?" Britt accepted her tablet then headed for the door. "Might as well, just in case we freeze."

"But—"

The door swished open to Aldur.

Britt stepped aside on instinct. "Tell me, Aldur, how do you make it warmer in here?"

The poor man dragged his gaze from Mom to blink at her. "Place your hand on the panel." He tapped a hidden tile to the right of the door.

When he waited, Britt hurried to press her palm to the black screen. A white light scanned her, then beeped.

"It will adjust and maintain the temperature to fifteen degrees cooler than your core." He faced Mom, and Britt couldn't help the sensation that she was all but forgotten. "I wanted to see if you are...settled. If you need anything—"

The door closed behind Britt the moment she stepped into the passage. A grated floor ran the length of the ship she'd seen so far. Gray metal lined the walls, and a dim light lit the area, although, she couldn't find the source.

Sighing, she veered left toward the common. Someone there would be able to direct her to a 'star deck.' She snorted. How old were the novels Mom read that she didn't know that term? The common was empty, so she placed her tablet on the trestle table to order a bottle of water. Wherever she found herself, taking something to drink with her meant not having to abandon her privacy because she was thirsty.

Movement caught her eye. She stilled, the bottle of water halfway to her mouth. A mop of black hair on a small girl snagged her focus. "Um, hello?" she called, feeling like an idiot when her quaking voice echoed.

"Hello," the girl said, skipping across the blue mat to reach Britt.

She gaped. The *human* child, about five or six years old, had fawn-colored skin, shocking black hair, and blue eyes. She wore pink pajamas and bunny slippers. Something was smeared across her cheek and stained her fingers.

"I'm Britt," she managed.

"My name's Lily." The girl twirled on the spot, her focus on the floppy ears of her slippers.

"Are you lost? And what's on your fingers?" She captured Lily's hand to trace a finger over what looked like paint.

"I'm drawing a picture."

"Where are your parents?" Britt raised her head to scan the common and med-bay as she tried to recall seeing any humans when they ported.

"Daddy's far away." Lily swung their clasped hands, then twirled.

Okay. Cryptic much. "And where is that?" Britt twisted to follow when Lily danced around her, not releasing her hand.

"Earth."

Possible. Maybe her mom's on board? "And your mommy?"

"Dead, I think. I can't remember." Lily stilled, her gaze on the mat.

A touchy subject, so it seems. Then why is Lily on an Etterian ship away from her family? This makes no sense. "Are you going back to your daddy?"

At Britt's question, Lily curled her arms across her body and shook her head. "Nerxie says never."

Nerxie? Had the horrible man kidnapped this little girl?

Anger barreled through Britt until she was ready to kill. "How dare he do this? What gives him the right to help himself to a child?"

She paced the common, aware Lily sat at the table watching her. Escape options were few. Commandeering the ship when she didn't know how to fly it? Porting? She'd also have to convince Mom to come with her. Staying with child kidnappers was a hell-no. What did humans know about Etterians anyway, other than what the news said? All knew how the media sensationalized trivial info and changed it align with their agenda. What if Britt's rushed decision had placed her mom in danger? And now she had Lily to save, as well. How when they were trapped?

Were they even going to Etteria? Maybe their destination was some slave facility on an abandoned moon? Her only choice was to confront Nerx, to get him to do the right thing. That man deserved a piece of her mind, and he'd better turn this ship around. No way was she standing by while he separated a daughter from her father.

"Hello," she yelled at the ceiling, making Lily squeak. "Can anyone tell me how to find Nerx?"

"I can." Lily bounded off the bench to grab Britt's hand. "This way."

Britt was dragged along the passage past her quarters to another door at the far end. It swished open when they reached it, probably triggered by movement. Though she couldn't be sure without investigating and looking like a peasant. Nerx and Matir swiveled to look at her, while another man stared at a massive screen filled with stars. Buttons flickered across a console without lettering to tell her what each color meant or did. So, no, piloting this thing was out of the question.

"You," she pointed at Nerx, "need to take this girl back to her home." She stomped across to stab him in the chest with her forefinger, barely noting how good his pec felt when she poked him through his bulletproof vest.

"And why would I do that?" he demanded, dipping to widen his arms for Lily to leap into. "She is my daughter."

"What?" Britt roared. "You kidnap a girl and think you have the right to? That it's just fine and dandy because you're some powerful race?" She jabbed his chest, then again, while avoiding Lily's arm.

"Kidnap?" Matir laughed. "Supreme Commander Nerx adopted Lily. He *is* her father."

"Adopted?" Britt whispered, curled in her extended finger, and stepped back. "Her daddy's not on Earth?" She raised wide eyes to Nerx, hoping he'd save her from perhaps another blunder.

"He is," Nerx growled, his gaze on Lily. "The bad daddy." His eyes narrowed, and determination solidified his handsome features. Britt had no doubt, if he wanted to, Bad Daddy would die a horrifying death.

"Oh," she said, heat blasting her cheeks. She cupped them while offering the room a weak smile. "Sorry. I thought—" What could she say? That the girl led her to believe she'd been stolen? No, she couldn't place the blame on little Lily. "I jumped to the wrong conclusions."

"Something you need to work on," Nerx said, his voice hoarse.

Great, I've offended him...again.

She sidled back, aiming her ass for the door. The sound it made opening was music to her ears. She slipped out then hurried down the passage before anyone could chastise her for her wild accusations. And damn if she didn't owe Nerx another apology.

Wait until Mom learned about this. Aldur would blab, no doubt. Britt drew in a deep breath, pinched her brow, then marched to the table to gather the tablet and water bottle. Off to find a quiet place where no one would find her while she wallowed in her mortification alone.

Nerx lowered Lily to the floor by kneeling, his trembling knees too weak to hold them both. She scampered off, unaware that a white-hot ecstasy shuddered through his body. He squeezed his eyes shut against the burning pain. *No, please Maker, not her. Anyone but Britta.* But the powerful emotions squeezing his chest didn't lie. Nor did the vision imprinting into his memories the image of a naked Britta, her beautiful breasts unbound, her stomach contoured, her hips more than a handful. Her back was against the wall, her hands splayed on the Maloidian steel panels, even as she cried out, then whimpered. Her leg was thrown over his shoulder, her feminine folds before him glistening and fragrant.

And her expression was one he longed to see again.

He sucked in a deep breath, fighting for calm.

"Supreme Commander?" Matir rested his hand on Nerx's upper arm.

He shook him off, unable to bear the slightest touch. Holding Lily had been torture. Hiding his reaction in Britta's presence more so. He struggled to his feet, then opened his eyes to meet Matir's gaze. "Is it true?" he asked.

Ziot glanced over his shoulder and froze.

Matir opened and closed his mouth, no words escaping.

"Lady Britta?" Ziot asked, peeking at the door. "She is your Dar Eth?"

"Yes." That word encompassed delight at having found his female and agony that it was her, of all humans. Now he'd *have* to talk to her. And how would he convince her to stay with him when she couldn't bear to be in the same room as him?

"I like Britt," Lily said, clinging to Matir's hand as he swung her back and forth. "She's pretty."

Yes, she was. Joy swept through Nerx's chest, warming him. The way she'd been protective over Lily gave him hope. If she stayed with him, then Lily would have a mother. He couldn't mess this up, for both their sakes.

"What is on your hands and cheek?" he asked, able to speak and think now that the pain had subsided.

"Paint." Lily danced around him, then slipped her hand in his. "Come. Look."

Her fruitless attempts to drag him had him chuckling. Giving in, he let her 'pull' him down the passage. His chest constricted at the possibility of spotting Britta but there was no sign of her. Her cheeks had bloomed a brilliant peach color, which he knew to be embarrassment. He liked that she'd realized her mistake. The court was in her ball, as the humans said.

Never in Nerx's life had he painted anything. It was such an odd thing to do. Dip a brush into a pot of color and smear it across paper? Yes, odd. Although, the way the nib had spread the color was satisfying. Lily's images were that of a male and a little female beside him. The long black line had to denote his hair. The female wore pink, that had to mean Lily. Strange symbols decorated the edges: a yellow circle with arrows pointing outward, big loops that looked like flowers, and one-winged black-and-yellow-striped flying objects.

Realizing she watched him, he held the paper high and said, "It is well-done."

She beamed, settled beside the pots of bold color, and took up a brush again. He pressed a kiss to her temple, ordered her a juice and cookie, then left their quarters. The door remained open. He didn't want her to feel trapped or unwelcome. The way to the engine room was restricted to ensure she remained safe, but she had access everywhere else on the scimitar.

He strolled to the comm, visiting the common for a hot chocolate. Britta sat with her head on the table, her arms covering her head. She was muttering, "...stupid ship. Why does it have to be so small? Surely there's somewhere quiet on this blasted thing?"

"Lady Britta?"

At his voice, she groaned and tightened her arms. "No, this can't be happening," she whispered. "I'm not a bad person, I swear."

He rolled his lips, trying to smother a chuckle. She was amusing; he'd give her that. Her tablet rested by her elbow, a bottle of water beside that. Somewhere quiet, she'd said. "The scimitar is smaller than a battleship, but there is a viewing deck if you are willing to climb a ladder."

Her head shot up. The smile she blessed him with shot to two spots on his body: his chest and malehood. He hurried to adjust his suit when his temperature spiked, forming perspiration on his temple. How could one female have such control over him? And she had yet to touch him.

"Thank you," she said as she leaped to her feet. With tablet and bottle in hand, she strode toward him.

He swept a gaze over her body, knowing just what her garments hid. Without much effort on his part, he caught the gentle bounce of her breasts, the way her tunic cinched in at her waist, the sway of her hips his palms knew the feel of. He drew in a deep inhale, capturing her scent, the pure essence of her as a female... As *his* female.

He may have stared at her upturned face too long. There was just something fascinating about the tiny dots across her cheeks. A sensation built, uncoiled, looped and reformed, somewhere in the vicinity of his heart. His void had frozen, no longer pulsing and making demands to 'feel.'

This female had saved him, and she knew it not. Had she been Etterian, they'd be in a spare quarters, his mouth between her thighs.

"Is it far?" she asked, her plump lips forming the words.

His nostrils flared as he fought the urge to lower his mouth to hers. She had no idea what she was doing to him. And for now, he'd keep it that way. There had to be time to soften her before she learned the truth.

"This way." He led her to the comm, then faced a hidden panel opposite the comm's door. He pressed the side and the bulkhead gaped. Behind it, a light flickered on to illuminate the narrow ladder. "Up there. No one will bother you."

The gray of her eyes sparkled before she tucked the tablet into the back of her pants and scampered up the ladder. He watched, unable to drag his gaze from her enticing backside. With her out of sight, he shut the bulkhead and faced the comm.

At least he knew where she was.

Chapter Six

Now that was weird. The way Nerx had looked at her. Britt had experienced admiration from men. Yet with Nerx, she didn't want to punch him in the face. His gaze had brushed across her body, settled on her face, and gone no farther, as if he'd found heaven. She snorted at her silly thoughts. Sure, the same man who hated her?

Nope, he'd simply been polite, keeping his attention off her fine assets and on her face. Respectable and boring of him. She'd like a man to whisk her off her feet, despite her protestations, and show her what it means to be devoured—also known as kissing, naughty whispers, and screaming orgasms. It had been a while since she'd enjoyed any of those.

She studied the tiny room just above the communications room. It had a sort-of bench carved into the back wall and about a meter of space between that and massive screens. Stars sped past, none familiar. Not that she knew them well, but Jupiter or Saturn she could recognize. She stared at the tablet in her hand, her thoughts reeling. Here in the silence with the vastness of space forming a panoramic view, she struggled to grasp how quickly her life had changed. Despite it happening in a day, she should've been happy. Instead, sadness tugged at her heart.

Earth was behind her. Gone was her solarcycle, irritating job, useless ex-boss, and...Dad. He wasn't 'available' anymore. She couldn't visit his memorial plaque to talk to him, to tell him what she'd done or failed to do. How Mom refused to date, to face her life, to find joy in her old hobbies... Not anymore with Aldur in the picture. Britt hadn't seen her mother this lively in a long time.

Yet, Britt's future wasn't looking so rosy.

She sucked in a shuddering breath and swept aside an escaped tear. "Dad, I single-handedly offended an alien species. You always said I was a vortex of disaster waiting to happen. That I'd land myself in a situation I couldn't escape. Well, you were right." Her chuckle cracked. "At least Mom may have found happily-ever-after. Her shriveled ovaries can attest to that."

Britt squeezed the tablet, running her thumb across its smooth casing. Something would come up to brighten her existence. Dad would've said, "Peanut, don't sweat the small stuff when the big stuff will need all your focus."

She laughed, her shoulders shaking even as the tears flowed. If the small stuff was pissing off an alien man, then she didn't want to know what the big stuff was. She gazed at space, clutching the tablet to her chest. A shiver summoned goosebumps along her arms, but she was loath to fetch a jacket. Next time...

With a slow exhale, she activated the tablet and started.

Dear Diary,

You won't believe what happened today.

What time was it? She'd had dinner already, thanks to Sena. Judging by a steady thrum of exhaustion on the edges of her senses, bedtime would be soon. Shaking her head, she typed:

Got myself fired, and it felt good dong it. Next time, broken finger and all, Kev will think twice about touching women inappropriately. Hell, I should release what security footage I backed up. Might as well save all women from his lecherous advances.

My baby died on me, and I had to push her home. I really need to do some exercise, because, damn, she's heavy. As I sit here in my private 'star deck,' my inner thighs twang. Well, she's my baby no more.

Regret twitched her fingers. She'd abandoned her solarcycle as if she meant nothing to her. Five minutes would have had her baby safe in the garage. No, she hadn't given her solarcycle a thought until it was too late.

The real shitty part of my day was pepper-spraying a sexy-as-hell alien commander. Well, he was staring at my house like some stalker.

She'd been saying that repeatedly, and yet, it sounded as if she was trying to convince herself that her actions were justified. Nerx was a big guy; taking him on for someone of her size would've been impossible. She'd had no other recourse.

He's tall, broad-shouldered with a brooding intensity and deep blue eyes. I can't seem to hold my tongue when I'm in his presence. It's like my inhibitions fly out the window, and I say and do the dumbest things. Did I mention he's an Etterian? A supreme commander? And he hates me? Well, all of that, no doubt because I tazed him and accused him of kidnapping a little girl.

She winced. That did sound bad, but her diary wouldn't judge her.

I still don't know how long traveling to his planet will take. I need to find that out and plan my 'vacay' accordingly. Mom's probably going to stay in our quarters. That leaves the rest of this small ship for me, kind of. There's Nerx, Lily, Matir, Sena, Aldur, Edon, and the pilot guy. Dunno his name yet. So not really alone-alone.

She smiled at the stars. This was her haven, thanks to Nerx. It showed he could forgive her for her overreactions. That alone gave her hope her next apology would go well. Stifling a yawn, she hurried to finish her journal entry.

I'll let you know how tomorrow goes. Let's pray I don't say something stupid that requires yet another apology. I suck at those. Dad said that true repentance means swallowing one's pride and changing one's behavior. Well, I can promise to never pepper spray or taze Nerx again. That's as sincere as I get. What more could the man ask for?

PS: Need to find something to do while Mom helps Aldur. I'm no nurse.

She shut off the tablet and slid it onto the bench beside her. What this place needed was a stash of snacks, a blanket, and a pillow for impromptu naps. She'd do that tomorrow after she started some sort of exercise regime. Not that she'd brought gym clothes. Argh. Sweating like a stuffed pig hadn't been on her mind when she'd packed.

Groaning, she left her tablet and scampered down the ladder. Only to be faced with a solid door with no handle. When she stroked, punched, tapped the sides, no panel popped open.

She pounded on the bulkhead and waited. Nothing. More pounding left her sobbing, her throat hoarse from screaming, and her fists bruised. She rested her temple on the door, unable to slide down to the grated floor. There was space to stand and nothing more.

Here she'd thought it was sweet of Nerx to show her this spot. When he'd meant to trap her all along.

She climbed up the ladder and settled on the bench. Again a shiver swept through her, forcing her to rub her biceps to generate some heat. She'd have to spend the night here if no one searched for her. Would Mom worry when she didn't return?

Satisfied that it wouldn't be long before Aldur found her, she lay on the floor, tucking herself under the bench. She only had to be patient.

The next time she saw Nerx, she'd punch him in his smug face.

Nerx scowled at the bulkhead. It had been hours since he'd shown Britta the ladder. What could the woman be doing for so long? He'd tucked Lily into bed with a short bedtime story about dinosaurs—fascinating creatures. Yet sleep had eluded him. Restless, he'd cleansed and returned to the comm. While he waited for Britta, he'd commanded Ziot to retire.

A quick scan of the console confirmed all was in order. The sol and sludge storage was as expected. No approaching ships, hazardous asteroid belts, or comets were near the scimitar. Abandoning the comm, he opened the bulkhead and climbed up the ladder. A peek showed the viewing deck empty except for a tablet on the bench. A faint clatter caught his ears, and he pulled himself onto the deck.

Curled in a shivering ball was Britta. Her teeth chattering must've been what he'd heard. He kneeled beside her to stroke her arm, finding her chilled.

"Female," he growled. "How foolish must you be not to leave?"

She didn't answer, deeply asleep. He couldn't carry her down the ladder without banging her head. Opening the hidden panel, he adjusted the temperature of the space to suit her human biology. That would help her later, but for now, she needed warmth.

He should wake her...

Instead, he scooped her into his arms and sat with her on his lap. She moaned, pressing her body to his, her face tucked into the curve of his neck.

Maker.

He shuddered, drawing her closer. To hold her was...sublime. Despite wanting to rip off her clothes and taste every inch of her, a serenity engulfed his soul. He could embrace her for an eternity, just to experience this sense of peace she brought to him. Time slowed as he watched the star-filled display vids. It had been a while since he'd admired the beauty of space.

He ran his hand up and down her back, the pads of his fingers picking up her delicate muscles and bones. Humans were so fragile. It felt as if he could snap her in two. He gathered her against him, wanting her contours to meld to his. Even as he vowed that nothing would ever harm her.

Her breath huffed. She shifted in his arms then stiffened. As she scrambled off him, she touched parts of his body, summoning a sweet thrill of pleasure.

"You...bastard," she hissed. "You lured me here with promises of privacy, then locked me in." She pointed her finger at him, her cheeks a bright peach, while tears shimmered in her eyes. "I thought...like an idiot, that you were being nice, that we could start over." She wiped her cheek, grabbed her tablet, and tried to hurry past him.

He caught her wrist and tugged, using her momentum to drive her onto his lap. She squeaked when she sprawled across him, her face in his chest, her knees between his thighs. He wrapped his arms around her, trapping her there.

"I did not lock you in," he said.

"Right, with no door handle or panel-thingy to let me out?" She leaned back only as far as he'd let her. "I screamed..." She glanced away, hiding her eyes from him.

He pinched her chin between forefinger and thumb and forced her to meet his gaze. "Push on the center of the bulkhead, and it will open."

"I punched—" She snapped her mouth shut. "Just push?"

He nodded. "The fault does lie with me. I did not ensure you knew how to open it."

Her shrug was weak. "To you, it's common sense how your doors work so it wouldn't have occurred to explain it."

He tried not to smile. Had she just defended him? Justified his error?

"Um, would you mind releasing me...please?" She jerked her gaze everywhere but at him.

"What if I do mind?" He freed a grin. "You are cold."

She glanced down but whipped her gaze up. He did the same, then stilled at the sight of her nipples peaking her thin tunic.

"I would like a hot shower and a warm bed. Maybe even a cup of cocoa. Let's just forget this silly incident." She pulled away, and he let her.

Down the ladder she went with him close behind her. In the tight space, his chest pressing her back, he waited. His arm twitched with the urge to wrap around her waist and pin her against him. He forced himself not to move.

"Push?" she asked, then pressed the center of the bulkhead. It didn't move.

"Harder," he rasped.

With a shove, the bulkhead slid open.

She didn't step into the passage, nor did he nudge her. Instead, he ran his nose up the nape of her neck, amid her soft curls.

"Let me know if you need...anything," he said, gripping her elbows to keep her close.

Her breasts rose and fell with every jagged breath as the seconds ticked past. She twisted to meet his gaze, the gray of hers tempestuous. "Thank you."

Her footsteps thumped along the passage before disappearing into her quarters. He leaned against the ladder while adjusting his pants around his Fuyra-hard malehood. The scent of her hair lingered in his nose. The fleeting taste of her skin tingled his lips.

Alodon's balls, the Maker has chosen well.

He slid into the pilot's seat and stared unseeingly at the console. Lock her in? Oh, he wanted to but in his quarters. Why did she always leap to the worst scenario? That, in itself, intrigued him.

He stalked her mother.

He kidnapped children.

He trapped her on purpose.

The phantom sensation of her in his arms tightened his body. Her curves against his hard edges had been everything he'd hoped for and remembered from the visions. She hadn't noticed her backside pressing against his malehood. Nor had she realized how her fingers had dug into his chest like when she'd accused him of kidnapping. It was as if she hadn't considered he'd find her attractive and had been 'content' to sit on his lap.

And the way her nipples stretched the fabric of her tunic. He closed his eyes, recalling from his visions their sweet color against her paler skin tone. With hours left before Edon's shift-start, Nerx had time to take care of his morning chore and hopefully ease his throbbing arousal. Then he would attend to his tasks and perhaps write a poem about Britta and what she was starting to invoke in him.

Chapter Seven

ALDUR SAT IN A chair beside Mom, reading on her tablet. Mom stood in front of the wall-mounted screen, skimming through what looked like medical articles.

"Um, hi," Britt said, offering a weak wave.

"Where've you been?" Mom asked, pausing on an image of a woman giving birth, caesarian, if Britt hazarded a guess. She averted her gaze. It was too late to have that fixed in her mind.

"On the star deck." She eyed the bathroom, desperate for a shower.

"We're going to be a while. Will that bother you?" Mom crossed for a hug, then leaned back to rub her hands up and down Britt's arms.

Could she sleep with these two discussing what-nots and procedures? She grimaced. She could try, for Mom's happiness.

"Or use my quarters in medical," Aldur said, setting the tablet on the table to rise. "Let me grant you access."

Britt flashed him a smile. "That would be wonderful. Thank you."

She hurried into the bedroom to grab a baggy T-shirt and a fresh set of clothing for tomorrow. Clutching the bundle to her chest, she trailed Aldur into the empty common room. Beyond the bed in medical was a door. He led her there and gestured to her to place her palm on the panel. She did, this time knowing what to expect.

His quarters was a small studio apartment. A bed was tucked into the corner. A door beside it had to be the bathroom. To the left against a wall was a counter with a rehydrator and replicator, and two chairs were placed to the right, below a wall-mounted screen.

"I will set these to Earth English." He tapped on the counter while she dumped her clothes on the closest chair.

"Tell me, Aldur, how long does it take reach your planet?"

"Two weeks at full fusion pulse," he said, without facing her. "Order anything you need, including garments."

"Thank you again, and good night," she managed as the door closed behind him.

Two weeks? She slumped, leaning against the door to stare at her room for the night. How things were going between Mom and Aldur, this seemed like an upgrade. Here, she could sleep in, spend hours curled up in a chair reading or watching something on the screen. During the day, of course. Aldur had to sleep somewhere.

She shook her head, trying to clear the image of childbirth. What she needed was a hot shower. She stripped, tossing off her T-shirt, boots, socks, camo pants, and underwear before she reached the bathroom.

No taps had her stroking the walls for a panel. Damn aliens with their superior technology— She squealed when the water came on by itself. Grumbles followed as she stood there, letting it warm every inch of her. No soap, no shampoo, but at least the toilet looked familiar.

She stepped out of the spray and watched it, wondering if she'd have to call someone to switch it off. When it did it by itself, she grinned. *Nice. Okay, one task done. Now to dry.* Solid white walls held no towel rails. But there were two buttons. She stroked the top button in blue, twitched her fingers as she hesitated, then pressed it.

Hot air blasted her. She spun, trying to assess from where the air came from. Looking up forced her to squeeze her eyes shut. And she couldn't shut it off. Fine. Blow away. She hit the gray button and laughed when a panel slid open, showing folded towels. Flicking one out revealed a robe. She slid into it then squeaked when it adjusted around her body like the chair had.

"Gives a new meaning to one size fits all." Waltzing out of the bathroom, she made a beeline to the rehydrator to order a hot cocoa then two blankets from the replicator. A glance at Aldur's bed showed it devoid of comfort. She touched and patted the right side of the front door, found the panel, then let it scan her palm. Temperature sorted. Maybe the star deck had the same?

She snorted. Freezing for no reason. Serves her right for being slow to grasp their tech.

"Harder," Nerx had said in a gruff voice. The sound alone had bolted through like a love drug on steroids. Wow. She'd just stood there and let it wash over her, let the heat of his chest pour into her back, let him stroke her neck.

She shivered, left the cup on the counter, and slid onto Aldur's bed. As she drew the blanket over her, she muttered, "Don't let that sexy man get to you, Britt-baby. He's gonna break your heart."

Her nod was slow, deliberate. "They all do," she said, her voice carrying gravitas in her new quarters. The silence, warm blanket, and a belly full of hot liquid lulled her to sleep.

BRITT STUMBLED OUT OF Aldur's quarters to find Edon seated at the table. She relaxed her stiff shoulders, having half-expected to find a full-on audience because she'd slept so late.

"Morning," she said, hurrying past him to the rehydrator.

A bowl of fruit salad with yoghurt and a coffee were next on her agenda. So much for starting with exercise. When she stared at the blue sparring mat, she didn't know what she'd do anyway. Maybe Aldur could advise, as the ship's medic. And he was buff for someone his age which meant he had to be maintaining that physique somehow. One narrow wall held weapons that could cut you just by looking at them. There had to be other things or activities to do to remain fit while in space.

When she sat opposite Edon, his nostrils flared. He grabbed his plate, and with a tiny bow, abandoned her. Had he sniffed her? There hadn't been soap or shampoo in the shower? Maybe she stank? She raised her arms to draw in deep whiffs of her pits. Nope, no stench there, just pure Britta.

Nerx strode past her to the rehydrator. He didn't greet her, and after their last inter-action, she was hesitant to say anything. But desperation made her stupid things.

"Um, Nerx?"

"Yes?" he said, but not glancing at her. She could imagine his eyes narrowing, just hearing her voice.

She grinned. "Two things. Soap. Does the replicator have that on its menu?" She could've checked this morning but asking him seemed to irritate him.

A steaming mug of something appeared on the rehydrator's surface. He wrapped those long fingers of his around it. "Why?" While sipping what smelled like hot cocoa, he faced her.

"To wash my body, hair, face." The existence of bathrooms proved Etterians cared about cleanliness so having to explain her need for soap seemed stupid. Her tone might have implied that. She shrugged. What he perceived in her tone was on him.

"Such is provided in the water." His focus shifted to his cocoa. So, not meeting her gaze, and Edon reacting a little over the top?

"Okay, then do I stink?"

He tried to leave then halted. "Is there a point to this conversation?"

"Edon almost ran from the common like a herd of sweating and huffing wildebeest sat beside him. Why would your man avoid me?" She folded her arms, waiting for Nerx's response. If he so much as took a step to leave, she'd be on his ass.

"Male for Etterian. Man for human."

She rolled her eyes. "Thanks for the lesson, Professor Smarty Pants."

He growled. "I am done discussing this."

"Wait." She leaped to her feet, looping around him to block his way. "I need reading material. Books or something."

"Any display vid will have archives of every species known to Etteria." With his cup, he gestured to the wall-mounted black screen. "Your Earthian data is there too."

"It is?" She squealed and crossed to the screen. A few taps had her finding the folder filled with books, movies, music, and documentaries.

"I do not lie. To imply so is rude."

She ignored him as she perused the genres. "How do I get it onto my tablet?" She tapped the device to the screen for a transfer without success.

Warmth soaked her right shoulder and flung out a wave of tingles when he leaned around her to flick a file at her tablet. It dinged, confirming receipt. She laughed, dancing on the spot just like Dad had taught her. Yup, she knew all his moves.

"Thanks, Nerx. You're the best."

With her focus on the tablet, she sank onto her pre-warmed seat by her untouched meal. She didn't hear Nerx leave and only when Lily clambered onto the bench did Britt look up.

"Whatya doing?" Lily asked.

"Breakfast and reading. You?" Britt tried not to smile at the pink furry onesie she was wearing.

"Nerxie said to find something to do."

"So you're asking me?" Britt placed the tablet face down and scooped a grape into her mouth. "Mm," she said while chewing. "We could play hopscotch?" She chuckled. *That counts as exercise, right?*

"Can we?" Lily bounced on her backside, clambered to her feet, then leaped off the bench to dance around the common.

"Sure. Let me finish eating. We'll need chalk. I suppose this is the only area big enough?" To the left was a narrow passage that led to an impenetrable door. She didn't know what was beyond that. To the right was the passage to her mom's quarters, the star deck, and the communications room. The other way was a door she hadn't tried to open, yet.

"Harder," Nerx's voice came to mind.

She focused on Lily but found her gone. With a shrug, she finished her breakfast and was sipping her coffee when Lily slapped chalk on the table. Her cheeks glowed a bright pink.

"Fetch your brush; let's braid your hair first."

And again Lily bolted, turning right to the untried door. So, her quarters was that way. She returned with a brush and a hair band. Britt circled the table and sat on the bench, tapping it to ask Lily to come closer. As she ran the brush through the girl's long hair, she threw ideas at her.

"We need a stone or an object to throw onto the squares. It's got to be something we can order from the replicator."

"Oranges?" Lily said, while swinging her hips.

"Too big and squishy. What will Nerxie say when the mat's all sticky?" Britt bit her tongue to hide a chuckle. Maybe she should start calling him that, just to irritate him.

"A tiny ball?" Lily twisted to smile.

"A cube or an odd shape that won't bounce or roll away." Britt leaned in as she finished braiding and tied the end.

"I have old data cubes," a man said.

Britt jerked back, having not heard him approach. She knew that face—the other man sitting at the console when she'd accused Nerx of kidnapping. Great, a witness.

"How big are they, Uncle Ziot?" Lily crossed to him to grab his hand.

He kneeled and tugged on her braid playfully. "About the size of my thumb." He wiggled it.

"That could work. Want to join us?" The idea of a big alien skipping and hopping had Britt swallowing her laughter.

"Certainly and my thanks for the offer. How many cubes do you need?"

Britt held up three fingers. "One for each player."

Lily trailed Ziot, leaving Britt alone. She swept a stick of chalk off the table and began to draw squares on the blue mat. They couldn't be too big otherwise Lily wouldn't make the jumps, and they couldn't be too small for Britt and Ziot's feet. One square, two on top, then another one, and two again, until she hit the end. She wrote '10' in that block, then added the numbers going down to '1.'

Lily raced into the common and thrust a three-inch cube at Britt. The thing was iridescent and too pretty to be tossed around. Old, he'd said.

"This is perfect. Thank you, Ziot." Britt stood before '1' and dropped her cube on it. "The goal is to make it to '10' and back without lowering your other foot on a single square. Those side by side like '8' and '9,' you use both legs. You toss your cube in each square as you progress. If it touches the chalk, you lower your foot, or step on the chalk, you lose your turn." She hopped over '1,' spread her legs for '2' and '3' next to each other, then hopped on one foot to '4.' When she reached '10,' she swiveled and hopped back, bending to pick up her cube. She beamed at Lily. "Want to show Ziot again?"

Lily placed her cube on '1,' then went through the motions, almost perfectly. She did touch the chalk once, but Britt let it slide. This was a demonstration, after all.

"Wanna try?" Lily asked Ziot, who'd watched them with puzzlement furrowing his brow.

"Yes," he said, then stopped at '2' on the way back. "And I pick up my cube?"

"To finish you turn, yup. Technically, a successful completion means you get to carry on by throwing your cube onto the next numbered square. Trust me, it gets harder the farther away the numbers are."

The poor man threw his cube to '2' and hopped along, his braid swaying violently and almost wiping the chalk off the mat. He picked up the cube, hopped over '2' then swiveled to aim his cube at '3.' He missed and scowled at it.

Lily scooped it up and placed it in his hand before standing at '1' to throw her cube at '2.' By the time they all reached '6' and '7,' they were laughing, swaying on the spot, teetering over, and generally smearing chalk dust everywhere. Cubes flew every which way in attempts to land it dead center of each square.

Britt's thighs and calves burned, her breathing was ragged, but she found air to laugh.

"Shall we try again tomorrow?" she asked Lily, who'd sprawled on the mat beside the hopscotch blocks. "I could do with a soda."

"Me too," she squealed, leaping to her feet to race to the rehydrator.

"That was...enjoyable," Ziot said as he settled at the table. "We do not have such activities as *damu*."

Nerx had used that word before, when Britt accused him of being a baby. "This builds motor co-ordination, sportsmanship, and how to count, all while having fun." She tapped the rehydrator when Lily slid her fruit juice off the surface. "Soda, water, beer, what's your preference?"

"Whatever you are having is fine, Lady Britta."

She huffed. What she should do is order a Bloody Mary, just to teach him that letting her choose wasn't wise. But then he'd given them data cubes and played with them. "Soda it is." She placed the chilled can in front of him then sat on the bench next to Lily.

"What's next?" she asked the girl.

"Lunch with Nerxie," and off she bolted, leaving Britt alone with Ziot.

He stiffened and rose, taking his can with him. "I did not realize it was that late. Please, do excuse me. I must attend to my tasks."

She blinked at the empty common, alone again before she'd taken her first sip. A moan slipped out as she downed the cold soda. Sweat stuck her T-shirt to her body, and the mat was a mess. This ship had to have a mop and bucket somewhere. And she could do with a shower. She pushed off the table and placed her glass next to the rehydrator, not knowing what to do with it.

"The waste receptacle converts it back to sludge," Sena said, striding into the common. He tossed a glance at the hopscotch pattern but didn't comment. Instead, he waved his hand over a dark circle, and a hole opened. In it, he shoved her glass. "Your quarters has one too."

"Thanks, Sena. Tell me, what do you for...fitness?" She tried not to glance at the man's bulging biceps and muscled shoulders, bared by his sleeveless armor. But he couldn't have gotten those by doing nothing.

He touched a panel. It glided up and disappeared at the top of a boxing pad. "We punch this or spar with or without weapons. I suggest you not touch those, Lady Britta. They are made of Maloidian steel and can slice through bone with ease."

"And you practice with them?" Having the medical close made sense. Speaking of which, she'd better tidy up, both the common and Aldur's quarters. Because he was smitten with Mom didn't mean they'd be getting it on just yet.

"Yes." He glanced from her to the mat. "Do not worry. The auto-servos will clean it. Though, if you want to keep the data cubes, it is best to rescue those."

She did just that, scooping up the cubes then stacking them on a nearby shelf. "When is the common the quietest? I want to exercise but not be in the crew's way."

"Before six and after nine in the morning." Sena ordered a plate of meat and dark sauce then settled at the table.

It felt awkward to force her company on him but also to leave him alone. He didn't help her make up her mind either way, just sat there, eating.

"Thanks," she said, rocked on the balls of her feet and headed for Mom. Might as well find out first if she was to move permanently.

Walking into her quarters was met with Mom kissing Aldur like they were teenagers. Britt spun on her heel and exited post-haste. She pressed her flaming cheek to the closest metal panel while squeezing her eyes shut. That imagery was worse than the caesarian. Yup, she was staying in Aldur's quarters for the duration of the trip.

A peek through the door Lily always used showed a narrower passage with doors going off it in both directions. This had to be the staff quarters, or in this case, the barracks? She closed the door then peeked in to find the common empty. Once inside Aldur's quarters, she showered and dressed in jeans, a T-shirt, and sneakers she had to order from the replicator.

Time to kit out the star deck. She'd already ordered the blanket. Next would be a cushion, since a pillow wasn't on the menu. Popcorn, crisps, and biscuits followed. She stared at her choices then wondered how she'd get them up the ladder. The cushion flew through the hatch when she threw it for the fourth time. The snacks she'd trapped in the blanket and slung over her shoulder. Climbing the ladder was difficult with one arm to hold the rungs but as soon as she could, she pushed the bundle through. Her tablet sat where she'd left it.

Memories of Nerx holding her came to mind, bringing with them a frisson of awareness. She shivered in remembrance. He'd swept her anger aside with directness and the unwillingness to release her. His unemotional responses had sucked the air out of her sails. Yet, he had an intensity about him that made her hyper-vigilant in his presence.

Not willing to think about him, she returned to Aldur's quarters to order a jacket and another bottle of water to join her half-empty one she'd left there. The star deck hadn't been as cold as last night, which was odd. Still, she'd find that panel and set the temperature. Rather safe than sorry, or worse, land herself in his lap again.

She settled on the floor, her back against the wall, the blanket over her legs. While nibbling on popcorn, she flicked through the novels she'd downloaded. Before she could blink, she was elbows deep in a fantasy romance and loving every word.

Chapter Eight

"Why are you so...flushed, Lily?" Nerx touched his daughter's cheek.

"Britt played hopscotch with me and Ziot." Lily bit into her hotdog with gusto before Nerx could ask her another question.

His O.D.I. explained the meaning of the word and its rules. He ate his fourth hotdog, desperate to find the sec vids from the common. Just like that, Britt had become a part of Lily's life, and all it had taken was a day. Lily was fearful of strangers, yet Britt had won her over with ease. He should see this as a good sign, but until his Dar Eth committed to him, he didn't want Lily becoming too attached to Britt. Although, if she rejected him, he'd die and orphan Lily.

What have I done?

He stared at his daughter, his chest cinching. Winning Britt was paramount, now more than ever.

"Ziot too?" he asked.

"We're going to play again tomorrow." Lily slurped her juice, unable to sit still.

He caught the tail end of her braid, running his fingers along it. *Britta.*

Lily jumped to her feet to clear her plate and glass, then she shoved her paints and paper into a bag.

"Where are you going?" He blinked at his untouched giyua juice then gulped it down.

"To find Britt." The door closed behind Lily, leaving him alone.

He cleaned up, not even bothering to finish his last hotdog. Tonight, it would be kreso for him, and he was looking forward to it. His teeth itched for the texture, if that made sense.

Tapping the display vid in his quarters, he summoned the sec vids from the common. His focus shifted between Britta and Lily. Their joy was breathtaking, their interactions inspiring. How easily Britta had charmed his Lily made his soul sing. His Dar Eth was more beautiful to him than an hour ago.

He made it to the common before a sobbing Lily found him.

"I can't find her, Nerxie."

He caught her into his arms for a cuddle. "Where did you look?"

"Her mommy said Britt wasn't there. And she's not in the common or with Uncle Edon." Lily's eyes widened. "Did the sharks take her?"

Nerx bit back a laugh. Lily must have heard about the sharklike Yithians from Lady Ava. "Come, let's look for her together." He strode to the ladder and called up, "Lady Britta?"

"Yup?"

Lily squealed, scrambled out of Nerx's arms, then up the ladder. He followed, but hesitated, even as Lily settled on the edge of Britta's blanket.

"I hope she is not intruding," he said, remembering Britta's desperation for privacy.

"Not at all. This will be mine and Lily's treehouse, right, squirt?"

Nerx absorbed every feature of the woman before him. Yes, she'd been a pain in his backside since she'd sprayed his eyes, but now, she was nothing short of extraordinarily entertaining.

"No boys allowed," Lily called, giving Nerx an adorable glare.

Britta laughed. It filled the small space with joy and vibrancy. "You can't chase away the captain in his own ship."

Lily giggled. "Nerxie, I stay with Britt. Okay?"

"All right, *minus susa*." He dipped his head as he turned to leave. "I shall fetch you...*both* for dinner."

He met Britta's gaze and held it until she nodded. Her easy acquiescence gave him hope. He stole glimpses while descending through the hatch, wishing he was the one sitting at her feet.

He strode into the comm, debating with himself whether he should eavesdrop on the viewing deck. Settling into a comfy, he tugged the tablet across the table and stared at it. No, he had to trust to be trusted.

A bright light, tiny, in the distance,

Creates more hope than a shooting star.

For the light is constant,

A beacon promising everlasting reprieve.

As awe-inspiring the fleeting star,

As portent and mystical,

It cannot compare to a life without darkness.

That is what you are to me, blossoming hope in a pointless existence.

His last poem was meant for Lily, but it applied to Britta as well.

He drew in a long inhale then focused on his tasks. On a scimitar, communication and requests weren't endless. Usually it was to note a defect in an engine part or the low reserves he himself had checked last night. If any of his males onboard needed to discuss something, they spoke to him, face-to-face. He had to admit, he preferred that to sifting through mails.

"Comm Advisor Kanzo," he said to Edon.

"Yes, Supreme Commander. Linking you through."

Nerx leaped to his feet and assumed position in front of a smaller display vid mounted above the console. "Advisor Kanzo," he greeted when Kanzo answered. "Just an update for the queen. We have her doctor on board and are en route to Etteria. Expected arrival is thirteen days."

"Excellent news. Well done. The king is informed." Kanzo shoved his face into the vid, his eyes widened and so did his grin. "You found your Dar Eth? Is it the doctor?"

Nerx chuckled, accepting the joy as his due. "No, Lady Dahlia is Aldur's."

"Aldur? My king, Supreme Commander brings good news." Kanzo disappeared off vid, but still his voice carried. "Aldur is saved, Nerx too."

"Both?" King Xeus stepped into the vid, stared into Nerx's eyes, then laughed. "What a remarkable species humans are." A frown faded his smile. "If not the doctor, then who?"

"Her daughter," Nerx said. "Lady Britta."

"Wonderful. I am sure to meet them both soon. All of Etteria is with you." The king ended the comm from his side, as expected from a warrior with a higher rank.

"Foresee any obstacles?" Nerx asked Edon.

A quick tap of his fingers zoomed the vids from all angles around the scimitar and along the comm stations on their trajectory. "Nothing, Supreme Commander."

"Good." Nerx sat and grabbed his tablet.

"The problem with these tactical missions is how to fill one's time," Edon offered, sliding a glance at Nerx.

"Indeed. Up for a sparring session?" Nerx smirked. "Summon Ziot to the comm room."

A grinning Edon did so, then jumped up. "Swords, staves, daggers?"

"Grappling," Nerx said, for it would exhaust him the most.

"Mm, challenge accepted, Supreme Commander."

Ziot strode in, also wearing a smile. "If I did not have to man the comm, I would enjoy the sport."

"Watch," Edon said, gesturing to the display vids. "When Sub-Commander Matir or Sena start their shift, perhaps they would spar with you."

"Suggest a roster," Aldur said, appearing at the door. "Has Lady Britta been found?"

Nerx squeezed his shoulder in passing. "Britta and Lily are in the 'treehouse.'" He pointed at the ceiling to the viewing deck. "That is if Lady Dahlia is concerned."

"She will be overjoyed to hear this. My thanks, Supreme Commander." Aldur swiveled away, then spun back, his mouth gaping. "Your eyes..." His widened. "Lady Britta?"

"Yes, though I have yet to inform her."

Aldur stilled. "I am in the same predicament. Had Dahlia been Etterian..." He tapped his O.D.I., no doubt to adjust his suit. Nerx did that way too often in Britta's presence.

"Indeed," Nerx said. "Now is the time, before we reach Etteria. They cannot leave the confines of this ship even if they wish to." Wise words he needed to follow. Yet, his situation was complicated. He had to win Britta over first. Telling her she was his salvation while she still hated him was a definite path to death.

"You are correct to mention this," Aldur said, then beamed. "I am learning much about the human physiology, specifically a woman's. Remarkable." He left, muttering to himself about hormones.

Thumping his chest released his armor which Nerx shrugged off, letting it fall to the floor beside the mat. Edon did the same, then circled, his gaze focused.

Nerx stood in the center of the padded mat, designed to cushion the inevitable falls. Tension thickened the air with anticipation. He kept his posture relaxed, but he calculated possible moves before they happened.

"Supreme Commander." Edon bowed, his fist on his chest above his heart. A confident smirk played across his mouth. He was younger and faster, but Nerx had experience and strategy on his side.

"Pilot Edon." Nerx thumped his chest.

Edon lunged, aiming a swift punch at Nerx's midsection. Nerx sidestepped, grabbing the pilot's arm and using his momentum to flip him over onto the mat. Edon rolled to his feet, undeterred. He launched a series of rapid strikes, each one aimed to test Nerx's defenses.

Nerx blocked and parried with precise movements, using minimal effort to counter the pilot's attacks. He saw an opening and took it, delivering a quick elbow strike to Edon's side, making him grunt in pain. The pilot responded with a kick, which Nerx caught mid-air, twisting his leg to unbalance him.

Edon fell but flipped back up, this time more cautious. He tried a different tactic, attempting to sweep Nerx's legs. Nerx jumped, avoiding the move, and landed a powerful knee strike to Edon's chest, sending him sprawling back.

"Well done, Supreme Commander," Edon said, wiping sweat from his brow. "But I am not done yet."

Nerx nodded, respecting the younger male's tenacity. "I should hope not. We have just begun."

Edon charged again, this time feinting left before aiming a right hook at Nerx's jaw. He'd anticipated the move, ducking under the punch and slipping behind the pilot. In a swift motion, he wrapped his arm around Edon's neck, locking him in a chokehold.

Edon struggled, trying to break free, but Nerx tightened his grip, applying just enough pressure to prove he was in control. Edon's movements slowed as if he'd realized he was caught.

"Yield," Nerx commanded, his voice calm but firm.

Edon hesitated, then tapped Nerx's arm, signaling his submission.

Nerx released him, then offered a hand to help him up.

"Good fight," Edon said, his breathing labored as he took Nerx's hand.

"Not bad," Nerx said with a smile. "You have much potential."

"My thanks, Supreme Commander." Edon thumped his chest, gathered his armor, and left the common.

Nerx stilled, his gaze landing on Britta hovering in the doorway. Her face was that adorable peach color he liked seeing on her. Her focus shifted down his sweat-soaked chest then she lowered her head, hiding her thoughts. Without a word, she headed to the rehydrator, tapping with rapid fingers as if time was an issue.

He wanted to cleanse but hesitated. Any chance to gaze upon her was to be grasped with both hands. So he settled beside her, ordering a towel from the replicator. He too said nothing, though he snuck glances at her profile, admiring the way her hair curled around her face, her earlobe peeking out, the angle of her jaw, the flash of her tiny white teeth nibbling on her bottom lip.

Heat of another sort fired through him, heightening his senses and hardening his malehood. Just a look; that was all it took. With towel in hand, he dabbed at his face and chest, rolling his lips to hide a smirk when her gaze shifted to him, then away, then back again. She sucked in a shuddering breath, grabbed the pile of colorful packets she'd ordered, then raced from the common.

And in her wake, the luscious scent of her arousal lingered.

He laughed, delighted by that revelation. His Dar Eth finding him attractive was a good thing. He could work with that.

TWO HOURS BEFORE DINNER, Lily appeared in the comm, demanding to climb onto Nerx's lap. He lifted her and settled her against his chest.

"What is it, *minus susa*?"

"Britt said she had to take a nap. I didn't want to." Lily raised a pleading gaze to his. "I don't have to, do I?"

"Of course not. Unless you are tired." He rubbed her back. "Do you want a pink milkshake?"

Lily nodded, yawned, then sank into him when he lifted her into his arms. Before he reached the common, she was sound asleep. He grinned and continued to their quarters to tuck her into bed. On the way to the comm room, he ordered two hot chocolates, handing one to Edon. He sat, pulled the tablet closer, then stared at it. He'd written the first word of his next poem when Lily had interrupted him.

Fire!

He blinked at it, then added the imagery that one word inspired.

She fires my blood.

My senses tumble along,

Sparking a newness that is breathtaking.

Britta...

Oh, how the Maker has blessed me.

It didn't encompass this roiling, volatile, and growing ball of emotion that now resided in his chest. Matir grinned at him when he crossed the comm room to the war room on the side. His humor deepened Nerx's scowl. Matir tended to push the boundaries on acceptable emotions and usually Nerx didn't mind. Yet this afternoon, it worried him. To feel is to fail, the Etterian motto, was there to ensure they lost no males to the void. Before he could reprimand him, for the male had yet to find his Dar Eth, silence descended on the comm room, no longer peppered with Edon's tapping. Nerx's head shot up. On the display vid set to the common where Sena and Ziot sparred, it was easy to locate Britta coming out of Aldur's quarters in a state of disarray. *What is the meaning of this?*

Nerx was on his feet before he knew he'd risen. He stormed to the common to find her watching the sparring match. Unsure why fury fired his blood or hazed his vision in red, he grabbed her by the elbow then ushered her into Aldur's quarters, closing the door behind them.

A thorough search revealed the quarters to be empty. Where was Aldur? Nerx would kill him.

"He's with my mother," Britta said, dropping into a comfy as he rushed around the room. "I sleep here now."

"You sleep...?" Nerx drew to a halt.

"Yup," she snapped. "It's better than the cold treehouse."

"Why did you not come to me, Britta?"

"Would you have listened, Nerx?" She shrugged.

His gaze shot up to meet hers in alarm. He would have, yet she believed otherwise. She jumped up, presenting quite an enticing package in a baggy tunic that slipped off one bare shoulder and tight pants hugging every curve of her legs. He took the time to admire her well-toned calves and thighs.

"It doesn't matter, I made a plan, and this suits me just fine. So, thank you for your *concern*."

"Britta?" He paused, uncertain what words he could speak to alter her perception of him. They'd been making good progress.

She flashed him a look with her cool gray eyes, her hair tumbling around her. "What? What do you want from me, Nerx? Yup, I'm sorry I hurt you, but please understand. I'd do it again in a heartbeat. She's all I have after my father died. I would do anything to protect her. I'd taze your ass every day for a week and not regret it." She marched to the door and waved at him. "Now, if you'll leave, that would be great."

"Very well, but I shall collect you for dinner." Considering that settled, he did as she asked.

"I'll think about it," she said.

When he faced her to somehow convince her, he met steel instead. So much for her softening toward him. He returned to the comm in a daze. "I will be in the engine room," he said, desperate for something to occupy his mind. Perhaps an in-depth analysis of all systems would do.

Chapter Nine

THE FOLLOWING MORNING, BRITT awoke, having slept well. She swung her legs off the bed then stretched. Today, she planned to stay couped up in Aldur's quarters. Time passed as she switched between watching movies or reading books while surviving on pizza, popcorn, ice cream, and cotton candy. Her stomach ached by mid-afternoon. She pushed aside the half-eaten bowl of jelly beans to order a bottle of water before settling on her bed.

"*Ensa*, are you well?" A text from Nerx popped up on her tablet.

She blinked at it, not bothering to wonder how a superior race could access her contact info. "I'm good," she typed.

"Prove it," was his response.

"Huh?" With an unnatural smile, she commanded the tablet to take a photo.

A minute later, the door to Aldur's quarters opened. To Nerx.

"What the hell?" she cried out, scrambling to her feet while trying to tug her baggy T-shirt over her bare legs. The hem hit mid-thigh only if she bent a little but nothing could help her feel less naked underneath. "Knock first."

He stared at her legs then met her gaze. "Aldur asked that I check up on you. His Dar Eth...your mother is concerned."

She harumphed at him ignoring his rudeness. "Does Dar Eth mean lover?" She waved her hand, changing her mind on needing an answer. "If it does, that makes sense. I got passed over like I'm not her daughter. All for a lay." She glanced at her bare toes. "I get it. Maybe Aldur's a stunning lay, but still, family comes first."

"What's a lay?" Lily asked, peeking from behind Nerx's legs.

"Um...friend?" Britt dropped her head in her hands. Why hadn't she noticed Lily? Nerx was gorgeous, but she wasn't the type of woman to be addled by looks.

"Aldur is Nerxie's lay too," Lily said as she poked the colorful candy in the bowl.

Britt snapped her mouth shut. Swallowed laughter cramped her cheeks. "I bet your dad's the best lay ever."

"Britta," he warned.

She met his gaze and caught the fire burning in his ice blue eyes. Something whispered across her mind, but she dismissed it.

"May I have these?" Lily clasped the half-full bowl of candy.

"Go share with Edon." Nerx ushered her out of the room before facing Britt.

She sank onto the chair, curling her legs under her ass, while preparing for a lecture or a reprimand.

"I apologize for the intrusion." His gaze lingered on parts of her, and she'd swear, she tingled as if he'd touched her.

Instead of leaving, he ventured deeper into her room, then slipped his hands under her armpits to hoist her to her feet.

She bit her tongue to smother a gasp, having not expected him to touch her, never mind manhandle her like she weighed nothing. When he didn't step away, she raised her chin to meet his gaze. Emotion burned in the depths of his eyes.

"What?" she asked, meaning it to sound irritated. Instead, desire hoarsened her voice.

"You do not stink." He buried his face in the curve of her neck for a deep inhale. His nose brushing along her skin summoned a shiver. "You smell good," he growled. "Artificial scents hurt our noses. We find them offensive."

"Ah," she said, just to respond somehow. "Well, um, thanks for checking on me."

He swept aside her hair falling across her temple. Electricity trailed where he touched. He pinched her chin, holding her still while he studied her face.

"Nerx?" She frowned at his odd behavior.

His gaze met hers. His nostrils flared seconds before he feathered his mouth across hers. She gasped, freezing on the spot. Her thoughts ricocheted, pinging between outrage and humming like a horny teenager.

"My apologies again." He pulled away from her, dropping his hand. "I should not have done that."

She winced. He regretted kissing her, and with their history, she could understand why. Still, embarrassment scorched her cheeks.

"I should have asked first," he said, cupping her neck. "I find I cannot think clearly when around you."

"I...I didn't mind." She ran her fingers down the center of his bulletproof vest. "I mean... Permission granted."

His eyes widened. His focus shifted to her mouth, then he yanked her against his hard length. "Britta," he whispered, before kissing her again.

His taste curled her toes, like sticky toffee pudding with custard. She dug her fingers into his pecs when he deepened the kiss. A mewl escaped her, and more followed when he splayed his fingers across her back to crush her to him.

Oh, yes, please.

"Maker," he mumbled, breaking the kiss. "You fire my blood, *minus cesu.*" He snatched a hard kiss then buried his fingers in her hair to hold her still for a long perusal. "If I was not honor-bound to inform Aldur or see to Lily, I would be learning every inch of your body."

Whoa. What? Britt blinked at him. A kiss or two, no matter how steamy, didn't mean sex. Despite wanting another taste of him, perhaps him leaving was for the best. Especially when disappointment sank deep, like cinder blocks tied to the feet of a corpse. A little morbid, but she'd been binge-watching old crime movies.

"Duty calls," she managed.

"Soon, you will be my duty and my honor to protect, *ensa.*"

"Okay." *Whatever that meant.* She watched him retreat, desire making his eyes glow. Then it hit her what her inner voice had been trying to tell her. "Nerx. Wait."

Stilling, Britt frowned and crossed the room to stare into Nerx's eyes. She brought her delicious spicy scent to engulf him.

He fought the urge to inhale it deeply. This close, her skin appeared smooth. Tiny lines fanned out from the corner of her eyes as if she'd had much to laugh about. And her lips... She'd let him kiss her and expected many more.

"Your eyes were dark blue. They're lighter. Shit, did the pepper spray do that?" She stumbled backward, lowering herself into a comfy, her face pale, her eyes wide in horror. "I'm so sorry, Nerx. I never once considered what the spray could do to your physiology."

He was too stunned to respond. Her body trembled, even her bottom lip, and a suspicious sheen of moisture filled her eyes. He didn't like her so distraught. She was strong, bold, and not a cowering female, not by any standard. Yet, he couldn't lie to her and say she hadn't caused his eyes to pale when she had.

"Your pepper spray did not do this, Britta." He kneeled before her, raising his hand to brush the tears slipping down her cheeks. He tried to be gentle and must have failed when her breath caught. Her gaze met his.

"It didn't?" Before him sat a young woman in need of reassurance, in need of...him.

The feeling was indescribable, that she could *need* him. But telling her the truth was so risky when much rested on her accepting him. Still, it was dishonorable to lie.

"No, finding my Dar Eth did."

"You found a lover?" Her expression hardened.

He chuckled. "Dar Eth does not mean 'lay.'"

"Then what *is* it? What is Aldur doing with my mom?" Her chest rose and fell with her agitation. Her fingers crushed the fabric of her tunic.

"Spending time with her."

"Good, I guess, but I'm still confused. Does Dar Eth mean companion? And if so, do you have another woman on board?" Her eyes narrowed, with her thoughts flitting across them. She was wondering why she'd yet to meet his woman.

"Yes, a close companion, as in inseparable. And no, no other woman. Just you," he said despite the gravel texture to his voice. His other hand shook when he brought it up to caress her collarbone.

"Me?" Her lips parted; the dark pink depths of her mouth called to him. "But you hate me."

He focused on the spots splattered across her cheeks. "I feel many things for you, Britta, but hate is not one of them."

"Oh." She hesitated then brushed her fingertips over his eyebrow.

He shivered, unable to prevent the reaction from slipping through his defenses. Her touch was better than when she'd cupped his cheek in medical. He'd been too angry to cherish that moment. He gripped her hip. She was so soft. *Alodon's balls, she tempts me.*

She leaped to her feet, sprawling him backward. "What the hell does that mean? A companion for a short while, for this trip?" She danced away to pace in the tight confines. "I can handle a casual affair. But my mom... I will not have her hurt, Nerx. I won't stand for it. Sure, she's happy now, but if Aldur's hoping for something short and sweet, it's not happening. Does she know his intentions?" Britt rested her fists on her hips and glared at him. "Spill, Supreme Commander Nerx. Tell me exactly what being a Dar Eth means."

"There is nothing casual about Eths and Dar Eths." He grinned, enjoying how her mind worked. "According to Etterian law, when you triggered the Ethera in me and my eye color changed, you became my wife."

She squeaked, threw back her hand to catch the bulkhead, then slid down. "What?" she whispered.

With her obscured by comfys, he stood, not wanting to miss her expressions. "For an eternity. Etterians do not divorce."

She gaped at him. "No effing way."

"Your term would be soulmate, though it does not encapsulate all you invoke in me."

"Right," she muttered. "So my mother and I don't get a say? Our opinions don't matter?" She scrambled to her feet to shove her face into his. "I'm stuck with you?"

"Yes," he said.

"And when were you going to tell me?" Again, she met his gaze, not backing down.

"The Ethera does not like delays, driving lust through me even as it builds the bond between us. It would have been soon." He rubbed his jaw. "I cannot harm Lily."

Britta's puzzlement knitted her brow. Without thinking, he ran a fingertip over the creases, soothing them.

She swatted his hand away. "Why would Lily get hurt?"

"If you reject me, which is a possibility after what we have been through, I will..." He sucked in a sharp breath. "Die."

She gaped, closed her mouth, then sank into a comfy. "How?"

"As my Dar Eth, you save me from the emotionless void building in my chest since birth. If you do not stay with me, the Ethera, along with the void, will drive me to sacrifice my life in some sort of battle." He met her gaze, trying to judge her expressions. Yet failed. "Just to *feel* anything."

"So, each Etterian has a ticking time bomb inside them?" She arched a brow, asking him to confirm she understood correctly.

"Yes, in a way."

"Just this morning, you and I weren't sympatico." She winced, no doubt remembering her accusations. "So why me, Nerx?"

"I do not know. We have no annals that explain the Ethera, how it chooses, or its effects. All I know, when I am not near you, thoughts of you consume me. When I am in your presence, it is like basking in sunlight."

"But you hate me." She shook her head, sending her hair swirling around her. "I've said that already, and you claim you don't, but hatred doesn't just fizzle out."

"I admit I was angry, yes, but I understand why you attacked me. Your mother is your only blood-bond, yours to guard, as Lily and now you are mine."

She exhaled, slumping her shoulders. "So, if I buy into this soulmate stuff, what's next?"

"Dinner," he said. "Despite everything within me wanting to know you intimately—"

Her eyes widened, and her heartbeat skittered, pounding loud enough that he need not sharpen his hearing to listen.

"We take it slow." He grimaced. Already, the Ethera demanded he claim her. The only times it hadn't was when she'd cupped his jaw or poked his chest. "If you touch me often, I can resist the compulsion despite the pain."

"Pain?" she yelped. "Aldur—"

"Should be suffering too. There is no cure, only consummation can 'heal' me."

"Sex?" She laughed, her expression incredulous. "Talk about the worst pick-up line I've heard. Fuck me so I don't die?"

He growled. Not needing her to add dirty talk and its imagery to his already strained control. He strode toward her. She inclined back, squaring her shoulders but meeting his gaze. Leaning over her to bring his face inches from hers, he gripped the comfy's armrests, sliding his thumbs between her thighs and the upholstery.

"I have had visions of your body," he glanced down, lingering on the curve of her breasts, "beneath me. Here, now, it is taking every ounce of my strength not to kiss you again."

Her lips parted, her cheeks glowed peach, then her gaze shifted to his mouth.

"Britta," he warned.

She cleared her throat. "Yes, dinner sounds good."

When she cupped his hands, his world tilted. Peace descended, the agony faded, but lust weakened his knees.

"Is that helping?" she asked, her expression innocent.

When he didn't respond, his tongue tied, she slid her soft fingers along his forearms. It was as if she ran Eiltur fur over his skin.

He squeezed his eyes shut for a moment, wanting so much to close the distance between them, to taste her lips. "The pain...is gone," he rasped, gritting his teeth at the partial lie. The Ethera had ceased its demands, but now his malehood throbbed.

"Good." She shifted in the comfy, her breasts jiggling.

This was foolishness, placing himself in this situation. He should succumb, force her to accept him sooner. She liked the look of him, found him desirable. That mattered to humans.

"Nerx? You all right?" she asked.

He met her gaze, then smiled. Yes, he was more than 'all right.' "Dinner in the common?" That seemed safest.

"Sure."

He pushed off, sending himself away from her too-tempting lips. "See you in an hour."

Exiting Aldur's quarters, he leaned against the bulkhead, drawing strength from its cool Maloidian steel. *Maker, that was close.* That she'd willingly touched him sent warmth through him. She wasn't opposed to being his. He just prayed the Ethera would be happy with that for now.

Chapter Ten

Britta stared at the door. Her fingers tingled from touching him, her thoughts whirled, while her emotions danced around like jumping beans. What the hell had just happened?

Dar Eths, soulmates, voids, and sex? Sure, trust her mind to lock onto the last item. She shivered. Who was she kidding? Sex with Nerx would be mind-blowing. She had no doubts about that.

Still, to be his forever? She didn't have a choice, and neither did he, by the looks of things. This Ethera-thing had chosen by changing his eye-color? She called bullshit. Part of her wanted to flip her finger at fate's interference. She didn't appreciate anyone but herself deciding her future. Another part whispered that he'd never have looked at her twice if it wasn't for this stupid soulmate shit. And despite his protestations otherwise, he hated her guts, so this switch was...unnatural. But it was different for Mom. She and Aldur hadn't fought from first sight. Quite the opposite. A firehose would've come in handy.

Britt swallowed a hysterical giggle. Should she warn Mom or let Aldur tell her in his time?

She was torn. Not once had she interfered with Mom and Dad's relationship. Doing so now with Aldur when Nerx had said they're already married would be awkward. But if Mom found out Britt had known all along and hadn't said anything? Groaning, she rose then swayed, her knees weak.

Nerx, a sexy-as-sin Etterian, the very man she'd pepper sprayed and tazed, was her husband? She gulped, her stomach rising to choke her. No white wedding for her. No declarations of love. Just an instant husband and family.

Bright joy exploded like fireworks in her chest. Lily was her daughter now.

Laughing, she tried not to think about her kidnapping accusations. How had Nerx not lost his temper? That man might just be strong enough to handle her sass. She smirked. Tonight, she'd test his acceptance of her. There was no way she'd hide that part of her from him. She was who she was, and if he didn't like her that way, he could eff right off.

Why wasn't she super pissed about all this? Had she changed from the Kev incident? She prodded her soul. Was it because Nerx was as trapped as she was? Wait a minute, no way would she trust his word without question. She'd done some dumb things once or twice... Okay, maybe many times. But he couldn't spin some story and expect her to suck it up like a gullible idiot.

After yanking on leggings and slippers, she marched through the common to her old quarters but hesitated at the door. Rolling her shoulders back, she walked in then released a grateful sigh at finding Mom not in Aldur's arms.

"Aldur, could I speak to you...please." Britt hitched a thumb at the door. They could 'chat' in the passage.

"Britt?" Mom frowned.

"I need him to show me something in his quarters," she lied.

"Oh, of course, Lady Britta." Aldur placed a tablet on the table and ushered her out, shutting the door behind him.

"Just Britt will do, Aldur, considering that Mom's your Dar Eth."

He froze and released a long breath. "Nerx told you? And you are not furious?"

"I should be with this Etterian nonsense."

"I understand why you might think it so. If you bear with me, I shall explain. We were unruly warriors centuries ago, killing each other without care. Our king at that time approached a superior race known as the Durn. They engineered our genetics to calm our more volatile natures. The Ethera came into being. At first, all was well. Then fewer females were birthed, which impacted the number of matings. Until Princess Oriana, Dar Eths were considered a myth." He glanced at the door. "Not anymore."

His ice blue eyes did match Nerx's, when just a few days ago, his had been a dark blue like Ziot and Sena's. She folded her arms across her chest, trying to squelch the truth cinching her heart. "Why haven't you told my mom?"

"I do not know how. And I cannot lose her. For a warrior as old as I, to find my Dar Eth is a gift beyond measure." He glanced at the closed door. "She is incredible, Lady Britta."

"Britt," she said. "What will happen if you never tell her?"

He jerked back. "Etterians do not lie or deceive; it is dishonorable. To do either might cost me a foot of my hair."

A race that doesn't lie? She fought a snort and won. "Your hair?" *What an odd thing to value.*

"Yes, it is an outward indication of our obedience, discipline, teamwork, and authority. Only *damu...*" He met her gaze. "Your word would be children. They are still earning their honor." He flicked his braid and caught its tail to run his thumb over it. "I must tell her. The Ethera demands we mate." He offered a smile. "I never expected it to be this potent—the emotions she summons in me. Nor did I know the Ethera would be so merciless."

So far, he'd confirmed everything Nerx had said. "And when she touches you?"

His expression became dreamy. "It eases the pain the Ethera inflicts, but to kiss her is beyond my ability to endure." He cleared his throat. "You do not mind that we are—"

"Married?" Britt teased. "You better tell her soon, Aldur. Omission is deception."

He stared at her. "You speak truth. Shall we head to my quarters now?"

She laughed. "No, I lied to get you out here. Once you tell her, then we'll have nothing to hide from her. One more thing. What will happen if she rejects you?"

His eyes darkened with sadness. "I die. The void will grow until it consumes what makes me Etterian. I will become reckless, desperate to feel a drop of joy. Death would be a kindness."

He abandoned her, returning to Mom. Britt had no doubt he'd be spilling everything soon enough. So, all true and an insight into how Nerx suffered. Right. So she could throw a tantrum, act as if the universe conspired against her, or she could embrace this. Rejecting Nerx meant he'd die and orphan Lily.

Britt's heart twanged, and tears pressed at the backs of her eyes. This was a horrible predicament. It wasn't fair. After decades of studying planet after planet, she'd hoped to, at least, meet a biologist. She'd wanted the meet-cute, dates, wild sex, and love confessions or the minimum mutual affection. Instead, she had this. Although, dinner tonight could be considered a date if she treated it as such. And she couldn't get a cuter meet-cute than tazing her future-husband. She swallowed a giggle. Sure, the stuff of romantic comedies everywhere.

Should she wear something fancy? She nibbled on her lip while entering Aldur's old quarters. Starting on the right foot might be wise, but she didn't want to look like she tried too hard. For her husband, she should be giving their relationship her all. She'd do that for a boyfriend, why not for Nerx?

She ran her hands from her waist to her hips. Something slinky would have her 'beneath' him sooner. She shivered. *Oh, yes, please.* Or another kiss or four. She could settle for that. Browsing the clothes available had her choosing a cocktail dress. A sleeveless blue silk body-contour, with a plunging neckline, ended just above her knees. Simple, stylish, and not too sexy. A sheer demi bra in sky blue lace with matching G-string were next. Navy blue three-inch peep-toe mules would complete the outfit. Since she'd be crossing the common and not walking along their metal-grated passages, these shoes should do fine.

After a quick shower, she diligently stood under the wind tunnel to dry. She studied her reflection in the mirror above the basin. Her hair fell in curls to her shoulders, with amazing volume when she had yet to brush it. Her skin glowed as if she moisturized regularly—she didn't. Underwear was easy to put on, sliding into the dress a little trickier, but zipping it up the back...

Shit. After huffing and wiggling, she got it halfway up, then slumped into the chair. Slipping the mules on gave her a sense of accomplishment even though she wasn't ready.

The door chimed. It had never done that.

"Enter," she called, praying the visitor wouldn't mind helping her.

When the door stayed closed, she crossed to it, careful not to take too-wide steps lest she tore the dress.

Nerx stood before her in his military uniform and big boots. Lily chatted to Ziot by the rehydrator.

"I need your help." Britt grabbed Nerx by the arm and yanked him inside.

He said nothing but ran his gaze up and down her body, lingering on her cleavage and bare toes.

"Nerx." She stomped her foot.

He whipped his gaze to hers. "You look magnificent."

Heat warmed her cheeks at his compliment, and his stunned reaction boosted her confidence. "Thanks." She spun and offered her back. "Please zip me closed. I can't reach."

His breath hitched. Warm fingers snuck between the fabric and her skin to clasp her waist. He tugged her against his chest while sliding his hands around to her belly. Nudging her hair aside with his chin, he feathered his nose from her earlobe down her neck to her collarbone.

"Do you wear this for me?" he asked, his voice like butter along her senses.

"Yes," she said, unable to think of something clever to say.

"*Ensa*," he growled. "It is not wise to tempt me so." He pulled away to stroke the back clasp of the bra. "And this?"

"Lingerie," she said when she should have said 'bra.' Yes, she was playing with fire and loving every moment of it.

"Maker," he rasped. Spinning her to face him, he settled his fingers at the top of the dress, threatening to pull it down to expose her. He skimmed the silk to her cleavage then up, his touch feathering along her skin. "I ache to rip this off you."

She swallowed hard. Damn, if she didn't want to arch into him. He peeled the silk away a little, revealing a sliver of lace.

His nostrils flared, something like the gruff of a bear lodged in his throat—the sexiest sound she'd ever heard. Again he turned her. With one tug, the zip was up and he was rushing her to the door.

A sense of loss cocooned her heart, as if disappointment and yearning had taken up residence there. She forced a smile and let Nerx guide her across the common with his hand burning the base of her spine through the silk.

"Oh, you look so pretty." Lily clapped.

"Why thank you, Lily," Britt said and slid onto the bench beside her. "What's for dinner?"

"Pizza," she squealed.

Nerx was already ordering from the rehydrator, his back ramrod, his ass glorious in his military pants. Why hadn't Britt noticed that before?

"Please, excuse me," Edon said, abandoning them with a pained expression and a grumble.

"See. I do stink," Britt said to Nerx when he placed a small pizza in front of Lily.

"I can smell you," he whispered, holding her gaze.

Britt sniffed her shoulder. She was a little hot and sweaty but not so much that it would drive a man away. "I did shower."

"No." A sexy smile curled Nerx's lips. "Your arousal."

She gasped, snuck a glance at a distracted Lily, then said, "You can't be serious."

"Indeed. What would you like to eat?"

She shifted on the bench, trying to ease the burn between her thighs. No wonder these poor men were in pain. "Tagliatelle Alfredo, please."

Again, he blessed her with the fine view of his ass before setting a deep bowl of pasta before her. He joined them moments later with a steak bathed in dark sauce.

"Yours looks yummy," Lily said to Britt.

"I'm sure it is. Wanna try some?" She twirled a little on her fork and offered it to Lily.

Britt laughed when a piece of pasta slapped the girl on the chin. She smeared the sauce off and popped her thumb into her mouth. She hummed at the rich creamy flavor. *So good.* "Do you like it?"

Lily beamed. "I want that next, Nerxie."

"Very well, *minus susa*," he said, though his gaze remained on Britt, watching as she spiraled pasta onto her fork and shoved it into her mouth.

"What are you eating?" She smirked as she said, "Nerxie."

He stilled, his eyes glowed, then he focused on his plate. "Kreso meat with momaberry sauce." When he met her gaze again, something intense pooled in the depths of his eyes.

Heat rushed to warm her cheeks, and she choked on her pasta. "Something to drink?" she said, leaping to reach the rehydrator.

"I will get it," he said.

They slammed into each other. Without hesitation, he looped his arms around her and took the brunt when they bumped into the counter. Pressed against his length, every one of his hard edges registered. He was solid muscle with strength pouring off him. She reacted on a visceral level; her thoughts faded, drowned by sexual urges. Like seeing him shirtless yesterday, all bronze-skinned and glistening, his muscles rippling. She'd swallowed her tongue, unable to say a word. Forever, the sheer masculinity of him would be imprinted in her memories.

"Water, please," she whispered when he righted her, his fingers skimming over her hips.

On shaking knees, she returned to Lily, who was her cheerful self, humming to the fourth pizza slice she nibbled on. He placed a small pink milkshake and a bottle of water on the table, then returned for a cup of pale-yellow liquid.

While sipping his beverage, he peered at Britt over the rim. His eyes promised something sensual. Not wanting to finish her water in case she forgot again how to chew, she picked at her meal, her appetite for food gone.

She tried to hide her trembling fingers while sipping from the bottle, but his sex-appeal rattled her. "Hopscotch tomorrow, right?" she asked Lily.

"Yes, please." With boundless energy, Lily bounced, almost spilling the milkshake in her hand. Thankfully, she slid the shake onto the table before Britt had to lunge for it.

"Good, if Nerxie can spare Ziot." Britt offered him an innocent smile.

"I will join you, *minus cesu*," he said, his voice hoarse.

"Yay," Lily squealed, jumping off the bench to dance across the blue mat. She didn't hide her yawn when she climbed up beside Britt minutes later.

"Hand in front of your mouth," Britt said, tugging Lily against her.

She nodded even as she nuzzled into Britt's side.

"I hear it's quite a long journey to reach Etteria," she said, then swallowed hard at the heated expression Nerx leveled on her.

She wanted to fan herself or empty the water bottle down her cleavage. She'd read somewhere that space was cold; well, she was far from it.

"Fourteen days."

"And I used to complain when something took longer than fourteen minutes to drive to." She smiled. "Aldur told me about your hair." All right, she was desperate for safe topics. Especially when Nerx stared at her like he'd been doing since he'd seen her in this dress.

He caught his braid and unclipped it. "*Malia pado.*"

She gaped when it began to unravel itself until it swayed around him as if he was underwater. "It moves?" she whispered. Squeezing her eyes shut as if she was seeing things, she opened them to the same scene. "It's beautiful." She caught a strand, then squeaked when it wrapped around her wrist like silk sashes caressing her.

His chuckle was husky. "It likes you."

"Oh?" She arched a brow, meeting his gaze before hastily looking away. "How can you tell?"

"It is trying to draw you closer." He cleared his throat. "To me."

Yup, it was, tugging on her wrist as if to drag her across the table. Visions of his hair tying her hands and feet to the bedposts dried her throat and sent a spasm of pleasure to her core.

"*Malia pa,*" he said then waited as it rebraided itself. He caught the ends and clipped it.

"Um, thank you...for showing me." She took a gulp of water.

"Come, it is time for bed."

"What?" she gasped, a warm flutter exploding from her chest to much, much lower.

He scooped a sleeping Lily into his arms, his hands brushing parts of Britt in passing. Alone in the common, she stared at the table. Just like that, dinner was over. No goodnight kiss for her, but the 'date' had been a decent start. Not once had they argued. She cleared the leftovers, tossing them into the waste receptable before heading to her quarters.

Once inside, she leaned against the door while kicking off her heels. Her efforts hadn't gone unappreciated. Though, she doubted she'd be able to sleep anytime soon. With a cry, she spun on a heel and opened the door...to Nerx.

"Thank goodness. I..." She hitched a thumb at her back. "I need to be unzipped."

He crossed the threshold, nudging her aside. She offered him her back and waited. Nothing happened. Peeking at him over her shoulder froze her in place. A tsunami of need crashed against her resistance, crumbling it. That intensity was still in his narrowed eyes. His nostrils flared, his jaw clenched.

He gripped her zip and ripped it down, cool air rushing across her shoulder blades.

"What's wrong?" she asked, facing him.

"Wrong?" he rasped. "You in this garment, your undergarments, that footwear, and scenting of arousal while calling me Nerxie?" Each step he took pushed her back until she bumped her ass against a wall.

She grinned. "Yup, well, Nerxie has a nice ring to it."

"Oh." A wicked smile twitched his lips. "When I want you screaming it. Demanding I thrust harder, faster."

She swallowed past the lump in her throat even as her cheeks burned. Okay, maybe testing his boundaries wasn't such a good idea. He splayed his hands beside her ears, trapping her in the circle of his arms. His focus remained on her face, not once dipping to her cleavage.

"These dots fascinate me," he said, before pressing a soft kiss to her cheek.

This close, his cologne filled her nose, warmed by his skin and smelling of wildflowers, damp soil, and apples. She ached to feel him against her, to have his mouth on hers. Unable to hold off any longer, she closed the distance, pinning her chest to his even as she gripped his braid and pulled, arching his throat. He stiffened, but she was too gone to care. She feathered a kiss along his Adam's apple to under his jaw, the taste of his skin addictive.

He growled, lowered his arms and crushed her against him. "Do that again," he demanded.

She did, then followed it with a sweep of her tongue.

He shuddered. "Britta, please…"

She dug her fingers into his pecs and hooked a leg over his thigh. "Kiss me, Nerxie."

When he leaned back to slash his lips across hers, her senses sang. He didn't hesitate to dominate her mouth. She couldn't keep up, could only cave to his kissing abilities. *Damn.* Air? What was that? To hell with breathing.

Without breaking the kiss, he grasped her under a knee, his touch hot and potent. With his other hand, he buried his fingers in her hair, his palm holding her cheek. This was the stuff of romance covers. She clung to his biceps, bending into him to give him access to her neck when he broke the kiss and ran his soft lips to her earlobe. He nipped her there, shooting bolts of sensations lower.

Her breasts swelled, aching for his exploration. She whimpered, unable to voice how desperate she wanted to be beneath him.

A vibration traveled along his forearm and into her cheek. He froze, groaned, then held his temple to hers while he fought for breath. "Alodon's balls, what now?" He tightened his arms around her, grasping her across her bare back.

"What's wrong?" she asked.

"I have been summoned to the comm."

"Is that bad?" She straightened, sliding her leg down his within his tight embrace.

"Let us hope not." He huffed. "I do not want to leave you."

"I'm not going anywhere." She cupped his jaw to run her thumb over his chin.

He flashed her a smile, dimpling his left cheek.

She blinked, dazzled by his beauty. No man had the right to look this good.

"Give me five minutes." He released her and bolted for the door, then paused when it opened to toss her a heated look. "Do not change."

She squealed when she was alone. This was insane. They'd hated each other just yesterday, and now she was on the cusp of getting laid...by her husband. She hurried to the bathroom to check her reflection then marvel at her flushed cheeks, sparkling and lust-filled eyes, kiss-swollen lips, and heaving breasts, thanks to her ragged breathing. The dress gaped, flashing a little sky-blue lace. Nice.

She twisted, checking how amazing she looked from the side too. Best decision she ever made.

She chuckled, almost gleefully rubbing her palms together.

Chapter Eleven

Nerx splayed his fingers on Britta's closed door, trying to wrangle in a decent breath, while willing his Fuyra-hard malehood to quit throbbing. *Alodon's balls, if this is not important, I am going to kill Edon.* With murder in mind, he sprinted to the comm room.

"You had better have valid reason—" Nerx stumbled to a stop at the sight of a battleship dominating the display vids.

It was like nothing he'd ever seen. Despite having the sheen of Maloidian steel, it was a deep metallic blue. An elongated code to a point made it clear which was its bow from its stern. A glowing green came from the far end—perhaps their propulsion engines? Tiny lights scattered across its jagged surface, as if they were windows. Narrow slits shone white.

"Did you hail it?" Nerx asked, not wanting to blink.

"Yes, and had Ziot begin a full scan."

"No response?" He frowned. "No identification markings?"

"None to both. And they are blocking our comms." Edon threw Nerx a glance. "We will have no assistance from our battleships should we need it."

Maker. Isolated, vulnerable, with two Dar Eths and a *damu* on board? Nerx gritted his teeth. "Comm the king."

The display vid didn't even flicker. No connection formed.

"The comm stations?" Edon stiffened. "Do you think this thing—"

"Let us not leap to conclusions, Pilot Edon." Nerx sucked in a shuddering breath, then touched his O.D.I. "Ziot, are you able to read—"

"Yes, Supreme Commander."

"Which means they can scan us. I will hide the humans in the engine room, close to the power source. Perhaps they do not know how many are on board. Sub-Commander

Matir, Ziot, and Sena, get down here." Nerx studied the star charts on the display vids while racking his brain for solutions. He waited for his males to arrive, then granted them a few seconds to gape at the battleship before saying, "Edon and Ziot will pilot while gathering what data you can. Matir and Sena, I need you on the viewing deck, directly above this position. If anything happens to us, you two can fly this ship to Etteria, saving the females...and Lily."

He spun and tapped a panel, opening a mini armory. Blasters, swords, daggers, spare med-guns made their way to various parts of their anatomy. He carried an extra blaster for Britta. He'd rather have her armed than vulnerable.

"Surely a male guarding the females would be wiser?" Matir asked while arming himself. "After all, the engine room can hide more than a few heat signatures."

"True, but what if you are injured defending the females? Who will fly the ship?"

"If we are killed as the last bastion, then the scimitar and the females are lost. I will guard them. Double tap your O.D.I. should you need aid. Sena, stay in the viewing deck. That will place you closest to the comm. Aldur will remain in medical as expected of a medic."

"A good plan. I concur." Nerx placed his palm above Matir's heart. "May the Maker bless us." With Matir trailing him, Nerx raced to the officer's quarters. He barged in, uncaring in what state he might find the pair. "Aldur, arm yourself. Lady Dahlia, with me."

"What is it?" she asked, looking up from her tablet.

Aldur squeezed past Nerx to reach the common where additional weapons were stored.

"Matir will explain." Nerx crossed to Britta's door where moments ago his only concern was claiming her.

He entered and held out the blaster, grateful that she was still in the dress and not naked. Although, that imagery would be something he'd die for. "An unknown battleship approaches; it will be passing too close to this scimitar. I need to hide you and Lily." He glanced at Lady Dahlia, clutching a tablet to her chest. "And your mother. Take the blaster. Tap the yellow for stun, red to kill, and do not touch the white." He ran his thumb along a slider, setting stun to maximum. "Come, let me close your garment."

She offered him her back. Her skin looked so soft that he stroked a finger from the nape of her neck to the base of her spine. She clutched the blaster to her chest but said nothing, despite the tiny bumps forming. Sighing, he guided the zip up.

"Go, get Lily," she said, brushing past him to reach her mother.

Fetching Lily, still bundled in her pink blanket, was the easy part. With her in his arms, Britta, Dahlia, and Aldur followed Matir through the locked door to the shuttle bay, storerooms, and engine room beyond.

Britta shivered. The engines released warmth, so none of them would be cold for long. She didn't barrage Nerx with questions he couldn't answer. For that, he was grateful. In the engine room, he took them to the closest fusion drive at the center of the grated floor—its pulse hummed too loud for his ears. Other drives lined the walls with conduits traveling between them, fueling each other. More tubes networked across the bulkheads and ceiling for sol harvesting.

"I apologize," Nerx muttered. "It will not be comfortable to hide here, but I need them not to know you are on board."

"Makes sense," Britta said, gesturing for him to lower Lily into the only comfy available—locked in place in front of the diagnostic console. His daughter didn't stir when he did so.

While Aldur hugged Lady Dahlia, Nerx took Britta aside.

"Not where I wanted to be," she said, offering him a shaky smile.

"Indeed." He cupped her cheek, pressed a kiss to her temple, then crushed her in a hug, taking a second to inhale her scent. "I will collect you if all goes well."

"And if it doesn't?"

"Matir and Aldur will protect you."

She tapped her bare foot on the floor and tried to fold her arms with the blaster in the way. If their situation wasn't so serious, he'd smile, at least.

"And if they die? I don't know how to fly anything, Nerx."

He caught her hand and ushered her to a panel. "Touch here at the side." It slid open to reveal a pod big enough for three Etterians. One of four on this ship. Its door shot up revealing two benches facing each other. "Inside is a white lever. Buckle Lily and your mother in, yank the lever down, then strap yourself in too. I *will* find you."

"Nerxie, I—" She swallowed and raised wide eyes.

"You, as a human, can survive my death, but I cannot exist without you." He brushed a kiss across her lips. "Lily is yours now."

Britta glanced at their daughter, squared her shoulders, and nodded. "You better be all right, or so help me, Nerx, pepper spray will be the least of the things I'll do to you."

He laughed. "It will not matter if I am dead."

She glared at him, despite a teardrop forming on her lashes. "Just...live, okay?"

He hesitated, not wanting to promise he'd survive this. It would be a lie when he had no idea what could happen. Aldur strode to the engine room door, snagging Nerx's gaze. He touched the panel, shutting it—the thunk of the pod door confirmed it closed too.

"What will you do?" Britta asked, hurrying after him when he headed to Aldur.

Nerx glanced at her, memorizing her face in case it was for the last time. "Learn who they are and what they want. Listen to Matir, please. Now is not the time to be reckless."

She scoffed. "Attacking you was calculated."

He chuckled. "Fine, do not do anything calculated."

It took all his strength to walk away, the swish of the engine room door like a death knell. It didn't help that scalding pain radiated outward from the center of his chest. His future, everything that mattered to him, was behind him. Ahead lay trouble. He couldn't say how he knew this, but instinct drove him to be cautious. Rather have his family be safe than endanger them because he didn't anticipate and prepare for the unexpected, that worst case scenario. Thank the Maker for Matir's advice. If they lived through this, Nerx would recommend all his males for promotion.

Aldur grimaced, then withdrew his blaster. "I assume no help is forthcoming?"

"Yes." Nerx clenched his jaw as he headed for the comm.

"Nothing, Supreme Commander," Ziot said the moment he entered. "The scans are at twelve percent. This could take a while."

"Keep trying to comm the king or the nearest battleship, hell, the closest comm station will do. And do not change trajectory or increase the speed, Edon. I want nothing to alarm them." He stared at the ship, focusing on the massive canons running the length of every second row of lit rectangles, and the odd way the entire ship spun with its nose remaining static.

"It is most ominous," Aldur said. "Each canon is aimed at us. What kind of a threat do they think us? We are in a scimitar with but a few chokaars."

What if Etteria's most powerful canons couldn't compare to the might before them? How would Etteria defend the weaker races? "What are they waiting for?" Nerx asked the comm in general. "They could obliterate us, and no one would know."

"Perhaps we are first contact?" Ziot said, his fingers flying over the console. "The metal is a derivative of Maloidian steel but different. I do not know if a chokaar will have any impact."

"How different?" Nerx unsheathed a dagger and blinked at the blade. "We have never met an empire more powerful than Etteria."

His mind reeled. They'd lived invincible, perhaps overly confident. But they were honorable and appreciated culture, differences, and diversity. What if this new species didn't share their values? What if their agenda was to kill, to dominate, to destroy? Etteria, no matter how many ships Xeus had in his armada, might not be able to win if a war was on the horizon.

"Hail, strange ship." A delicate face with a square jawline flickered on the display vid.

Nerx blinked at what looked like an Etterian youngin except for the copper-scaled skin and shaven head. Black eyebrows denoted what the hair color would've been.

"Greetings, I am Supreme Commander Nerx," he said.

"Regent Kaara."

When they remained silent, Nerx asked, "Are you lost? From where do you travel?"

The regent laughed, his black eyes crinkling around the edges. "We are where we planned to be."

Behind him was a wall of lights, though the symbols denoting their purpose were unknown. Mechanical noises and chatter droned in the background. The purple armor he wore didn't reveal much either.

"Welcome, Regent Kaara." Nerx bowed. "It is not often I meet such a high-ranking personage."

"Flattery? How quaint." Kaara held up a thin finger, black rings as jewelry rested below each knuckle.

So much for diplomacy, though Nerx had never claimed to be good at it. "How may we assist?"

"I grow weary of this conversation," the regent said. "Prepare to be boarded."

Nerx scowled. "For what purpose?"

The display vid went black.

"This is not promising." Aldur held the blaster to his chest.

That was an understatement. What could Nerx do? To deny them access could start a war with an unknown species and their untested capabilities. But to allow them entry might endanger Britta and Lily.

He rubbed a hand across his face. "Send the hatch co-ordinates, Edon."

"Wise. A narrow entry point and far from the engine room." Aldur nudged his head at the common. "I will wait in medical."

A speck shot out of a lit slit, aiming for the scimitar's port side.

"If we run, where to?" Nerx gripped the back of Edon's comfy.

"An asteroid belt is not too far. We might lose them there. A battleship cannot navigate through it."

"Unless they launch fighter craft." Pain pulsed up Nerx's neck to throb behind his eye. "No nearby planet?"

"The gas giant Aberdus is close enough. Though flying into its volatile atmosphere may not be wise."

"All right. First chance we get, bolt for the asteroid belt. Perhaps we will be out of range of their comm dampener and can call for aid." He stepped into the passage. "Seal yourself inside the comm room. And activate all sec vids. If the ship survives and we do not, then whoever finds it will know why."

Striding to the common felt like a sentencing, with a waiting Adviser Kanzo sharpening his sword to slice off a foot of Nerx's hair. His boots thumped when his approach should have been silent. Not knowing what to expect cinched his chest tight. He couldn't plan, couldn't anticipate, which meant dealing with this blindsided. They didn't train for this, and should he survive, he'd suggest a change to the curriculum on Gikaet.

Facing the external hatch in the common, he spread his legs, clasped his hands behind his back, and waited. His hearing prickled, picking up every sound: the steady hum of the engines, the movement of air along the ducting, and Aldur's faint inhalations. The clunk from the outside of the scimitar boomed in his ears. He didn't flinch.

The hatch slid open to the bright white interior of a shuttle of some sort. Soft benches lined each side; the smooth surface of the floor and the padded bulkhead said luxury. Still, four blue-suited individuals filed into the common to circle him. Their features were hidden behind tinted helmets, elongated in the back to connect to a pack at the base of what he would imagine was their spines. Two legs and two arms made their physiology seem similar to Etterians. They were almost as tall, yet far too slender.

He said nothing, hoping to appear unbothered by their intrusion.

"This is what they fear," a cloaked male strode into the common and spun to grimace at the interior. "Way too primitive for my tastes."

"Welcome," Nerx gritted out, then frowned at the fruity fragrance tickling his nose.

"Supreme Commander, is it not?" Purple armor accentuated a body hardened by war or the preparation of it. Yet his face was too...soft, as if he had yet to reach malehood. That they sent their youngins into battle said much about their mindset. "Primary Shioll, though my name should be of no consequence to one such as you."

"How may I assist, Primary Shioll?" Nerx asked, forcing his shoulders to relax.

"I have been tasked to 'introduce' your people to mine." The smile he offered Nerx curled with enough venom to confirm his instincts had been correct.

He glanced at the warriors, their odd-shaped blasters no doubt lethal. Dipping his head in a bow, he said, "I am Etterian and, on behalf of the Global Council, welcome you to our universe."

"*Your* universe?" Again, derision drenched Shioll's almost-lyrical voice.

"Well, we do share it with many species and cultures. You will find we are quite diverse and at peace, for the most part."

Shioll's laugh sounded like sucking noises instead of huffs. "Peace we despise for it does not force change, Supreme Commander."

"True, but to constantly battle cannot build the might of an empire." Nerx relaxed his arms by his sides, close enough to reach for his blaster. "War needs warriors, does it not?"

Shioll jerked back. "You still *birth* your young?"

Nerx clenched his fists, the only outward sign of his irritation. This male had yet to attend to his imperial task, and the sooner he did so, the quicker he could leave the scimitar. "And you are?"

"Viqrian." Shioll clasped his left forearm, below the elbow, then released it in some sort of salute. "On behalf of Regent Kaara, the ruler of the *Bronvol*, we demand you submit to our superiority and give us your planet."

As he struggled to focus, anger burned Nerx's nostrils. He choked down the retort curling his tongue. "I am a supreme commander," he managed. "You will need to address your demands with my king."

"I see, then escort us to your king."

What madness is this? "Why would I lead you to my homeworld?"

"For my regent to negotiate with your king." Shioll shrugged.

"No, when a comm will do." What firepower did this battleship have? No, he refused to endanger his Etteria.

"We expected you to resist." Shioll flicked out his cloak in a mini-tantrum Nerx had seen the children do. "I am to insist by leaving a message only Etterians will understand." He raised a finger with fewer black rings adorning it.

His Viqrian males closed in on Nerx, who shook his head when Aldur tapped the red of his blaster. Two Viqrians grabbed Nerx. He hesitated before letting them twist his arms behind his back. They forced him to kneel. He didn't fight them, unworried about dying, as long these males never ventured into the engine room.

Shioll unsheathed a dagger from his boot and approached. "Something as silly as your hair has importance to you?" He scoffed. "For us, the shorter it is, the higher the rank. Surely as supreme commander, yours should reflect as much."

Nerx stilled, heat sliding down his spine at the threat. He clenched his jaw, not willing to offer any information. Besides, Shioll had revealed how much he knew of Etteria and their culture. When he'd been sent to introduce his kind? Wanted to negotiate with King Xeus? The sentences implied diplomacy yet something seemed...off.

Shioll tugged on Nerx's braid, tucking the shimmering blue dagger under it. Aldur roared a battle cry any battle-bond would be proud of. The remaining two Viqrians turned as one. Despite Aldur's blaster shot nicking one Viqrian's shoulder, they fired, forcing Aldur to dive behind the med-E.D. A gasp and his slumped body sucked the air from Nerx's lungs. No, his soul cried out. Aldur couldn't die, not when he'd just discovered his Dar Eth.

He tried to focus on Aldur's breathing, his heartbeat, but with so many males around him, his attempts were futile. A Viqrian ventured into medical to nudge Aldur with his boot.

"Why?" Nerx demanded, shifting on his knees to make it easier to lunge at Shioll. "You have no right—"

"Search this ship," Shioll commanded his males except for the two still holding Nerx.

Fear seized his chest. He roared, wrenching his arms free. With a slash of the dagger, the glint on its steel the only warning, his braid pooled on the floor. He stared, unable to believe it. No. He couldn't deal with that now. Not when he had to stop them from finding the females. He wrapped his fingers around the hilt of his greatsword sheathed down his back. With one lunge, he cleaved two Viqrians in half. He held the tip of the blade to Shioll's throat but kept his focus on the remaining warriors. They had their blasters aimed at him.

With one command from Shioll, Nerx would die. He'd take Shioll with him, but that left those in his command and his females at the mercy of these Viqrians. Think. Could he take Shioll hostage? Force them to leave the scimitar? He was outnumbered.

Movement to his left snapped his gaze. Horror, pure fear, and sorrow gripped him, far surpassing the loss of his hair. He shook his head, even as anger flooded his veins. These potent emotions bombarded him, stiffening his body while time slowed.

Britta marched into the common with the blaster yellow and ready.

Chapter Twelve

Just by Nerx's expression, Britt knew something was wrong. Handing her a gun confirmed it. The damn thing was heavy, but she didn't question why he'd given it to her. Rather be armed than sorry. She sucked in a sharp breath, her gaze fixed on Lily still fast asleep in the chair. Britt was tempted to carry her into the pod, strap her in, then let her sleep in safety. Here, she was still in the open, vulnerable.

Mom gasped, tapped her tablet, then cupped her mouth.

"What is it?" Britt crossed to her then leaned over her shoulder. Matir did so from the other side.

On the tablet, images played, of Nerx speaking to a man, whose soldiers circled him. That didn't look good, especially the way they clasped their guns, like law enforcement did back home. Movement in the medical snagged her gaze. Aldur tapped the yellow button and preparing to fire.

She glanced at the strangers, who hadn't yet noticed his presence.

Nerx was grabbed, his arms twisted behind his back, and forced to kneel while the man unsheathed a wicked-looking dagger. The way Nerx's braid was touched meant only one thing.

She froze, horror dawning. "No, not his hair." Losing it would devastate him. The pride on his face when he'd unclipped his braid revealed as much.

"Why not?" Mom asked.

"The length is a measurement of their honor, like a medal." Britt palmed the yellow button, not actually wanting to kill anyone, even a baddie. She hurried to the door. "I'm just going to peek, to make sure Aldur and Nerx don't need backup."

"Britt, no," Mom said, flicking a glance at Lily still fast asleep.

"I forbid it," Matir said, stomping toward her.

Britt scowled. No man forbade her from doing anything she damned well wanted to do. And Nerx losing his most precious hair was a hell-no in her book. "I can do this. Working at Stay Alive taught me much."

"On how to be stupid." Mom scoffed, her gaze on the tablet. "Nerx said to stay, and dammit, that's what we'll do."

"And watch him and Aldur die?" Britt planted her feet when Matir tried to nudge her out of the way without touching her.

"He's got everything under control," Mom said, but her voice quavered. Then she paled; the tablet almost tumbled from her hands. "They shot my Aldur."

Matir leaped across to confirm this on her tablet.

Now was Britt's chance. With him distracted, she opened the door and bolted, sidling along the side of the shuttle far from the common.

"Stop, Lady Britta, I beg you." Matir rushed after her, while casting glances ahead and behind them.

She ignored him, ducking between crates to listen for approaching footsteps. None came.

When Matir lunged for her, as if he had every intention of throwing her over his shoulder, she jabbed him with the muzzle of the gun. Right in his ribs. He grunted and staggered back, clutching his side. "This is foolhardy. You will only endanger yourself and the supreme commander. I also have my orders," he snapped.

"You're wasting precious moments." She slid over the crate. "Then come with me. Take down the one with a cape. Do something other than waste my time." She snuck through the door that had been sealed shut just yesterday, not even waiting to see if Matir followed. Along the short passage, she plastered herself to the wall, clasping the heavy gun and trying to keep her breathing quiet.

A peek locked her tongue in place. On the floor at Nerx's knees was his braid. Already his hair, now past his shoulder blades, darted out like knife points, as if in attack-mode. Then in slow motion, he lunged forward, a massive greatsword in hand, and swung, slicing the closest soldiers in half.

Blinking at the spilled guts and blue blood, she swallowed the bile pooling at the back of her throat. It was now or never. She strode into the common, hefting the gun.

Nerx's eyes widened. Fear contorted his expression. It was too late to rethink her life choices, so she shot twice. From hours of testing Stay Alive's demo weapons, her aim was true. When she spun her arm to stun the man who'd cut Nerx's hair, fire exploded in agonizing white heat in her side. She stumbled back when Matir ran past her, his gun extended. He shot once sending the purple dude flying. He sprawled on his back even as Nerx charged her.

"What did I say?" he roared at her. "And you, Sub-Commander? Willingly endangering my Dar Eth. I will have your hair for this."

She dismissed his anger while running an admiring gaze over him. The sword hung at his side as if it weighed nothing. Muscles bulged in his arm though. "He tried to stop me." She skimmed her fingers down his bicep, her touching not softening his scowl.

Mom scampered past to reach Aldur.

"Is he—?" Britt called, not taking her focus from Nerx. He'd swung that greatsword like an ancient warrior.

"He's breathing," Mom cried out, joy claiming her face even as her tears flowed.

"Matir, get Aldur in the med-E.D. We will discuss your disobedience later." Nerx caught Britt's free hand, then dragged her to the communications room. The door opened before they arrived.

"Edon, prepare to get us to the asteroid belt but do not hide. I want you to fly along its field, weaving between its largest debris. I do not want to find out firsthand what that ship's canons can do."

"Acknowledged, Supreme Commander." He stared at Nerx's hair, then spun on his seat to hit the many buttons on the console.

Nerx tapped his forearm, summoning holographics. "Sena, get down here. And you, my silly, brave Dar Eth, may have helped me start a war with an unknown race."

On the black screens was a scary-looking ship, like an ice pick with bits plastered to its pretty-blue sides. Gigantic tubes shaped like canons were easy to spot amid the flickering lights. Something cinched her chest. Had she really started a war with...that?

"Unknown? When they look Etterian? And to hell with war, Nerx. They attacked first when they shot Aldur and...y'know." She gestured to his head.

He barked a laugh that was by no means warm. "For Aldur, I would kill them again. For my hair... It is but a slight."

"I thought it mattered to you. Next time, I'll let them shave your stupid head." She huffed and slid the gun onto a nearby table. "And what did you expect me to do? Watch you die?"

His nose twitched, then he dropped his sword and yanked a black box out of a pants pocket. "I scent your blood, *ensa*."

"Oh." That's right. She'd been shot. Only now did the incessant pulsating pain register. She cupped her side and blinked at the red staining her palm. "They've ruined the silk," she muttered.

"Supreme Commander," Sena said from the doorway.

"Toss the dead into their shuttle except those stunned—lock them in an unallocated quarters in the barracks but make sure they know how the rehydrator works. We need them alive. And see if you can set their shuttle to return to its bay. Failing that, we need to jettison it off the scimitar and explode it. I can deny any involvement as the 'inferior' race." He grimaced at her when Sena left. "Your garment is not conducive to healing, *ensa*. I must remove it."

"Ninety-eight percent," Ziot said.

Nerx grunted, then hoisted Britt into his arms, one hand under her knees, the other above her wound.

"I can walk." Although, she was grateful. For some strange reason, her knees were weak.

Ignoring her, he carried her to Mom's quarters and waited at the door for Britt to palm it open. Once inside, he lowered her to her feet, then kneeled. He gripped the hem of the dress, his touch hot where he brushed her skin. With one yank, the silk split up the side. Cool air rushed in, sending a flood of goosebumps all over her body. She swayed as nausea blossomed in her stomach. Catching herself on his shoulder, she forced herself to inhale and exhale slowly while he ran the black box over her. His hair reached for her, the strands stroking any part of her they could reach.

"Foolish woman," he chided, sliding his fingers up her inner thigh to hold her still. "You could have died."

"So could you have." She squeezed her eyes shut and swallowed hard.

"I am trained for war."

Was he angry that a woman had come to his aid? "So I cannot save you?"

"No. You had one task, Britta. To protect Lily. Where is she now?" He flicked a glance at her, made sexier by his narrowed eyes.

"She's where you put her. And… And I didn't leave her alone." Her face flushed then chilled. Was this thing healing her or what?

He arched a brow at her, made more compelling by the beauty of the black-winged slash against bronzed skin. "I have to trust you to do as instructed. I cannot worry you will endanger yourself and *our* daughter."

Her heartbeat stilled then bounced. He *had* trusted her wholeheartedly to care for Lily, and she'd abandoned the girl the first chance she could. She opened her mouth then snapped it shut with a wince. "You're right. Lily comes first." She twitched her fingers. "Give me the device-thingy. Go get Lily before she wakes up alone."

He hesitated.

"Scan complete, Supreme Commander," Ziot said from Nerx's wrist. "The shuttle has launched and the hatch sealed."

"Good." Nerx stood and cupped Britt's cheek. "Aldur will complete the healing when the med-E.D. is done with him. You need synthetic skin to ensure no scarring."

He marched to the door. "Stay here. I mean it, Britta."

"Fine." She folded her arms across her chest and glared at the door after he left. The pressure crushing her chest didn't ease. Would those men have stopped at cutting Nerx's hair? Her instincts screamed no. Still, diplomacy had fallen to the way side. Her fault? Perhaps. But Nerx and Lily were alive. That was all that mattered.

She paced the quarters, wishing she could shower then wear something with a little more coverage. But doing so would put her at a disadvantage. Until they were far away from that battleship, she wouldn't chance a distraction.

When the door opened minutes later, Nerx carried a bundled Lily in his arms. He'd tucked the blanket over her face, probably to hide the carnage around them.

"Hello, sleepy head," Britt said, holding out her arms for him to transfer Lily. He did so without hesitation. She nuzzled the girl, tucked her face into the curve of her neck, then nudged her chin at the door. "I'll put her to bed. You deal with the rest of this."

"Oh?" A smirk teased his gorgeous mouth. "Stun two males then take a nap?"

She smiled. "I thought you wanted me not causing trouble? I could follow you—"

"No, you are wise to excuse yourself." He wrapped his arms around them both, snatching a kiss. "I shall come for you when we have escaped them."

"I'm sorry if we started a war, Nerx. That wasn't my intention when I rushed in." She met his gaze when he pulled away.

"I know, *ensa*." He stepped into the passage and waited for her to pass him.

She glanced over her shoulder then headed to the barracks.

Nerx's raised voice halted her. "What do you mean...gone?" he demanded, his focus on the common.

She peeked around the corner. Bodies still littered the floor. A glance confirmed Lily still asleep and shielded by the blanket.

Sena gestured to the hatch where the shuttle had been. "Medic Aldur, Lady Dahlia, and Sub-Commander Matir...are gone."

"Ziot," Nerx bellowed at the ceiling.

"Checking sec vids now." Seconds ticked past as they waited.

Britt held her breath as fear bathed her senses in ice. A deafening roar dominated her hearing like she was underwater, distorting and slowing sounds. No, no, no, Mom had returned to the engine room. She had to have. No way was she *not* on this ship. But Aldur not lying on the floor of the medical or dominating the big bed screamed otherwise. *My Aldur*, Mom had said. Nor would she have stepped into that shuttle willingly. Mom was the most reliable and predictable woman Britt knew.

"Nerx?" she squeaked past the tears she couldn't stem. "Not my mother."

"The vids reveal Primary Shioll forced Matir by blaster to carry Aldur into the shuttle. Lady Dahlia tried to stop him and threw herself into the shuttle before the hatch sealed."

Mom reckless? Britt snorted through the tears. That didn't sound like her at all. Still, how to get her back? What could they do? They'd be lucky to survive this. Perhaps going with Aldur had saved her life? Or it hadn't.

This ship was dead in the water if they couldn't hide. And firing upon it would be like shooting fish in a barrel.

"Edon, the asteroid belt now." Nerx met and held Britt's gaze.

"No," she whimpered, squeezing a sleeping Lily against her chest while crying into her blanket.

"I cannot fire upon the battleship, not with Matir, Aldur, and Lady Dahlia on board. Not to mention the chokaar might do minimal damage and fuel their anger. We need reinforcements, *ensa*. To call for aid, we must escape the comm dampener."

She pinched her lips to smother a wail but nodded at him. It made sense. What could they do against that...thing? Never had she been this helpless. And it was all her fault. She'd decided they'd travel to Etteria. Instead of staying put, she'd abandoned Mom in the engine. They'd been safe. Hell, she doubted these aliens had known they were even there.

"Ziot?" She raised her gaze to the ceiling. "Please show me the way to Nerx's cabin. Oh, and grant me access."

"Of course, Lady Britta," he said through hidden speakers. Lights flickers, directing her. Without hesitation, she spun on her heel and walked. All she could do was take care of Lily and trust Nerx to do everything within his power to get her mother back.

NOT ANYTIME SOON WOULD Nerx forget the elation, fear, and fury engulfing him when Britta had stormed in and shot two males. He'd never felt the like. Ice had drenched him, freezing every muscle in his body. He'd caught her movement when she'd peered around the edge of the bulkhead, but in her distraction, she hadn't seen the slight shake of his head, warning her not to reveal herself. Anger had followed, so violent and bright, he'd frozen. Unable to stop whatever the foolish woman did, he'd have to watch her die.

Nor had he planned for her to witness his death. Without a strategy, he'd reacted on instinct. Despite the two Viqrian males who'd lost their lives, the others were at least stunned.

But now, her devastation at her mother's absence tore through him when he could do nothing to ease her pain. The constant tickle of his unbound hair reminded him of his failure. Memories of his disappointed father added to his sorrow, for surely nothing would displease his father more than Nerx's loss of honor. If he cut his dead braid from his mind, he could think.

He only hoped these Viqrians didn't kill their hostages. Primary Shioll had taken Aldur and Matir for a reason. Odd that. Yithians would only have abducted the human. Did the Viqrians think they could use Aldur and Matir as bait? Perhaps. If they knew the Etterian culture as well as they'd revealed, then they'd know King Xeus would throw everything at them...for Lady Dahlia and Aldur. A pairing mattered. Yet Nerx doubted Primary Shioll had been aware of that.

Once they fled possible retribution and could comm the king, whatever data Ziot had gathered might mean they could track the battleship. "Ziot, can you lock onto Matir or Aldur's O.D.I.?"

"The signals are faint and unsteady, but if I port either of them and Lady Dahlia is not touching them, we risk stranding her."

"Indeed." As injured as Aldur was, Matir's presence might be needed to ensure Lady Dahlia lived. "Let us hope we do not lose the signal."

"I have sent them both a message. I pray they receive it."

Nerx gritted his teeth. His battle-bonds might not survive this. No, he couldn't think like that. There was still time.

"Approaching the belt now. They do not seem to be pursuing us," Edon said.

Nerx strode to the comm, settling behind Edon as he navigated toward the asteroids larger than the scimitar. "Ziot, can you comm the king yet?"

"No. I have been trying since Edon set our escape into motion." Ziot's fingers flew across the war room's console against the far wall. In a battleship, the war room, though adjoined to the comm, was far larger. On a scimitar, it was but a console and a holographic panel.

Edon tapped a button and called forth two levers. He gripped both, swerving the scimitar with ease. Thankfully, having trained in all aspects of Etterian life, Nerx didn't flinch when a boulder dominated the display vids as it came within inches of hitting the scimitar. Trust, the key to all this. Had Britta not trusted him? Or had something else driven her to intervene?

Admittedly, they'd known each other for days. Trust was earned, yet, he'd not once given her the idea that she couldn't rely on him. Had he?

"Supreme Commander, you better see this." Sena spoke through Nerx's O.D.I., his voice grave.

Now what? "Keep me posted on progress," Nerx commanded Edon and Ziot.

When he reached the common, Sena was standing over the bodies. "What is the problem?" Blue blood stained the mat, as would Etterian blood—just as blue.

"This," Sena flicked a visor back, exposing the delicate features of a female.

"Alodon's balls," Nerx growled and staggered. He thrust out a hand to catch himself on a nearby bulkhead. "I killed two females?"

"What male allows females to go to war?" Sena nudged a blaster aside as he picked up a discarded dagger in their blue Maloidian-like steel.

Nerx grimaced. "Regardless of whether they were compatible with Etterians, I *killed* females."

"My point is, Supreme Commander, we know what being a warrior entails. So too did these females. They came armed; one wounded Aldur." Sena offered Nerx the dagger. "It was them or us, and with Dar Eths on board, you made the right choice."

Nerx released a shuddering breath. He prayed his king and Adviser Kanzo thought so too. "My thanks, Sena," he said, accepted the dagger then pointed to the bodies. "Bag the dead...for research."

"Supreme Commander," Sena called, halting Nerx's exit. "Would you like to...keep this?"

The way the long braid dangled over the male's palm made Nerx wince. His heart ached at the loss. He'd worked so hard on his honor, especially after Kyerx died. And yet, in one act, he'd lost years of growth. He took the braid, ran his hand along its thickness before catching the ends to remove the Maloidian clip. He half-expected it to unravel, to swirl around him, instead, it lay there as lifeless as human hair. With determined strides, he crossed to the waste disposal and tossed it in. He slid the clip next to three data cubes on a shelf.

"Their game is strategic," Sena said. "They knew how to weaken an Etterian. This does not bode well when we know nothing about them." He glanced in the direction of the barracks. "Thanks to Lady Britta, we have the means to find out."

Questions burned Nerx's tongue. 'Where were their males' being the most important. Regent and primary were androgynous titles. Did they intentionally hide their femininity from him? Or was it a non-issue for them? Despite needing answers, he couldn't risk setting off a death trigger. He didn't know their level of technology or whether they used such organic devices planted in the victim's brains. Speaking the keyword could kill a female, and they had to live.

"Do not interrogate the Viqrians without back up." Nerx scowled. "It might be best to wait for an operative. Once we reach Operations Commander Malo, I suspect he would want his males to interview them."

Sena pursed his lips. "Very well, Supreme Commander. Let us pray time is on our side."

Chapter Thirteen

Britt awoke to the sensation of floating. She'd read a book to Lily who drifted off to sleep with the ease of a carefree child. After this day, Britt longed to be as unburdened. She'd showered, donned a baggy T-shirt she'd ordered from the replicator, then climbed into bed beside Lily. Self-recriminations, solutions, and what-ifs circled her mind. She blinked her eyes open, trying to stay awake. Nerx could come by at any moment to say he'd found her mom.

But now, he carried her out of Lily's room and into his.

"Nerx," she whispered, cuddling into his warmth. "Any news?"

In the minimal lighting, his expression didn't soften. "The comms are not reliable. We managed to transmit some data, but cannot get a response. Aldur and Matir's O.D.I.s are active which is hopeful."

"O.D.I.?" Using his shoulders as leverage, she pulled herself up to meet his gaze.

He settled her on his bed. "Let me cleanse, then I will answer all of your questions."

She slumped. How long would that take? But having showered herself, she'd let him do the same. The hot water and a good cry had gone a long way to calming her. Not to mention giving her perspective. She scrambled to the replicator for a blanket. Then around him she darted to sprawl on his bed.

He watched her, his eyes narrowed, his focus sharp. Without a word, he disappeared into his bathroom. She lay back, snuggling deeper under the blanket while musing over what he'd revealed so far. *If* the data reached his king, the armada would be en route. If it didn't, they were still weaving around rocks, hoping the battleship didn't shoot them or worse, vanish.

She swallowed past the lump in her throat then sucked in shuddering breaths, willing the tears pressing behind her eyes to stay away. Mom would be fine. She'd have an adventurous story to tell, one they could all laugh about. For now, Britt only had to live through this agonizing uncertainty.

The blower came on, announcing Nerx would join her soon. He appeared all too soon, wearing one of those bathrobes. Shit. She pinched her lips together so she wouldn't gawk. The deep 'V' of the neckline showed way too much of his sculpted chest. And with his hair undulating around him, his electric blue gaze on her, the blanket became a little too warm. He settled on the far end of his bed, his leg half-extended. The robe parted from shin to mid-thigh, highlighting muscles she wished she knew the names of.

Mom would know.

"The two females you stunned are—"

"Females?" Britt dragged her gaze off his fine physique.

"Yes, they are female, these Viqrians."

"Is that what they call themselves? But didn't the purple dude have no hair?" She waved a dismissive hand. Women could have any hair style they wanted. "Never mind that, do you know what they wanted?"

"Primary Shioll..." His lips twitched into a smirk. "The purple 'dude'...wanted Etteria...as in the planet. Failing that, to meet King Xeus, no doubt to kill him and assume his position."

"Shit." Britt fixed her gaze on Nerx's eyes and no lower. Well, she tried to. Damn, did he look lickable. "Just up and ask for a planet? That takes balls."

He chuckled. "I suppose so. What is curious is that they have yet to send fighter craft after us or to fire a cannon. Nor have they commed us again. If they did not have my males and your mother, I would have headed to Etteria posthaste."

"So we're like an unruly child waiting to see what our punishment will be?" She sat up, letting the blanket pool in her lap and the chilly interior of his room cool her. "So, what's an O.D.I.?"

He touched his wrist, summoning holographics. "An implant powered by your body's internal energy and with a path to your brain. It is how I know Earth English." He dipped his chin to his chest. "It is protocol for all women to receive one. And you would have, either today or tomorrow. I just never expected this mission to go to hell so quickly."

She patted his shin, the closest part of his body to her. It was rock-solid. "Why would an O.D.I. make a difference?"

"We can lock onto it and port you."

Her mouth fell open. "Thus saving my mom. *Shit*." She gazed across his room, her thoughts in a whirl. "And you aren't porting Aldur or Matir because of my mom?"

Nerx nodded. "If she was touching Aldur, she would port as well."

That explained how they'd arrived on the ship without having an O.D.I. "Except you don't know if she's near him."

"Nor is the signal strong enough to avoid mishaps, otherwise I would port a male across to bring them back." A pulse ticked at the base of his clenched jaw.

He'd considered every avenue, something she was so grateful for.

From Nerx's wrist, Ziot's voice filled the room, a little tinny but recognizable. "I have reached Adviser Kanzo. King Xeus commanded all nearby battleships to rendezvous at our co-ordinates. He is en route in the *Celeeri*."

Nerx tapped his O.D.I. "My thanks, Ziot. Take turns finding your rest. Who knows when next we will have the time."

"As you command, Supreme Commander."

Britt grinned. "This is good news, right?"

"It is." He fisted the edge of the blanket and tugged, peeling it off her legs. "Do you wish to return to your quarters?"

She wasn't sure if his voice was huskier, but the way it stroked over her senses made her shiver. Or it could be the cool air hitting her bare legs. She didn't want to be alone now, not with this hanging over their heads. Hours-ago-Britt would've jumped his bones like it was nobody's business. The new her was taking their relationship a little more seriously.

She opened her mouth to say yes. "No."

Her heart thudded in her chest, trying to escape the sex-mad-and-desperate-for-affection she'd become. He studied her, not revealing his thoughts, nor putting her at ease. She squirmed, torn between self-consciousness and the heat pooling between her thighs. A part of her wanted to know what he was thinking; the other part savored the brooding intensity he leveled on her.

"Leave your hair down," she said, running a gaze over the swirling mass.

His fingers were hot when he circled her ankle. With a yank, she sprawled backward, blinking at the ceiling like an idiot. She glanced at him crawling over her, his robe still on.

With his hair caressing her skin and his face hidden, she couldn't read his expressions or intentions. Something soft touched the skin behind her ankle, along her calf, then tickled her behind her knee. Her leg jerked, spreading her thighs.

His head whipped up. He locked gazes with her even as his breath hitched. His nostrils flared. "*Ensa*," he rasped, his focus dipping to where the T-shirt had ridden up, exposing her sex.

Heat exploded across her cheeks at what he must perceive as a blatant invitation. She tried to close her knees but trapped his hand between her inner thighs.

"Oh, no, you do not," he said, flashing her a smirk. "The scent of you drives me to taste you."

She gulped back a gasp. He hadn't just said that. Unfurling his fingers, he stroked her, inches from the pulsing need. She wanted to whimper when he ran a featherlight touch up her outer thigh with his other hand.

He caught the hem of her T-shirt. "Lose this."

If she obeyed, there was no going back. This would be consummating the Ethera thingy, and right now, with the endorphins flooding her body and her mind on vacay, she could see nothing wrong being stuck with Nerx. She didn't hesitate, not one to consider the consequences. In this case, the new her had warned her, even if it was briefly. Her fingers trembled when she peeled the T-shirt off, tossing it on the floor beside the bed.

Her nipples puckered, pulling tight enough to shoot sensations to her core.

He took in his fill, admiring every inch of her from her face to her sex, lingering for long moments on her cheeks and breasts. Again, his eyes burned with something dark and potent. He lunged, catching the backs of her thighs on his shoulders and pushing her knees up.

She laughed but swallowed it when he ran his tongue over her sex. "That feels...so good," she hummed, burying her fingers in his affectionate hair.

He growled, then latched his mouth over her clit, devouring her. She arched off the bed, the sensations too intense with every flick of his tongue.

"Your taste is better than I remember," she thought she heard him say.

It hurt her brain to think, so she dismissed his mumbled words and succumbed to the ecstasy coursing through her. He had a masterful tongue, lapping and circling, then thrusting into her. She whimpered, her world spinning. Squeezing her eyes shut only focused everything that defined who she was on what he made her feel.

Then it slammed into her. She let go, falling off the edge of sanity into the abyss of bliss. "Nerx," she cried out and splintered, uncaring what he saw when she came apart.

As she descended from the best euphoric high she'd had in ages, a movement of air caught her attention. He'd stepped back and slipped off the robe, showing her that her imagination couldn't match reality.

Shit. He was perfect with those broad shoulders, bulging biceps and pecs into a ripped torso to.... Her core thrummed in anticipation. His cock, so hard, was bronzed with a darker base, and hairless which made visible the ridges along its length. She almost threw her legs wide and declared he was free to take her.

"Britta, *ensa*, now is the time to leave...if you have changed your mind." He kneeled on the bed, his body taut, as he waited for her decision. Not once did he reveal how he'd feel if she up and left him. Honor, Aldur had called it.

"I'm staying," she said.

His smile crawled onto those gorgeous lips. He landed on top of her but caught his weight on his hands, keeping him inches from touching her. Still, warmth poured off him. He ran kisses along her throat to her earlobe for a quick nibble. She looped her legs around his hips, trying to pull him onto her. When he didn't budge, she arched into him, pressing her breasts to his chest. A hum slipped past her lips at how incredible his velvety skin caressed her taut nipples.

"Behave," he said, leaning back with a smirk. He captured her lips in a kiss, plundering her mouth. She clung to him, driving her fingers into his hair to scrape her nails along his scalp. Strands locked around her wrists and yanked her closer.

He broke the kiss to laugh, then, while gazing into her eyes, he grabbed behind her knees and raised them. Glancing down, he angled his hips until the head of his cock pressed at her channel. She moaned, wriggling her hips to hurry him.

"Patience, Britta, my *ensa*." He pushed in, taking his sweet time to conquer her inch by inch.

"Dammit, Nerx, if you don't hurry up—"

He thrust into her, shoving her back. She mewled as every nerve in her core pulsed. Incredible heat curled around her belly, traveled up to her chest, and settled in her heart. Something, like ribbons of energy, wrapped around her soul. She blinked at Nerx, his gaze on her. He was so beautiful, his commitment too much yet just right. Nothing made sense yet it did. A rippled of pleasure, of need traveled along her channel. He hadn't moved, just drowned in her eyes. A sweet smile tugged at his top lip, and that damn dimple peeked.

"*Ensa*," he said, his voice barely a whisper. "Do you feel that?"

"I feel your hard cock *not* moving," she whined.

He laughed but still didn't budge. Surely by now his arms should be trembling from holding his weight off her. She harumphed, wanting him to sprawl over her, to crush her to the bed with delicious warmth and intimacy.

Grazing her nails down his arms she met a scar from wrist to elbow. She hesitated, then carried onto his shoulders and back, but touching him did nothing to urge him on. She tried gyrating her hips. That didn't work either.

When she shoved her hand to her sex, eager to finish the job, his breath hitched and he growled at her. "You are mine to pleasure."

She huffed, retracting her fingers. "Then get on with it, or so help me, Nerxie—"

"There we go," he said and grinned.

Oh. She snapped her mouth shut then chuckled. "Will Nerxie make little ol' me scream his name again?"

As he withdrew, those ridges rubbed all the right places. She couldn't control her hips now, their swirling and tilting. His second thrust arched her off the bed. She keened. It, no, *he* was too intense. She almost pleaded with him to stop but would kill him if he did. He kept a steady pace, his focus on her. Rivulets of tingling heat swept through her. Her core tightened, a deep ache growing until she couldn't think, could only experience.

"Nerxie," she whimpered, on the cusp of something incredible, then stilled.

Shivers and warmth bathed her, as if he'd dipped her body in pure ecstasy. An orgasm slammed her, so hard, she forgot to breathe. She held onto him, needing his touch, yet too sensitive to it.

"Maker," he gritted out as each thrust slowed, marked by his grunts until he collapsed on top of her, finally pinning her in place.

She hummed, wrapped her arms around his torso, and pressed her face to a pec. The scent of his skin engulfed her, his body heat almost too hot to bear, but she clung to him, not wanting him to move.

He did, falling beside her to sprawl on his back. But he kept her close, ensuring she was comfortable even as he crushed her against him. His breathing was ragged, and his expression had softened. A smile twitched his mouth when he dipped to snatch a kiss.

"*You are mine, ensa.*" He brushed a curl off her temple then stroked down to her jaw with the barest of caresses.

The air thickened with tension, and again those white ribbons closed in, like they wrapped around her heart. She prodded them, each poke triggering an explosion of light and color.

She swallowed and forced a chuckle, not willing to address the 'elephant' in her chest. "Forgiven me yet?"

"For?" His raised one eyebrow.

Without hesitation, she stroked it, admiring the silkiness and its shape. "For everything, I suppose."

He grinned. "Would that be blinding me, calling me a kidnapper, or disobeying me?"

Listing it like that kind of looked bad. She scrunched her nose. "All were justifiable actions...at the time. But I want an O.D.I. and maybe you should teach me how to pilot one of these things." She twirled her finger, indicating the ship.

He chuckled. "Perhaps. Yet I am wary. As is, unarmed, you are a force to be reckoned with."

She beamed. "I'll take that as a compliment." She splayed her fingers over his right pec and snuggled closer.

He drew her tight against him, cupping her hip as he did so. She studied his handsome face: the sharp angle of his jaw, those lips that had brought her such pleasure, and the depth in his eyes that tugged at her heart.

Could she fall for him? Could she trust him not to break her heart? She swallowed and shut her eyes to hide her thoughts. It was too soon to think about this. Afterall, three days did not a relationship make. Hell, it wasn't even long enough to form a friendship. She exhaled slowly, perhaps for the first time in her life, considering letting her control slip. They could be friends with benefits.

Her eyebrows knitted, and she rubbed her nose across his chest. This was for eternity, as he'd said. Which meant, she'd gone and tied her life to his anyway. To Lily. There was no going back from that. She clenched her teeth, wanting to slap horny-Britt for succumbing.

Shit. Since she'd gone and trapped herself, the sex better stay good. And she'd need to find something to do because boredom was a hell-no. Learning how to pilot might fill her time.

"What will happen the moment the O.D.I. signal's strong?" She sat up to meet his gaze, needing to catch every expression.

He glanced at her breast peeking from behind the blanket. His nostrils flared. He lunged, gripped her hips, and dragged her on top of him, nestling her ass at the juncture of his thighs. With long caresses, he ran his fingers from her collarbone, down her cleavage, to her bellybutton, then up. Her sex and nipples zinged with anticipation, but his touch didn't drift to the parts aching for it.

"I will port over—"

"No." Something akin to the insidious slither of fear gripped her. When he blinked at her, she hurried to say, "Um, send Sena or Ziot. Don't risk..." She bit her lip. "You have Lily to think of."

His eyes narrowed, the intensity back. "Very well, Sena and Ziot will port to Aldur and Matir's location. I am hoping Lady Dahlia is with one of them. I do not want to search the Viqrian battleship to find her."

Britt's breath shuddered out of her. She pressed her forehead to Nerx's chin, hoping to hold back tears. "I blame myself. I put Mom in danger, Lily too."

"And yourself." He ran his hand up and down her back, drawing her nearer with every stroke until he crushed her breasts against his chest.

"I...never think of myself. When Dad died, my mom did to. In a way. It took two years to get her out of her shell. Since the funeral, only her happiness mattered." She leaned back to press a kiss to his chin. Within an inch of his face, she feathered her fingers along his jaw to his hair swirling around him as he lay there. She forced a smile. "I don't know how to focus on me."

"Your mother's life is with Aldur now. Yours is with me and Lily." He said it with such finality that a door shut in her mind, its reverberating bang echoing through her soul. "Once we have them safe and on Etteria, I would like to show you my home." A sadness flitted across his eyes. "I have not seen it in decades. Not since I let my brother die."

"Your brother? Is he behind your scar?" she asked, stretching across him to touch his wrist.

Chapter Fourteen

Nerx grimaced, having not wanted to think about Kyerx, not while his Britta pressed her beautiful body against his. She squirmed, unaware of how she aroused him. *Maker.* If only she knew how magnificent it had been to thrust into her, to have her beneath him, but more than that, for her to commit to him. The bond was complete, and yet, he still ached for her.

Some part of him expected this craving to never diminish. He inhaled her scent, relishing the brush of her cool lifeless hair across his face. Her sex was hot where she rubbed his malehood, too tempting for him to ignore. He gripped her hips to hold her in place, trying to still her movements. She pushed up, rubbing herself along the length of his arousal, even as she filled his vision with her breasts.

"Nerx?" she asked, concern in her eyes.

Desperate not to discuss Kyerx, he dipped his head to capture a nipple between his lips.

She gasped but didn't draw away. Instead, she arched into him, offering both breasts for his devotion. Her breathy rasp of his name sank into his ears like birdsong. She wiggled up, then, as if she had the right to, she impaled herself on his malehood. He shuddered, savoring each inch of him she conquered. From breast to breast, he licked a path, tasting her skin, her scent, and memorizing her flavors.

He moaned when she pulled away, sitting up. She splayed her fingers across his chest, her gaze locked on his. In slow motion, she swirled her hips. The sensations she invoked tore his breath from him. He couldn't look away, not from her face, the bounce of her swollen breasts, and the glimpse he caught of her sex as she tormented him.

Never had he seen anything as exquisite as Britta.

"Supreme Commander," Edon's called via the O.D.I.

Nerx tapped his wrist then gripped Britta's hips to keep her still. "What is it?"

"Three more Viqrian battleships just arrived."

Nerx blinked. "I am on my way."

When Britta made to climb off him, he flipped her onto her back, instead. She squeaked, clasping his biceps.

"I am not done with you, *ensa*." He caught her lips with his, then swept a tongue into her mouth as the training vids has shown. And, Maker, was he glad he'd taken the time to learn. Her taste was indescribable.

"But—"

He withdrew and thrust into her. Her eyes widened, and she moaned, hooking her legs around his hips. She dug into his backside with her heels, urging him on. Heat rippled over his length in a gush of liquid. His arousal pulsed in response, sending bolts of sensations to his balls. In and out, he pistoned, unable to slow the pace, not wanting to, and driven by the urgency of danger.

He tried not to think about the new threat but to savor this moment with his Dar Eth. She cried out, digging her nails into him. The sharp pain jettisoned him into a supernova of ecstasy. He grunted with each slowing thrust as he found his fulfilment—the joy almost too much to bear. Sucking in a ragged breath, he rested his temple on hers even as their pounding hearts aligned in beats for a few seconds.

Pulling out of her took all his strength of will. He shivered, forced himself to stand, to put on pants and boots. She watched him, her eyes hooded, cheeks flushed that wonderful peach color, and her lips redder than normal. Tiny bumps ran along her skin. He tugged the blanket over her, bending to steal a kiss.

"Get some sleep," he said as he slipped on his chest armor.

She scrambled off the bed, standing naked before him. "I'm coming with you." She hesitated. "If I may?"

"Of course." He grinned. "With garments on."

"Oh." She laughed as she ordered pants, undergarments, and footwear from the replicator.

As she covered her body with each item, tension built between his shoulders. He planned to undress in the same order. Later. If they survived the Viqrians.

"Supreme Commander, they are hailing us."

At Edon's voice, Nerx leaped for the door.

"Go, I'll follow." She flicked a dismissive hand.

He bolted. To linger would lead to more mating and would delay this further. "Patch them through," he said the moment he entered the comm. He flicked his hair off his shoulders, wishing he'd grabbed his clip from the common.

"Supreme Commander, or so I am told." A face appeared on the display vids. Now that he knew to expect females, the curve of her cheek, the angle of her jaw, and her delicate brow were obvious. Before, he'd assumed the regent was male for someone in a commanding rank.

Nerx was cautious, anticipating more trouble. "Greetings." He tapped the console to silence the comm. "Keep hiding us behind debris," he said to Edon. Glancing at the Viqrian female with short hair and solid black eyes, he had to assume they were all similar in appearance. He opened the comm. "How may I be of assistance?" He hid his grimace.

"It is I who must apologize on behalf of our empress." The female clenched her jaw as if apologizing didn't sit well with her. Nerx had to agree that doing so did irritate. "The *Bronvol* has gone rogue. When news reached us of your galaxy and the existence of males such as yourself, well...those opposed to our code stole a battleship..." She stiffened her shoulders.

"Forgive me, you have yet to introduce yourself."

Her cheeks darkened. "Regent Haiz of the *Kunakar*."

He nodded. "Our first contact may not have been a fortuitous one, but I am hoping your empress and my king can smooth any future interactions." He clasped his hands behind his back. "Unfortunately, two Viqrians lost their lives in the encounter which I deeply regret."

She bowed her head, touching two fingers to her temple. "May the goddess welcome them."

"How do you plan to resolve this?" Nerx asked then glanced at Britta who appeared in the doorway. He held out his arm, inviting her to join him. "Especially when Primary Shioll kidnapped three of ours."

Haiz studied Britta, running her gaze over his Dar Eth. "Well, I *was* planning on destroying the *Bronvol*, but hostages change this." She glanced to the side. "I will send a retrieval team to free your people."

"My thanks. My king is en route, as is an armada. And we have two of your females in a quarters. After the last incident, I am wary of opening my ship for another 'visit.'"

"Fair enough. We shall meet on the nearest habitable planet to exchange. Again, my empress is most apologetic."

"Once you have my people on board your ship, what then? Surely not all the crew on board the *Bronvol* deserve to die." All those females lost. Not that he knew whether they were compatible with Etterians, still, the possibility was there. A warrior female would suit any male. For their prowess, they were as respected as Lady Quinlan and Princess Oriana.

"We do not tolerate disobedience. Death or servitude is a choice each female must make. I will comm you with news as and when I receive it." Haiz waved her hand, and the screen went black.

"May I say, wow? She's formidable." Britta's smile faded. "I suppose we have to wait?"

"If we are to trust her." Nerx glanced at Edon. "Are the signals stronger? Can you locate their positions?"

"Yes and no, I cannot confirm Lady Dahlia is close to either." Edon typed across the console then gripped the lever to navigate around an approaching asteroid. "Matir has responded to his message, stating he is alone. Nothing from Aldur yet."

"We cannot wait a moment longer. Summon Sena and Ziot." After Edon did so, Nerx commanded him to draw nearer to the *Bronvol*. The act of doing so might make Haiz believe he trusted her.

When his males stepped into the comm, Nerx laid out his plan. "I want to hit this hard and fast. Sena, Edon will port you to Matir. Get in and get out. Ziot, you have Aldur. If Lady Dahlia is not with him, find a way to reach her."

Ziot stiffened, tightening his hands behind his back.

"As data officer, you are the best suited to figure out their systems. If not, then try and discover where Lady Dahlia is being held before porting back...with Aldur."

"What?" Britts snapped, pulling away from Nerx. "You'll be leaving her alone—"

"He is imprisoned, wounded, and perhaps far from your mother." Nerx caught Britta's hands, holding her in place. "If she is elsewhere, she *is* alone and without hope."

A tear slipped down Britta's cheek. "I understand. Save your men...males, but tell Haiz that she only has one person to rescue."

Nerx caught the droplet with the pad of his thumb. Helplessness cinched his chest, when all he could do was draw Britta into his embrace.

"I will do everything I can to save your mother, Lady Britta."

At Ziot's vow, she gave his forearm a squeeze.

"Thank you, and try not to get yourself killed." She forced a smile. "My mother wouldn't like it."

"Arm yourselves," Nerx said, pulling Britta closer and out of the way of the armory.

When they were ready, they nodded at Edon.

In the blink of an eye, they were gone.

Britta dug her nails into Nerx's armor, tension radiating off her. He ran his hand up and down her back, hoping to convey his faith in his males and that she had nothing to worry about. Except, this could go wrong in so many ways.

"Two to port," Sena commed.

Within moments, Matir and Sena appeared before them. Sena had thrown an arm around a bruised and battered Matir, who couldn't stand on his own.

"Get him to the med-E.D. And well done, Sena." Nerx gripped Matir's forearm. "It is good to have you back, my battle-bond."

"I have much to tell you," Matir managed, then nodded his head at Sena to lead him away.

Again, Nerx glanced at Edon, as if he'd know what Ziot had discovered. Seconds passed at an excruciating pace, with worry darkening Britta's eyes as time passed.

"One to port." At Ziot's voice, she threw a glance at Nerx but nibbled her lip, not saying anything

When Ziot appeared, he'd drawn his blaster and nursed his left arm. "Aldur is in their medical. Lady Dahlia is not near him, but neither has she gone far. She is in the next room, making demands. I had a few moments to access a terminal."

Nerx whipped out his med-gun to scan Ziot's wound. "You did well. What did you discover?"

"I have schematics of their battleship, though they do us no good now. My initial suggestion would have been to port back with Sena or yourself to snatch Aldur and Lady Dahlia." Ziot grimaced as Nerx scanned him. "But they spotted me and will be on high alert."

Nerx clenched and released his jaw. "Can you locate them on the schematics? We can inform Regent Haiz of this."

Ziot swung his healed arm when Nerx stepped back. "I will get on that."

"Stay locked onto Aldur's signal in the meantime, Edon." Nerx laced his fingers through Britta's and escorted her to the common. "Order me a hot chocolate, please." He glanced at Matir on the bed in medical.

"Okay," she said, pulling away to cross the common. "Though I could do with something stronger," she muttered.

Nerx stared after her, then headed to the medical. "How is he?" he asked Sena who tapped the med-E.D.'s console.

"Burns, cuts, bruises, and a cracked rib." Sena pursed his lips. "Impressive for female warriors. I have induced sleep to aid the healing. I should be able to wake him in an hour or two."

"My thanks, Sena." Nerx headed to Britta carrying the hot chocolate toward him.

"Hot cocoa has too much sugar. But I guess, cocoa, steak, sauce, pizza... With your advanced medical technology, whatever you do to your body can be cured. Except for a broken heart." She offered him a cup, then sank onto the bench to sip her hot chocolate.

Nerx grinned at that bit of nonsense. "Our hearts cannot break."

She chuckled. "No, it's a metaphor, silly."

"I am not silly." He drew his cup closer.

She ran her tongue over her bottom lip, catching a droplet of hot chocolate. "I didn't intend it as an insult, babe."

His focus snagged on her mouth, remembering how incredible it was to kiss her. "I am not a *damu* either. You will cease with these endearments unless they have meaning to you."

She opened her mouth then snapped it shut. "You're serious?" She grinned. "So only Nerxie? What about 'honey?'"

"No." He snorted at her absurd idea that he was sweet.

"Sweetheart? Sugarplums? Sexy Stud?" She giggled. "Pumpkin? Dreamboat? Snookums? Darling?"

He swallowed a bark of laughter, raised his hot chocolate and peered at her over the cup's rim. "All no."

She huffed, although her pursed lips hinted at a smile. "Well, then no calling me '*minus cesu*' or whatever."

"Little cat?" He smirked, licking his lips.

"Yes." Her cheeks flushed. "None of that."

He placed his cup on the table, snatched hers to join his, then lifted her. Spinning her, he pinned her to the bulkhead. With her face so close to his, he caught and held her gaze. "I will call you whatever I want, *ensa*."

Her sensual smile hit him hard.

He snatched a kiss while layering his body over hers.

"Double standards, huh?" she said, trailing her nails down his upper arms.

"I mean *'ensa,'* you do not mean any of yours." He planted kisses from her collarbone to her earlobe, enjoying the way her body arched into him, her feathered breathing, her erratic heartbeat, and that beautiful explosion of peach across her cheeks. He pretended to kiss her but stopped an inch from her lips. Using the bulkhead to push off, he abandoned her, choosing instead to stride away, when what he wanted was her beneath him...again.

"*'Ensa'* means 'brat,' doesn't it?" she called.

"Get some rest. I will find you when I have news."

Her string of curses made him laugh.

THE GRIN NERX TOSSED at her and his laughter echoing from the comm weakened Britta's knees. She dropped to the nearest bench. Fainting would give him an idea of what he made her feel and garner a full medical check-up.

How could she explain her symptoms stemmed from madness? Finding Nerx attractive—though that word lacked oomph—stole her voice, burned her cheeks, turned her bones to jello, *and* made her shy. The latter the worst in her book.

When he'd given her a chance to run, she should've said yes, postponed the inevitable. Not knowing how good he was in bed meant she could function and wouldn't confuse lust with affection. Maybe if she rubbed out an orgasm, she wouldn't want to seduce him, to beg him to thrust into her, stroking her very insides with his ridged cock. She shuddered. But screaming in ecstasy so close to the common didn't sit well with her, either.

Nerx would come to the rescue, charging in to find her fingers between her thighs.

Her senses exploded into a thousand tingles at the thought of him...intruding. Would he lick her, dominate her with the power of his thrusts, steal a kiss when the taste of his lips unraveled her thoughts?

Yup, she was mad. It was official. Certifiable.

She should be worrying about Mom. Disappointment should be in control of her thoughts and emotions, like a rogue rollercoaster. Instead, the news that Mom was alive, well, and defiant had flooded Britta with hope and happiness.

She veered toward Nerx's quarters. Although Aldur's was closest to the communications room and Nerx, she'd be there if Lily awoke. Stripping off her jeans, T-shirt, and underwear, she slipped into the baggy sleepshirt and climbed onto his bed. She lay there, snuggled under the blanket. The silence was deafening. She left her warm cocoon to check on Lily, tucking in her leg where it hung off the bed's edge. She picked up a stuffed elephant and stacked it with its zoo friends.

No one knew, not even Mom, how much Britta wanted children. So how had the Ethera known to match her to a readymade family? She tiptoed to Nerx's bed and settled again, pulling the blanket to her chin. He'd been right to mention the future. Once Mom was safe, she'd be busy with Aldur, doing doctory stuff. Which left Britta twiddling her thumbs. And by the sounds of things, Nerx's home wasn't on Etteria. Where he'd let his brother die? Now that had been revealing. And since it had been decades since he went home, she had to assume that was when he lost his brother. He mourned still, that was clear. She'd be far from Mom, unable to make sure she ate, slept, didn't throw herself off a cliff... That sort of thing.

Britta's heart twanged like it had been doing way too often lately. Leaving Mom alone went against every ounce of her being. What had she expected? To marry a man and move in with Mom? No, she'd hoped Mom rediscovering herself happened before a Mr.-Right-For-Britta came into the picture. Though, finding Mr. Soulmates for them both and at the same time was a godsend.

When Mom was back on board this ship, Britt planned to have a heart-to-heart with her—a mother (Britt) to daughter (Mom) chat. And it was time to put her reckless side to bed. Her overreactions and gung-ho attitude had been a futile attempt to hold onto her inner child. Dad was gone, Mom was finding her mojo, which meant Britt could calm down, especially when her actions taught her new *daughter* how to act.

She grinned. But her sass she was keeping. Nerx loved it, if she judged his laughter well. And anything that summoned that man's dimple was enough of an incentive for her. Humming, she let sleep claim her with a hope-filled future filling her dreams for the first time in a long while.

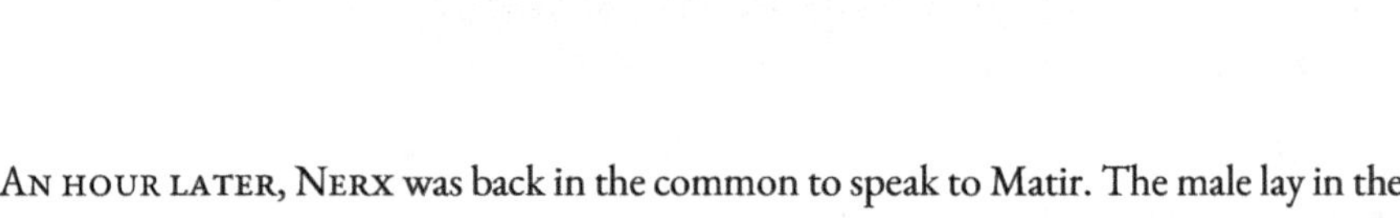

AN HOUR LATER, NERX was back in the common to speak to Matir. The male lay in the med-E.D. with his gaze focused. Already his bruises had faded even though he favored one side of his torso.

"Supreme Commander." He settled on Nerx's hair and winced. Only then did Nerx notice the short braid resting on Matir's shoulder.

"You too?" He lifted the ends then let it fall.

"Indeed. They find our long hair amusing." Matir closed his eyes, pain contorting his features. "They believe cutting it off weakens us...physically."

Nerx blinked, then chuckled. "That is preposterous."

Matir cracked a smile. "I know."

"Perhaps it is the way we react when our honor is threatened?" Sena said while tapping the med-E.D.'s console.

"What I gathered between beatings is that they're a rogue faction of female warriors, tired of their old ways of servitude or death." Matir frowned. "They spoke of ordering daughters from laboratories."

Nerx stepped back to lean against the bulkhead. "Do you mean they genetically modify their offspring?" He shook his head. "We attempted it once. I do believe those *damu* were too weak to live past the first month."

"I only saw females. And the one who beat me could've rivaled Garix in height and bulk."

Nerx gaped. "That is impossible. Garix is a rarity among us."

"Perhaps she is the same for Viqrians. Regardless, her punch carries much weight and power." Matir rubbed his mottled jaw.

"What questions did they ask?"

"The number of operational battleships. If it was true how many unmated males we have. Whether we have a patriarchal society. How much galaxy-wide authority did we have? Where could they find the most males? I thought, at first, they meant to conquer us. Or attempt to. But as the questions turned intimate, I figured out they mean to steal males."

"Steal?" Nerx snapped. "Is that why they kidnapped Aldur and yourself?"

"For compatibility tests and information. They are wary of harming Lady Dahlia. Not only is she a female, but she has ancient knowledge on child bearing." Matir held up a hand. "I vow, Supreme Commander, that was their words."

"And they know that how? Surely not before they took you three."

"She tried to plead with them, revealing her mission to Etteria." Matir offered a tight smile. "She fought like a sogair when they took her from Aldur's side."

"It is good news that they do not wish to kill her. Perhaps we should rescue Aldur..." Nerx settled his gaze on Matir. "I can confirm the *Bronvol* and its crew *have* gone rogue. Three Viqrian battleships surround it. I spoke with a Regent Haiz and negotiated a swap—two of her females for Aldur and Lady Dahlia."

Matir stilled. "They mean to breach their own battleship?"

"Seems like it. She was most apologetic and pretended fury when I mentioned how they'd mistreated you. If they take the *Bronvol* and leave our galaxy, I will not pursue her, as long as she is an honorable female. I want done with this."

"I agree. Better I not remember what I have endured. I did wonder though, with their copper skin tones and black hair, whether they were descendants of Etteria."

"And how would that have come about?" Nerx arched a brow at that nonsensical idea. "We do not have enough females to crew a battleship, never mind any Etterian male sending them into space without protection."

"Unless it was before the Durn's genetic modifications. Perhaps a few females commandeered a shuttle, tired of their males constantly at war?" Sena nodded. "My elder mother once mentioned leaving my elder father if he continued to argue with her." He smiled as if cherishing the memory.

"It is possible," Matir said, then lay back with a grateful sigh. "I suggest we test them, just to be sure."

Nerx glanced at Sena as Matir drifted off. "Take blood samples from the corpses while they're fresh. Have the system analyze it, then send the results to the medical council."

"It will be done, Supreme Commander." Sena took an injection gun from a drawer and headed for the shuttle bay.

Nerx stared after him. If the Viqrians were descendants, they might be compatible, or more so, trigger the Ethera in his males. He flicked his hair out of his face. If he'd stumbled upon more females for Etteria, it might go a long way to restoring his honor. And Matir's.

Chapter Fifteen

Nerx waited outside Britta's quarters. He'd announced his presence, but when she didn't answer, his body tensed as his mind whispered of foul play. Icy fear seized his lungs, blinded him, and pumped blood through his veins. With his security access, he forced the door open. One glance and a sense of emptiness confirmed she wasn't there. He hadn't re-sealed the door to the shuttle bay. Sprinting past the *kuta* to the engine room expended his pent-up energy, his hopes that he'd find her fueled him, even as he worried the Viqrians had stolen her.

Regent Haiz *had* studied Britta too long.

He hadn't wanted to chase her away when she'd come to the comm, and perhaps, if Haiz saw a female on board, she'd show mercy. The news of Matir's retrieval and condition had pursed Haiz's lips despite Aldur and Lady Dahlia's location being well received.

"Supreme Commander, just received comms the scimitar *Sasay* is only a half-day out." Ziot chuckled, his good humor so incongruent with the crushing weight on Nerx's chest. "Operations Commander Malo is as efficient as always."

"Good," Nerx managed. Though, he couldn't confirm the Viqrians would still be on board by the time the scimitar arrived.

A part of him urged him to question them before they were released. Malo would have, but Nerx lacked his skill sets. And if Haiz learned he'd done so and when, it wouldn't help King Xeus with talks of peace. As a supreme commander and an unwilling ambassador for Etteria, Nerx had to act above board.

"Pilot Ziot, locate Lady Britta."

Ziot's response was swift. "She has not left your quarters."

Relief flooded Nerx. Of course, she'd be there. He laughed at his ability to jump to extreme conclusions. "My thanks."

Using the few minutes it would take to reach his home, he worked on calming his breathing. But when the door opened to the common room between his bedroom and Lily's, the same emptiness along with the darkness sparked his concern. Not wanting to repeat his panic, he darted into his bedroom.

Finding Britta *in* his bed sucked the air out of his lungs. Again the constriction on his chest eased. He ignored his tumultuous emotions when they made no sense. Instead, he peeked in on Lily, her leg tucked under the blanket when it was always out. The toy usually clutched under her arm sat on a shelf beside the others. His chest swelled at the evidence of Britta's care, forcing him to take a few moments to calm his breathing. His nostrils burned when he returned to her, but he doubted it was from lack of oxygen.

He stripped, tossing his armor onto a comfy, then slipped between the blanket and bed, able to pull Britta snug against him. She mumbled something but didn't stir otherwise. As exhausted as he was, he lay there, content to hold her even as his thoughts pinged from scenario to repercussions. If Haiz couldn't return Aldur and Lady Dahlia, what could Nerx do?

He clenched his jaw, determination narrowing on the clearest solution. Port in, snatch Aldur, then with blasters set to stun, rescue Lady Dahlia. He was tempted to command Sena and Ziot to get it done. And yet, he hesitated. Granting Haiz a little time might cross the many bridges Regent Kaara had undermined.

Britta rolled over and nestled deeper into his embrace. She rubbed her nose across his chest, her breath warm. "Mm," she mumbled. "Any news?"

Her husky voice so like her throaty moans awoke his semi-hard malehood. He pressed an open-mouthed kiss to her neck, guided the collar of her tunic to the side, then brushed his lips across any exposed skin. She looped a leg around his, running her foot up and down his calf.

"We wait. Still."

She raised her gaze to his, not hiding her grimace. "Enough with this waiting. Couldn't Mom be grabbed from the other room, guns blazing?"

He grinned. The imagery of weapons on fire painted a vivid tale in his mind. "It is my next recourse. I shall give Regent Haiz until morning."

"For diplomacy?" Britta pounded a fist on his chest but not so hard as to hurt herself. "This is bullshit, Nerx."

"I know." He glided his hands down her back to cup her bare backside. With a firm tug, he drew her into the cradle of his thighs.

"We've...um, gone from enemies to lovers within days." She parted her mouth as she traced a path from his chin, down his throat, to his collarbone.

"You were never my enemy, *ensa*." *Maker*. Now, she was his world.

"I do not wish to speak to you, female," she said in a gruff voice.

He chuckled. "You did blind me."

She sat up, pulling away from him. He frowned, hating to release her. She crossed her legs, shuffling on her backside until her knees brushed his chest. With her soft hands, she cupped his face, her thumbs an inch from his mouth, only to peer into his eyes. "And look, all good." She smiled as she leaned forward to place the tiniest kiss on the tip of his nose.

"Thanks to Aldur." He caught her stray curl and toyed with it, spiraling it around a finger. "What would you do if you were the supreme commander?"

She narrowed her eyes in thought. "I'd be the guns-blazing-get-everyone-killed kind of leader. For me, actions speak louder than words. Sad? Let's cheer you up. Happy? We can find something to celebrate, even if it's just getting out of bed. Tired? Take a nap while I do your chores. Angry? Let's punch pillows, a boxing bag, or an ex-lover." She traced his eyebrows, his cheekbones, then his jawline, to pinch his earlobes. "This...kidnapping? It's taking everything in me not to lose my shit. Not to demand you and I port across. Give me a blaster and maybe some armor, just to be safe." She released a jagged breath. "News that she's well helped. I can bide my time. If Haiz doesn't come through, though, expect some hollering and a full-out tantrum from me."

He laughed, throwing his head back to do so. It was so damn good to give into the joy and vibrant emotions flooding him, to not care about the void. "My thanks for the forewarning."

"Now, do you want to sleep or fuck?"

His breath hitched, and his fingers dug into the soft flesh of her hips. "Do not speak so for I must indeed rest."

Her lips twitched into a sweet smile. "You choose sleep above me?" She faked a pout, then grinned and slid down to press her body against his. With her head on his upper arm, she met his gaze. "Night, Nerxie. Sweet dreams."

He brushed his mouth across hers. "Rest well, *ensa*." He pretended to sleep, even as his hearing narrowed on her breathing until it slowed. When he was sure she wouldn't catch him, he gazed upon her face. Without her eyes distracting him, he could spend as much time as he liked on every feature from her cheek spots to her nose and the black brows like paint smears across her forehead.

He drew her closer, once again content to hold her. He hadn't lied, needing to rest. Forcing his eyes closed, he willed himself to sleep. He jerked a moment later to find Lily scrambling over him. Exhaustion pounded at him, with a harsh word forming on his tongue.

"Morning, Nerxie and Britt." She squeezed between them, squirming to fit and get comfortable.

Morning? He swallowed at almost hurting her fragile spirit.

"Hey, pumpkin," Britta said, dropping a kiss on Lily's cheek. "How'd you sleep?"

"Good." She beamed. "I'm hungry."

"Same." Britta hummed. "I could do with French toast. Maybe with bacon and melted cheese?"

"Oh," Lily squealed, tossed aside the blanket to climb over Nerx as if he was nothing but a lump in her way.

Britta smiled at him. "And you?"

"I will try this French toast."

"No, silly, how'd you sleep?" She splayed her fingers across his chest, her touch sparking a malehood twitch.

"Silly?" He widened his eyes.

"Sorry, *honeybunch*." She pressed a kiss to his chin then crawled over him like Lily had done.

He caught and tucked her beneath him, just how he liked it. She laughed and writhed, pushing at his chest as if she could lift him. Her face was close enough for her breath to warm his chin. The longer he drowned in her eyes, the more her humor faded.

When he had her full attention, he kissed her, tilting his head to slant his mouth across hers, to thrust his tongue in to duel. She parried him without hesitation, digging her fingers into his hair. Her heartbeat thundered in his ears. When the pitter-patter of Lily's approach broke the kiss, he rested his temple on Britta's while he fought for air.

"Ready," Lily called, bending to peer at them both.

"Go find Uncle Ziot or Uncle Edon. Nerxie and Britta need a cleanse." He leaned to the side to smack a loud kiss on Lily's cheek. She giggled and danced off. "And save some French toast for us."

"Okay dokey." The door shut on her skipping along the passage.

"I thought you said I don't stink?" Britta sniffed herself. "Or do you want some *alone* time?" She wiggled her eyebrows in a way his O.D.I. couldn't explain.

"What does that mean?"

She jerked back, and her mouth parted on a gasp. "Alone-time?" Her cheeks flushed peach. "Um, when you're aroused—"

"No," he chuckled, "the thing you do with your eyebrows."

"Oh." She bit her lip. "It's usually tied to a sexual implication."

Realizing what she meant, he laughed. "Ah, time alone for me to attend to my daily chore."

She frowned. "And that is?"

"A morning fulfilment." He slid off her and offered her his hand.

"Like masturbation?" The moment she accepted it, he scooped her into his arms and carried her into the cleansing room. "I have legs, y'know," was all she said even as she wrapped her arms around his neck.

"I like holding you, *ensa*. It brings me joy."

She blinked at him. "Well, then carry away. Just know that at some point in your life, you're going to need both hands."

He flipped her, tossing her over his shoulder to rest his hands on her backside.

She squealed and squirmed, her fingers digging into his sides. "I'm not a sack of potatoes, Nerx." She huffed.

He swatted her. Her breath caught, and she pinched her thighs together. The scent of her arousal thickened. His malehood hardened and began to throb. He'd been serious about cleansing, but if she kept scenting so damn good, they'd take longer than five minutes. In the cleansing room, he set her on her feet, then whipped off her tunic. With another pat on one backside cheek, he nudged her to the spray.

When the water activated, she danced on the spot with her face raised. Black hair plastered to her head, and yet, he thought her beautiful. He stepped in behind her, nudging her back with his chest.

Looping one arm around her waist, he slid his other hand to cup a breast. He thrummed his thumb over her nipple until it tightened, then he stroked her stomach to slip between her thighs.

A groan escaped him seconds before he clenched his jaw. She was so ready for him.

"Kiss me," he whispered, pinning her to his front.

She angled her head to meet his lips while he tormented her until she trembled in his arms. Not once did she break the kiss, allowing him to swallow her whimpers and mewls. Against his hard arousal, she swirled her hips, rubbing her soft backside where he ached for her. Her fulfilment hit her, making her writhe. Her pert breasts filled his vision when he pulled away.

Spinning her, he hoisted her and pressed her back to the bulkhead.

"Nerxie?" she asked, clutching his shoulders.

"Wrap your legs around me, *ensa*."

When she did, he positioned his arousal at her entrance and eased himself into her. He closed his eyes as heated darts of pleasure rippled along his length. *Maker. Nothing feels as good as her.* He withdrew and thrust into her, the back of her head tapping the bulkhead, and drawing a startled gasp. With one hand behind her head, he gripped her hip as he pounded in her. She cried out, arching into him as her body trembled. She tightened her channel around him until it felt like the perfect grip of a glove.

He grunted when pure joy slammed into him, flooding his mind with white ecstasy, like the Ethera had triggered. As he struggled to catch his breath, he nestled his forehead between her breasts. Her heartbeat thumped, erratic and yet, somehow, musical. Warm tendrils wrapped around his heart while whispering her name in a tribal chant.

Stepping back, he released her, letting her slide down the bulkhead until her feet touched the floor. "Shall we?" He swept out his hand, gesturing to the blue button.

She laughed as she slipped around him to summon the dryer. Warm air bathed them both when he joined her. So close to her, he couldn't resist holding her even if it meant parts of him wouldn't fully dry. Just the bliss of Britta in his arms brought him so much contentment. He caught his image in the reflective surface above the waste receptable and grimaced. His hair...gone. Sadness warred with horror and disappointment. How could he face his father like this? If Father so much as spoke a vicious word to Lily, Britta, or himself, he'd deal with it like he should have too many years ago.

"Hungry?" she asked, offering him a robe.

"Ravenous," he rasped, running his gaze down the plunging 'V' hinting at her plump breasts while drawing his focus to her sex.

"Charmer," she said, activating the robe to close. "Let's not keep Lily waiting too long."

As he donned his armor, he watched without guilt as Britta pulled on tight-blue leggings she called jeans. The only undergarment she wiggled into was a bra. Above this went a sleeveless white tunic that ended mid-waist, exposing a sliver of skin when she raised her arms. Next were her thick boots missing the boosters and magna-locks in his.

She flicked her hair off her face with a puff from her mouth. "Ready?"

He nodded, staring at her while he followed her to the common.

On the table was a feast with Ziot's plate piled high. "Supreme Commander, Lady Britta," he said around a mouthful.

"Lily?" Britta scooped her into her arms and carried her around the table, giving exaggerated gasps at the food. "You did so well. This is exactly what I was thinking. Bacon, cheese, maple syrup? Boy, am I starving now."

Lily giggled then squealed when Britta planted kisses all over her face.

"What is that scent?" Matir called, swinging his legs off the side of the med-E.D. He inched off the bed then limped toward Ziot. Already his movements were smoother and the bruises almost faded.

Britta chose a spot, tucked Lily beside her, then patted the bench, her gaze on Nerx. Without hesitation, he sat while offering Matir an empty plate.

"Want some French toast, Uncle Matir?" Lily asked, scrambled up, then stacked the male's plate as if he hadn't eaten for days. Perhaps this was true.

"Syrup if you're craving sweet," Britta said as she drizzled golden liquid over a brown square. "Sprinkle cheese if you want a salty-sweet combination. Then add bacon for that wow factor."

She pushed the loaded plate in front of Nerx while sucking her thumb. "Here, have mine."

He forgot himself for a moment as he gazed into her eyes. With a sigh, he used a fork to cut off a piece. He stilled when the flavors exploded in his mouth. This was so much better than hotdogs and fish fingers. He said as much, relishing her untamed laughter.

"Supreme Commander, requesting permission to port the operatives?" Edon said from Nerx's O.D.I.

"Permission granted," he said, taking the time to lick a fingertip.

Hope conquered his soul. The operatives on board meant he'd have back up when they ventured planetside to collect Aldur and Britta's mother. With the delicious food before him, Britta warming his side, and Lily teasing Ziot with a strip of bacon, his world was complete.

Chapter Sixteen

Four men appearing in the common shouldn't scare the shit out of Britt. Still, this porting thing, though Edon had forewarned her, wasn't something she was used to seeing. People didn't just appear out of thin air. Well, not in her world. The tech to do that still blew her mind, though.

Their reaction to Nerx and Matir's shorter hair was better than Sena's. They didn't gawk or lower their gazes as if they were fearful of being caught staring. And yet, pain flickered across their eyes as if in sympathy.

"My apologies, Supreme Commander," a male said. "These females should be punished for their dismissal of your honor. Yours too, Sub-Commander."

Britt bit her tongue, squirming as anger burned through her. Unable to endure it a moment longer, she blurted, "My Dar Eth is honorable, long hair or not."

Nerx blinked at her, then laughed with that damn dimple peeking out. "You are *my* Dar Eth. I am your Eth."

"Potato, potahto." She harumphed.

He stole a kiss, smearing syrup across her lips. "My thanks for the defense."

"You speak truth, milady," the male said. "Supreme Commander Nerx et Tarx is renowned for his honor. None will think less of him for this slight."

"Malia pa," Nerx said, pushed off the bench, then collected his clip lying next to the old data cubes. He snapped it on the ends then let the short braid drape over a shoulder. "I must admit, it is light, as if a burden has been lifted off my shoulders."

Matir glanced up and grinned. "Indeed. Though I still move as if I might trip over it."

"When you are well, we shall spar. I look forward to the experience." Nerx kissed Britt's temple, tickled Lily's side then gestured to the men to follow him to the comm.

Matir grabbed his plate and hurried after them, leaving Lily and Britt with Ziot.

"Going to join them?" she asked, hitching her thumb at their backs.

Ziot shook his head. "Only if summoned. French toast? What is it made of?" he asked, a syrup-drenched chunk stuck to his fork.

As Britt described the ingredients and the cooking process, she picked at her meal. With the operatives here, the meet-up would happen soon. Mom could be back by dinner.

Her heart fluttered even as butterflies dive-bombed her stomach. Lily squirming beside her snapped her from the ever-spiraling worry coating her thoughts.

"How about a fruit juice?" she asked as she leaped up to order a coffee. "You, Ziot?"

"Whatever you are having, Lady Britta," he said, still staring at his overburdened fork. Syrup dribbled off it.

Again, she was tempted to order cider vinegar. Instead, she slid a cappuccino across to him and placed a grape juice before Lily. With her coffee in hand, she settled on the bench though facing outward. Nerx and his men would be deciding things that could be endangering Mom further. Old Britt would've snuck up to the communications room to eavesdrop. Part of her was tempted to, but Lily would tag along.

This is where trust came in, and it was damn hard. Her mother's life was at stake. Aldur's too. Then again, she wasn't military, and these 'operatives' would know what the hell to do. She'd be a fifth wheel—in the way. Despite knowing all this, she wanted to go with, to land on an unnamed planet, to welcome her mom with open arms.

She glanced at Lily, who had two animal-shaped strips of French toast attacking each other, with sound effects. "What do you feel like doing today, cupcake?"

"Mm," she hummed between growls, fake-screams, and threats of bodily harm. "Something fun."

"Like?" Britt asked while finger-combing Lily's black hair. "Marbles? Card games? Or...I can teach you how to crochet." She grinned, warming to the idea. "We can make hats, gloves, or handbags."

"A shirt for Ollie?" Lily's eyes widened.

Britt hesitated. She wasn't about to agree to make anything unless she knew the size of the wearer. "Who's Ollie?"

"My stuffed elephant."

"Oh, sure." Britt laughed. "We can make clothes for all your toys." There was bound to be patterns in the archives for Earth, and if not, she had no doubt that Ziot could source them for her. "Let's start by choosing colorful wools and crochet needles."

The wool was easy with the balls forming on the replicator like gigantic jelly beans. The needles, not so much. The replicator beeped every time she placed an order.

Ziot lowered his fork and rose. "It thinks it is a weapon." He typed in something, then boom, the needles appeared—the kind with the soft grip.

"Thanks," she said, snatching up the two needles.

Not that he heard. He sat again and lifted his fork for another mouthful.

She ordered a variety of marbles and two little bags. Stacking the wool and needles beside the data cubes on the shelf, she sank onto the bench to divvy up the marbles. She cast glances at the blue mat. They could take turns trying to get the marbles as close to a data cube as possible without knocking it off its spot. That could be fun, right?"

She nibbled her lip, explained her idea to Lily, who squealed and danced around the table, shaking her marble bag.

After every throw, Britta glanced in the direction of the communications room. More so when Ziot was summoned.

Lily screamed, "I won."

Britt grimaced. She couldn't recall a moment. Her inability to focus wasn't fair to Lily.

"Well done, squirt. Wanna grab a snack and head to the treehouse? We need to plan Ollie's wardrobe."

With a packet of crisps and a soda each, the crochet needles shoved in Britt's back pocket, and the balls of wool tucked under her arms, they headed down the passage.

"Regent Haiz is unavailable?" Nerx asked, his voice harsh.

"Yes, Supreme Commander. I am Primary Tarni, in charge for now. Regent Haiz and a unit of four warriors took a *yarva* to *Bronvol* under the pretense of negotiations. Some hours have passed, and we have yet to hear from her."

"Do you suspect foul play?" an operative asked.

"Of course. Rebels cannot be trusted when they've tossed aside their vows like petals in a breeze." Primary Tarni huffed.

"Do you require assistance?" Nerx asked. "My operatives can rescue your warriors and my people."

She pinched her lips. "My thanks for the offer. I will consult our strategists and revert."

"Alodon's balls," Ziot snapped, "I say we port across regardless. We've given them enough chance—"

"Britt?" Lily's puzzled voice snapped Britt out of her daze.

"Up the ladder you go, sweet pea," she hurried to say, then ushered Lily through the bulkhead. She tossed the wool up, unable to climb with her hands and armpits full. She didn't dare glance into the communications room, not wanting to be caught eavesdropping.

As Lily settled on the blanket, Britt dumped everything on the bench and grabbed her tablet. "Just going to get the patterns. Will you be fine alone for a few minutes?"

"Yup," Lily said, her hand in the crisp packet and her mouth stuffed.

Determined to be better disciplined, Britt managed to slink past the crowded communications room without listening in. Finding crochet patterns for toy clothing didn't take her long. She hurried back.

"Sena will retrieve Aldur while Karg collects Lady Dahlia. Ronin, Trav, Eriz, back him up and find the Viqrian warriors. Do not be heroic. A Dar Eth is in danger, but I need you all to live." Nerx grumbled something Britt couldn't catch. "Ziot has transferred to your O.D.I. the location of all the targets, but if something happens, then get Ziot access to their systems. Again, I reiterate, get in and out."

Britt clambered up the ladder, swelling her lungs until she exhaled long and hard. "Pants won't work, not on a four-legged animal."

"Ollie doesn't have four legs," Lily scoffed.

"He doesn't?" Britt tapped her chin as if in deep thought. "You better get him then. We need to measure him."

As Lily disappeared through the hatch, Britt flicked from one pattern to another. Finding the perfect elephant-shaped shirt pattern would be like stumbling on a diamond on a beach. She bookmarked possibles. It'd been so long since Mom had taught her the basics. Doing this with Lily would be a hard learning curve for them both.

"I suppose you heard?" Nerx appearing at the hatch made Britt squeak.

"Not much." She frowned. "How did you know I was listening?"

He laughed. "Even if you moved on silent feet, I would still know where you are. As my Dar Eth, I find your presence discernable."

Okay. She wasn't going to touch that. "I heard Haiz is missing, and you're sending the operatives." She forced a shrug she was far from feeling. Inside, she squealed like Lily would. At last, her mother would be rescued. Diplomacy be damned, right? "Lily and I have more important things to do."

He glanced down, then climbed into the star deck for a flushed Lily to dart around him to slump on the blanket. Poor Ollie was crushed to her chest, bulging his eyes.

"What do you think?" Britt asked, sliding her tablet over while flicking through the patterns.

"Oh, I love the flower one." With a delicate pinching of her brow, Lily bit her lip. "It looks hard. I don't know how..." She grabbed the closest needle and held it like a dagger.

"What are you doing?" Nerx asked, leaning down with a head tilt to study the image of a pink jacket.

"Making Ollie clothes," Lily said like it was obvious.

"Ah, good," he said. With a kiss to her temple and to Britt's lips, he disappeared down the hatch.

She released a pent-up breath, then grabbed the two balls of wool. "Which one?"

Of course, Lily chose the pink, leaving the purple for Britt. With patience she didn't know she had, she showed Lily how to start. Dad always said that keeping busy would make time fly. Britt was counting on that even as worry fiddled with the frayed edges of her mind. Operatives implied spies or agents. That meant they knew what they were doing. And if Nerx trusted them, then so would she.

Sending males to possibly die was the worst part of being a commander. Nerx was supposed to consider all scenarios, to mitigate any losses, and he'd done so on numerous occasions. But having met Britta, he couldn't bear for one male to die. He longed for his males to be as free of the void and their inevitable fates.

The silence wasn't helping. Edon managed the console, his fingers returning to the same button, forcing the system to refresh the scans when they were set to timed intervals.

Fear.

An uncontrollable flood of emotion.

Spiraling in ever-increasing concentric circles.

Down.

Until a physical manifestation takes over.

To fight.

To roar at the situation.

To save my males.

And yet, the mission is noble.

A must and a chance to earn honor.

Conquer the fear.

He opened his tablet to write the poem before he lost it. A distraction was what he needed.

Britta.

Except she was helping Lily make tiny garments. The replicator would've done that. Yet, their eyes had sparkled with excitement as they did this together. Perhaps it was the shared experience? He couldn't remember ever making anything by hand. Such skills were lost to them centuries ago when the replicator became common place and birthing females the main goal.

"Keep monitoring. I will make sure the med-E.D. is ready."

Edon swiveled his comfy to face Nerx. "We need Aldur. I do not know how to load a new species into the medical database. Ziot might but..."

Nerx smothered a grimace. He'd sent their only data officer to navigate an unknown battleship. If he was killed, they wouldn't be able to heal any injured Viqrians.

What they needed was stealth armor. He snorted at his *damu*-like imagination. All experiments had failed with the portable stealth generator being too unwieldy or exploding. They had, at least, self-healing, though it took a while, sensitive hearing, silent movements, and their regulating armor. That was the best they could do.

He strolled to the medical, checked the med-E.D.'s plasma tanks were full, then ordered two hot chocolates for him and Edon. He handed it to the pilot on his return, then sauntered over to the bulkhead to eavesdrop on Britta and Lily's conversation.

"Mine's messy," Lily whined.

"Mine too." Britta chuckled. "We can try again later or tomorrow, if you like."

"Awesome," Lily squealed. "I'm gonna play with my dolls."

"Sure, kiddo. I'll stay right here."

Nerx fought a sinking sadness that she wasn't going to seek him out. He snatched Lily as she scrambled down the ladder, sprinkling kisses all over her head and face. She giggled and squirmed, then swatted at him when he set her down. When she skipped along the passage while singing, warmth flooded his chest. She was *his* daughter.

What he should've realized was how traveling anywhere with her would endanger her. Not that he could've foreseen these events unfolded. Still, her future depended on him. And Britta's too.

Satisfied that Lily had headed to their quarters without getting distracted, he glanced at the hatch then at Edon focused on the console.

Everything within him compelled him to head up, to kiss Britta, and find solace in her arms. But he couldn't afford to when his males were mid-mission.

"Any news?" Britta's face appeared in the hatch.

"Four to port to medical," a male said via the console.

Nerx bolted to the common, Britta racing after him.

Sena was lifting Aldur onto the bed. His skin had taken on a darker hue, his eyes glazed.

"Thank you," Lady Dahlia said to Karg then limped toward the common.

"Mom." Britta veered around Nerx to hug her mother, who pulled out of the embrace.

"Not now, sweetheart," Lady Dahlia said, her focus on Aldur.

"Why are you limping? Is it your sciatica?" Britta wrung her hands.

"It feels like it." Lady Dahlia offered a tight smile. "Aldur was on the mend until he had to be heroic."

"Go," Britta whispered, her voice cracking. "We'll chat later. Just happy to have you back." She walked backward, spun and threw herself at Nerx.

He caught her on instinct, having not expected this.

She cried, her sobs muted even as she tightened her arms around his neck. "Thank you," she chanted. When she leaned back to meet his gaze, her cheeks were peach-colored and wet. "And you did it without letting me interfere. Mom will be in awe of your Britt-management skills."

He smiled. "I was selfish, not wanting you in harm's way."

The moment the fruity scents tickled his nose, Nerx raised his head. Viqrians had ported with Trav, Eriz, and Ziot. Only one male was missing.

"Where is Ronin?"

Trav thumped his chest. "Please honor Ronin et Brenin as having died in battle."

"Alodon's balls," Nerx roared, ice coating his heart. "What happened? Wait? As in Ambassador Brenin's son?"

"Yes, Supreme Commander. He was shot with a..." Trav glanced at Haiz clinging to his side. She held onto her ribs where blood stained her fingers.

"*Tagana*." Haiz grimaced. "A lethal weapon. My apologies. I did not factor in their desperation." She released Trav and inched toward Nerx, the corners of her mouth dipping. "I should have prepared better. I lost a warrior."

He lowered Britta and nudged her out of the way of his blaster.

"Thank you for taking the initiative." Haiz glanced at her remaining three females. "I fear the rebels would have killed us by end day." She swayed on the spot.

Britta lunged across and caught the Viqrian regent before she collapsed. "Wow, she's...uh, heavy."

Trav lifted the female into his arms and carried her to medical. Ziot waved his med-gun at Trav, then gestured to the fold-down bed.

"Now what?" Britta asked, sliding her hand in Nerx's.

He stilled, his nostrils flared, and he glanced at their intwined fingers. "We either dock on their ship, or we hand them over on a nearby moon."

"Which would you prefer?" she asked. "Can you trust them enough to dock?"

"In a way," Nerx said, despite having expected an attack from Haiz a moment ago. Where his Dar Eth was concerned, he couldn't be too cautious.

"I don't know, Nerx. They, or whoever, held my mother captive." She swept her gaze across the Viqrians, then inched closer to whisper, "I wouldn't trust them as far as I can throw them." Her lips twitched. "And they're damn heavy."

"So far, Haiz and her females have not deceived us other than to be vague." He drew her against him again. "I will be cautious though, taking with as many males as I can."

Britta exhaled. "I suppose you're going down. If it's the moon, I want to come with." She peered up him, a hopeful smile urging him to agree to anything she asked for.

"Absolutely not," he said.

"I don't accept your no," Britta said, facing him with her free hand on her hip.

"I *will not* place you in danger."

"Blah, blah," she snapped. "I've never been on any planet other than Earth. And if I get a chance to stand on some extraterrestrial soil, I'm going to take it."

"Britta," he growled, done speaking about this. "No."

She released his hand and shoved her face at his. "What? No? Like you and a few secret spies can't protect little me? And from what, exactly? A wild animal with a love for Britt-blood? Maybe a handsome prince desperate to find his forever-princess? Or... Wait for it, a bunch of nothing out there except dust and wind?"

He *could* ensure they landed in the open. That way he'd see danger approaching, and Ziot *could* monitor the air above them. That he was softening to the idea wasn't something he'd reveal to Britta. He liked this side of her: all fire, passion, determination, courage, and so damn lovable.

"And I could carry a blaster. It's not as if I haven't used it before." She ran a finger down his chest. "You can kit me in one of these too." She tapped his armor, then rose onto her toes to place a kiss on the underside of his jaw. "I can be very...appreciative." She licked her lips while hovering her touch an inch from his straining arousal.

"No..." He hesitated. "If you could give me a sample of your appreciation, I might think about allowing you to come with."

Her eyes widened, a peach hue stained her cheeks, then she cleared her throat. "Now?" she rasped, glancing around her.

He laughed, cupping her elbows to draw her closer. "*Ensa*, you cannot use our mating to bargain with."

She pouted, her adorable lips tempting him more than curiosity did. What would she have done? Images from the human mating vids hinted at many possibilities.

"I've nothing to barter with." She lowered her gaze.

Her words hit him hard. *Nothing to barter... Maker.* She'd saved him and Lily. For that alone, he'd spend his life making sure Britta never doubted her worth.

"Why are they staring? Is it your hair again?" She pulled out of his arms to glare at his males.

A few smothered smiles, their mouths twitched from the effort. Others averted their gazes.

He listened in to a few grumbles, too low for her ears. "My hair is shorter than honor-requires, yes, but I used to be grumpy," he said, amazed at how he'd abandoned a habit he'd worked hard to form. Guarding the void had been his core focus after Kyerx died and triggered a sharp expansion.

"You, grumpy? No, never." She chuckled. "You're the picture of sunshine and daisies."

"Is that so?" He smirked, loving her ease at teasing him. "I have found my Dar Eth—that alone is reason to stare." He swept her against him, startling a gasp out of her. "I would gaze upon you for your beauty alone."

Her cheeks flushed. She opened and closed her mouth without saying a word, then whispered, "Is it still a no?"

"If you wear Etterian armor, carry a med gun, and accept being chained to the interior of the *kuta*, then yes." He pressed his nose into her hair for a deep inhale. "*And* I want your vow to remain out of sight until I deem it is safe to exit..."

The smile she blessed him with swelled the light in his heart to such an extent that he half-expected his ribs to crack under the pressure. The Ethera had so many characteristics they hadn't known about: the visions, the excruciating agony, the clinching of his heart at odd moments, the addiction to her scent, the unbearable lust... And now, this light. If Aldur was well, Nerx would ask him if he'd experienced the same. A full medical assessment might be wise.

Chapter Seventeen

With victory making her steps buoyant, Britt left the haven of Nerx's arms to approach her mother, who stood to the side, out of the way of the men working on Aldur and Haiz. Worry furrowed her brow. Sadness lingered in her gaze. Not once did she glance away from Aldur.

"Mom?" Britt touched her mom's hands, calming the white-knuckled grip.

She jerked back and blinked in a daze. "Oh, honey," she said, dragging Britt into a crushing hug.

"Was thinking, while they heal Aldur in that pod thingy... A shower wouldn't go amiss and maybe something to eat?" She didn't pull out of Mom's embrace, letting her take as long as she needed.

"I feel so helpless," she sobbed. "Their tech is so advanced, I'm of no help. And I'm not an expert on their physiology, not yet anyway. But yes, I can't just sit here. A shower would be nice." She chuckled through her crying. "I could kill for an herbal tea."

"How's your hip? Did they at least scan you with their med gun?"

Mom nodded. "All good."

Britt slumped. "I'll ask Nerx to fetch you the moment Aldur stirs. Let's get you freshened up." She tugged on Mom's hand, almost dragging her from the medical.

With one stumbling step at a time, Mom followed.

Britt paused next to Nerx still standing guard at the entrance of the common, his brooding scowl in place. "Please—"

"I will, *ensa*."

She smiled. "And send Lily to me if she's done playing with her dolls." She stole a kiss, not sure why, but with her lips tingling, glad she did. There was just something potent about the man she'd hated days ago. Whatever this was, this alien attraction, she was helpless against it.

"What was that?" Mom asked when they entered her quarters.

"Same as you and Aldur, so it seems." Britt pinched her lips to swallow a laugh. "Who would've thought... Now, hop in the shower, and I'll get your clothes and tea ready."

Mom hurried to the bathroom; no doubt eager for that tea. Britt smiled as she gathered capris and a blouse from Mom's closet. She'd soon feel like a human again, and once she had tea and perhaps her favorite PB&J sandwich in her, she'd be ready to face anything.

When Mom emerged in her toweling robe, Britt gestured to the table. Her clothes were draped over the back of the chair. But Mom sat and cupped the mug.

She hummed after one sip. "They only eat fruit, which is fine, I guess."

Britt sank into the chair opposite her. "At least they fed you."

Mom harumphed. "Can you see Nerx eating fruit?"

Britt grinned. "So you're happy being Aldur's Dar Eth?"

Mom stilled, met Britt's gaze, and nodded. "I would've fallen for him even if there wasn't this Ethera-thing between us. Still, as a doctor, a chemical bond like this, almost sentient, blows my mind. My scientific brain calls bullshit, and yet..." She splayed her fingers across her chest. "I feel it here. A certainty, a warmth cocooning my heart." She shook her head. "My peers would think me insane."

Tears pressed the backs of Britt's eyes. To finally see her mom settled, in love, after all this time... She swallowed a sob.

Mom bit into her sandwich and moaned. "It's the texture—soft bread, crunchy peanut butter, and sweet jelly. They say it's called palate fatigue. I can believe it." She met Britt's gaze. "I thought you hated Nerx?"

"I thought so too. Turns out...not so much. And um... I dunno how to say this, but you're a grandmama now."

Mom choked on a bite, coughed, then took a desperate sip of tea. "Lily?"

"Yup." Britt brought her feet up to rest her chin on her knees. "You know how I longed for the ride-into-the-sunset kind of romance? Well, it ain't gonna happen. I have to spend my life with a man who doesn't love me. Sure, he's affectionate, but is that enough?" She tutted. "Not that I have much of a choice either. Another thing that irritates. But when I'm with him, I don't care about this Ethera. I...want him, I guess." She shrugged, happy to be talking to someone about this, and since Mom was going through it too, she'd understand.

"What would your father say about obstacles?"

"They're a bitch to climb over?" Britt wiggled her eyebrows while grinning.

"Nice try." Mom smacked her lips after another sip. "They're just illusions built up in your mind to resemble a brick wall."

"Find a way through, around, or over it." Britt sniffed. "He said that, I remember." She lowered her legs and tucked her hands under her thighs. "So, does Aldur love you too?"

Mom's cheeks flushed. "None of your business."

"Ah, come on," Britt whined then huffed when her mother stayed quiet.

"I half-expected you to elope. Dropping me a text saying how you're on your honeymoon." Mom grinned. "Your father called you a wild child."

Britt scoffed. "Well, I guess this makes you a mom-in-law. And Aldur my stepdad." She swallowed hard. Having wanted Mom to move on hit differently now that it had happened. She mumbled, "He's awesome."

"Your father will always be my first love, honey. He'll never be forgotten."

"I know." Britt wiped her cheeks. "It's just too fast." She caught her mom's hand. "I'm happy for you...and sad. I'm being silly." She offered a watery smile.

"It's been just the two of us for so long."

"The Swansons against the world." Britt raised a fist in triumph.

"Now we have back up." Mom patted Britt's hand then rose to pull on her clothes.

"Just... I went from single with no prospects to married with a daughter."

A slow smile bloomed across Mom's face, sparkling her eyes. "I can't believe I'm a grandmother. This...is incredible."

"Yup, me as a mother. Who would've thought it."

"I did." Mom gave Britt an awkward hug then stepped back to slip into her ballet flats.

"Want to talk about what happened on that ship?"

Mom pursed her lips. "Nope."

Britt released a long exhale. "Do you think Aldur will recover?"

"Of course. With our medical tech, nope. With theirs, yup. They can grow eyeballs, for Pete's sake."

The door chimed.

Britt leaped to her feet to answer it. Lily danced on the spot; the neon pink tutu she wore bobbed around her.

"Cupcake, come meet your granny."

Lily skipped inside then stopped. "I have a granny?" She faced Mom, her mouth slack jawed. With a squeal, she bounced around the room, then wrapped her arms around Mom's legs, hugging them.

Mom laughed, caught Lily's hand and twirled her. "Hello, granddaughter."

Lily giggled, pulled away, then stared at Britt. Tears spilled over her plump cheeks. "You're my new mommy?"

Britt's heart wrenched, and she stepped toward Lily. "Of course," she managed to say through the lump in her throat. "And Aldur is your grandfather."

Lily's face crumpled as she threw herself at Britt, who kneeled to pick her up. When Mom had been saved, Britt had thrown herself at Nerx—she'd expected him to catch her. With the sobbing girl cradled in her arms, Britt let her tears flow. Yup, she trusted Nerx when she hadn't felt like that with any man since Dad died. Something unraveled in her soul. His death had been a betrayal. It had taken her this long to realize why she'd never dated, why she was such a control freak, why she was too scared to love again, and why she had to let that all go.

"A new beginning for us all," she whispered, rubbing her cheek over the crown of her daughter's head. "Lily and I are on a mission. Aren't we, squirt?" Britt asked, trying to lighten the mood. "We're crocheting clothes for Ollie, a stuffed elephant."

"Oh, that sounds like a noble quest. Knights armed with crochet needles." Mom paused, a slight frown forming. "You remember how?"

"Sort of. We tried this morning." Britt chuckled, tossed Lily over her shoulder then spun, eliciting giggles and laughter from her 'captive.'

"I'll show you when I can." Mom hummed. "Might even have a try. Something to keep my hands busy." She glanced at the door.

"Go." Britt nudged her chin. "Check on my stepdad. Squirt and I will follow." When alone, Britt sank onto a chair, adjusting a heavy Lily to face her. "How do you feel about having me as a new mommy?" She tucked a stray curl behind Lily's ear. "Mm? You can call me whatever you want, sweetheart."

"Can I get a brother?" Lily asked, pressing her palms together.

Britt laughed. "God controls that. You'll have to place your order with him."

"Oh, He knows," she sang, scampered off Britt's lap and skipped to the door. "I've gotta tell Nerxie. He's going to be so happy."

Britt grinned and raced after Lily, eager to overhear *that* conversation. His men stared at Lily when she darted around the common, calling Nerx's name. She barreled past Britt to the communications room, her energy unparallel. This time, Britt was hot on her heels.

"I bring sad news, Operations Commander Malo," Nerx said.

Britt lunged and caught Lily's arm, dragging her back while pressing a finger to her lips.

"Elite Operative Ronin has been killed on an enemy's battleship."

"And his body?" a man asked. She had to assume it was this Malo speaking.

"Left behind," Nerx said. "Can we retrieve it, Edon?"

"Yes and no," Edon said, confusion in his voice. "His O.D.I. is active which is not odd for a male not dead for long. What I cannot reconcile is his request not to retrieve him."

"He is alive?" Nerx roared.

Britt winced and hoisted Lily into her arms.

"When were you planning on telling me, Pilot?" Nerx demanded.

"My apologies, Supreme Commander," Edon said. "It just came through. I was monitoring his O.D.I. signal as per protocol, expecting it to fade as his residual energy does."

"Is the signal stronger than expected for a 'dead' male?" Malo asked.

"Yes, but too weak to port. I do have his location on the *Bronvol* if you wish to ignore his request, Operations Commander."

"Mm, intriguing," Malo said. "Do as he asks, Nerx. I am most pleased the news is not as sad as expected. Informing Ambassador Brenin of the loss of his son would have fallen on the king's shoulders."

"Indeed. Which is why I commed you first as Ronin's superior," Nerx said.

Britt peeked into the room when Malo said, "Keep me posted on new developments."

Nerx glared at Edon. "Alodon's balls, I am pleased *and* furious with you."

"My timing could have been better," Edon said.

"So could Ronin's." Nerx smiled. "What is he up to?"

Edon shook his head. "Who can fathom how an operative's mind works."

"Indeed."

Sensing an end to the conversation, Britt released a squirming Lily to run into the communications room.

"Nerxie," she cried out, holding her arms up.

Britt trailed but leaned against the inside wall of the room, content to watch this big man handle his daughter.

"Nerxie, Britt says she's my new mommy. Did you know?" She tugged on his braid, flicking it back and forth. "And her mommy's my granny. And Uncle Aldur's my gramps. Did you know?"

Nerx glanced at Britt, staring at her until Lily hit him across the chin with his braid. "Yes, *minus susa*. Are you happy about that?"

"Yup, I've a family now. Britt says I must ask God for a brother?"

Nerx's head shot up to meet Britt's gaze. "Yes," he said without breaking eye contact. "You do not want a sister?"

"A brother would be more fun." Lily grinned. "I'm hungry."

"Come. What do you feel like?" Britt wiggled her fingers in a universal hurry-up-let's-go gesture. "Pizza?"

"Tag Afred," Lily called, running out the door as soon as Nerx put her down.

He caught Britt's wrist, pulled her toward him, then kissed her. Warmth poured down her body like stepping into a hot shower. She moaned, gripped his arms, and melted against him.

"We need to start on that brother," he whispered, his hoarse voice electrifying her senses.

Something heavy twisted her gut. "Let's be this for now. Just us three."

He jerked back, his brows knitted.

She cupped his face, holding him still. "I'm reeling from all this—becoming a wife and mother. I need time to expand my heart before I add more. If that makes sense." She pressed her temple to his chin, unable to understand why she couldn't explain how she felt. The words escaped her when they were within grasp, burning her tongue. "It's too much. Too fast. I have to let go of my childish hopes and embrace my new life."

"What hopes?" he asked.

"I guess... Falling in love, to start with. A wedding where—" Her voice cracked, but she pushed on. "My dad walks me down the aisle. Our first home, getting pregnant... In that order. Impossible, I know." Her chuckle lacked mirth. "Dad's gone. You're my husband, and I have a daughter now." She tried to shrug and failed. "I feel...like I'm losing parts of who I am. Like I don't recognize me anymore." She stepped back as far as he'd let her. "I better feed the bottomless pit that is our daughter."

He let her go, yet the darkness in his eyes haunted her.

Nerx blinked at the empty doorway, long after Britta left. 'Falling in love' had snagged all of his attention. Yes, he wanted that too. The Ethera played havoc with his emotions. He couldn't tell whether what he felt for his Dar Eth was this elusive love or something the Ethera inspired. He fully understood when she said it was too soon. His mind and heart grappled with each other, but where she was losing herself, he was growing, becoming the male he was meant to be.

"Wedding," he muttered. Having to speak the word to activate the O.D.I. had been his decision. Most Etterians left the default setting, but Nerx hadn't wanted to be flooded with explanations for every strange word uttered by anyone.

Images flooded his mind now. The ecstatic brides said it all. And his Britta deserved to have such a day. That was doable. Perhaps at Berrann Falls. His chest cinched. Yes, to include Kyerx and bid him farewell. If Britta was up to the idea. Lily could be a flower girl. A smile twitched Nerx's lips at his imagination. She'd love that.

He glanced at Edon, his head dipped as he worked. "Pray forming a relationship with your Dar Eth is not as complicated."

Edon grinned. "The Ethera will choose well for me as it did for you, Supreme Commander."

That it had. For Aldur too. Nerx headed to the common intent on the medic in question. Britta sat with Lily at the table. Aldur was awake, Lady Dahlia in his arms.

"I understand why your males ogle Britta, but why the youngin?" Haiz asked when Nerx strolled past her to read the med-E.D.'s results.

"*Damu* are rarely seen, and that Lily is a female adds to their awe." Nerx smiled at his males trying their hardest to keep their gazes off his wife and daughter. "A female *damu* is a miracle in their eyes."

"Ah, so it is true, that you cherish your females?" Haiz scowled. "That is far from what we were taught. All males disrespect their females. For this alone, we have for centuries only cultivated daughters."

"It depends on the species," Matir said, joining them. "Some worlds do not value their females or *damu*. Some do not value life at all."

Haiz's frown didn't fade. "My thanks for your honesty, Sub-Commander."

"There are Etterian males without honor." Nerx grimaced, trying not to glance at his braid. "Good and evil exists in all of us. Some lack the strength to resist their dishonorable nature."

"Something the *Bronvol* has taught me." She pinched her lips. "There is nothing in our archives similar to this. No betrayals, no mutiny, no rebellions."

"Odd, indeed. Great change comes through great discomfort. Come, let us comm your *Kunakar* and arrange a meeting. A neutral ground will be chosen." Nerx nodded at Matir, indicating he should join them.

"You do not trust us," she said as a statement.

Nerx met her gaze. "I do not because I have females on board. Had it been just my males, we would be arrogant enough to dock on your ship."

"You are mated?" She glanced around the common. "And your males?"

"I am an Eth gifted with a Dar Eth..." His gaze rested on Britta teaching Lily how to twirl the food using a fork and spoon. "Too many of my males have not been as blessed yet."

"Dar Eth?" Haiz made a clicking sound with her tongue against her teeth. "Our studies revealed as much."

Matir twisted to look at her. "Tell me, how is it you speak Earth English?"

"With our scans, we found the language to be common across most inhabited worlds in this galaxy. All our warriors were required to learn it during the journey here." She stepped toward the passage. "Shall we? I am eager to return. As entertaining as this adventure has been, I long for my palette. I could sleep a whole cycle." She laughed and trailed Matir to the comm room.

"Pilot Edon, comm the *Kunakar*," Nerx instructed once Matir settled behind him. "Have we chosen the location?" he grumbled.

"Of course. As per your security requirements," Matir whispered. "When do you want to head down?"

"Within the hour." Nerx clasped his hands behind his back as the screen flickered.

"Regent Haiz," Primary Tarni exclaimed.

"Good tidings, Tarni. I'm well." Haiz touched her brow.

"We have sixty minutes to meet on Luchur, one of six moons orbiting Aberdus," Matir said. "Should the time elapse, we will return to the *Surata* with your warriors. Pilot Edon, convey the rendezvous co-ordinates."

Edon tapped buttons, his focus acute. "Done, Sub-Commander."

"Excellent." Haiz beamed. "Send a *yarva* to collect us, Primary."

"As you command, Regent Haiz." Tarni tapped her temple. The comm ended.

"As easy as hitting *znorgs* in a basket." Haiz chuckled. "My thanks again for the assistance. And deepest apologies for your lost male."

Nerx bowed, not willing to reveal that Ronin lived. Whatever the male was up to, secrecy meant he might stay alive a little longer.

When they returned to the common, Aldur was kneeling, Lily hugging him tight. She jabbered at a steady clip amid Aldur's laughter. "Gramps, we did... and then Britt helped me... and I have a granny too. I won at marbles... God will give me a brother to play with... Gramps, are you still sore?"

Nerx met Britta's gaze. She smiled.

He grinned then glanced at Matir. "Sub-Commander, you have the comm."

"Very well, Supreme Commander."

Nerx faced the common. "Trav, Eriz, Karg, Sena, and Ziot to me. Arm yourself and the *kuta* for a trip planetside. We aim to deliver the Viqrians."

Haiz crossed to her warriors and was welcomed with grins and brow taps.

"And me?" Britta asked, placing her hand on his waist. "I had better be on that shuttle."

He grinned and laced his fingers through hers. "Of course, *ensa*. I made a vow." With a firm tug, he pulled her along. "Lady Dahlia, Medic Aldur, I place Lily in your care."

"That sounds official," Lady Dahlia said. "And quit calling me lady, Nerx. You're my son now. Mom or Dahlia will do."

Nerx froze, blinked at her while he struggled to understand the explosion of emotions in his heart. "As in Mother?"

She nodded and scooped Lily into her arms for a dance around the table.

Tears burned the backs of his eyes. His nostrils flared, and a tickle scratched his throat. He'd never known his mother, and now, thanks to Britta, he had one. He glanced at Lily, truly understanding her elation.

"A responsibility I gladly accept," Aldur said, resting his palm on Nerx's shoulder.

Britta sliced worried glances at Nerx when he ushered her into Aldur's old quarters. As soon as the door closed, she asked, "Did my mom say something wrong?"

"No, Britta, my Dar Eth. *Our* mom was perfect."

Chapter Eighteen

Britt could swear there were tears in Nerx's eyes. But he didn't give her a chance to find out why. Instead, he was undressing her faster than she dressed on chilly winter mornings.

She laughed, trying to swat his hands away. "What are you doing?"

"You have to ask?" he growled. Around him were the scattered clothes she'd been in a moment ago. Even her boots and socks were discarded.

"Maybe we should go planetside more often," she whispered when he tapped his chest armor to release it and whip it off. Molten bronze pecs and abs to his Adonis belt glistened in the unnatural lighting. *He is just so damn...lickable.*

"We do not have much time." He touched the waistband of his pants. It parted, revealing the tip of a very erect cock.

"Oh? We don't?" She arched a brow even as she hooked a finger between the thick fabric of his pants and his stomach. He gave off so much heat, and the velvet texture of his skin invited her to stroke him all over.

Standing there naked made her feel...well, more naked. Exposed. Vulnerable. Almost shy. While she drew on the floor with her toe, she tried to hide how tingles goosebumped her skin. How her heart pounded in her ears. The way her breathing labored as if she'd run a marathon when she didn't even run to the bathroom.

She blinked and found herself pinned to the wall. He tossed her left leg over one shoulder and thrust his face into her crotch. "Whoa. Going for the sweet spot already?"

He didn't say anything, just ran his tongue along her sex. She gasped at the bolt of fiery need shooting outward. To hell with words. His tongue had better things to do. With each lick, swirl, lap, tension built in her core. It twanged, making demands she couldn't focus on. His touch, his fingers digging into her hips... Then he had her right leg draping his other shoulder. Pinned to the wall, she didn't fear falling. And if she did, she didn't care. Not when he devoured her, drawing sweet pleasure with his mouth.

"Nerxie," she panted. "So close."

He growled. The vibration hit her sensitive clit, and she shattered, crying out as she spasmed and contorted. Not that he stopped licking, and it didn't calm her when he thrust a finger into her as she came. Quite the opposite. Her nipples tightened to snapping point when another orgasm hit. She reeled, savoring the multiple explosions of joy, light, colors...

He guided her legs around his hips, then thrust into her.

Too much. Too intense.

She whimpered.

Each plunge, every withdrawal, she experienced to the minutest degree, until orgasms blurred together. She trembled in his arms, her tongue stuck to the roof of her mouth, tears of bliss slipped free, and yet, if he stopped, she'd kill him.

She arched into him, rubbing her breasts across his chest for another frisson of delight to pool lower. Digging her nails into his shoulders, she clung to him, letting him have his way with her when there was nothing she'd rather he be doing.

He stilled, groaned, grunted, leaned back to rest his temple to hers, then sucked in a shuddering breath. "Britta," he rasped. "My sweet, fiery Britta."

He didn't pull out as she expected him to. Instead, he looped an arm around her waist and crushed her to him. For a few minutes, he did nothing but hold her.

She pressed her chin to his shoulder and hugged him back while her breathing evened out. Her heart swelled, somehow hitting her tear ducts. She cleared her throat and tried to break away. No way was she going to cry without reason.

"Come," he said, pulling out.

She shivered and slid her legs down until her toes touched the cold floor.

He didn't tuck himself in but left his pants gaping. The sheer look of him flushed her cheeks. With his back to her, she hurried to snatch up her bra. She clipped it on then froze when he shoved a pile of clothing at her.

"What's this?" She took it from him and widened her eyes when the texture registered. "You were serious? My own armor?" She squealed, dropping the stack to yank on the pants while her mind whispered, *'Don't forget about the chain.'* She'd thought he'd been joking.

He watched...no, ogled her as she slipped into every piece, then she stood there, her arms extended. Without her asking, he snapped each item until he gestured at her boots. She sat to peel on her socks while he cleaned himself and dressed. Not an inch of him looked untidy.

She stamped on her boots, then faced him. "Do I get a blaster?"

"*Thamani.*" Chuckling, he whisked her into his arms to cup her cheek, burying his fingers in her hair. His smile faded when he dipped to brush his mouth across hers.

He didn't answer her, just clasped her hand and led her from the room. She'd probably burned that bridge when she'd charged in and shot two people. No way would he trust her with another weapon. She huffed, even as he weaved through the crowded common to the bay. His males were boarding the shuttle along with three Viqrians and Haiz. They stood or sank into fold-down chairs, with Etterians opting to stand in the center.

"Supreme Commander, the battleships *Usaha* and *Kushin* have arrived," Matir said through Nerx's O.D.I.

"Patch me through," Nerx said as he strapped Britt into the chair closest to the pilot seat but farthest from the door. Then from a pocket, he withdrew a thin chain, no thicker than her pinky.

She gasped, wiggling to watch him clip it to her belt and to the chair's frame. "But—"

"Nerx, what do you need?"

Britt glared at Nerx, shaking the chain at him.

"Prince Citus?" He stroked her ear. "Matir, share the co-ordinates. We are en route to deliver the Viqrians, my prince."

Prince, she mouthed. Etteria had royalty? Oh, wait, Aldur had mentioned a king and queen. Although, she hadn't believed him at the time. Sure, *'I'm on a quest for my queen.'* When would that not sound bizarre?

"We will meet you there." The call ended.

"Ziot, take us out," Nerx commanded.

The shuttle's door shut with a defining thud.

Giving up on convincing him to unchain her, she leaned forward to watch via the front window how Ziot spun them then shot through the bay doors. Nerx inched closer, until her temple touched his stomach. She gripped his waist, giving him a squeeze.

Her breath lodged in her throat at the endless expanse of black space and stars. In a ship with just the treehouse and the communications room giving her glimpses of the outside, she hadn't grasped the full extent of where she was. A massive purple planet with multi-colored swirls loomed, but Ziot veered to the side, aiming for a tiny dot.

"We're landing on that?" she whispered, raising her gaze to Nerx's.

He brushed curls off her cheek and ran a caressing finger along her jaw, all while staring into her eyes. A sweet smile teased his lips.

Something in his expression resonated in her soul. She couldn't put her finger on it, nor truly understand what it meant, but she couldn't breathe, like air had been sucked out of her lungs. He said nothing, just stood there, their gazes locked. *Thamani?* He'd called her that instead of 'brat' or 'little cat.'

"Two minutes," Ziot said.

Nerx whipped his head up, narrowed his eyes on the window, then scowled. "Are we first to arrive?"

"Yes, Supreme Commander."

"Come, Britta." Nerx unbuckled her then gripped her shoulders, twisting her to face the front. The chain pooled on the floor behind her feet. "Look." He settled behind her, then wrapped an arm around her waist, while gripping a strap hanging from the ceiling.

Details formed on that dot: rolling hills, forests, waterfalls, gigantic lakes, and snow-capped mountains. She couldn't help the idea that this was Earth millions of years ago.

"It's beautiful," she said, cupping Nerx's hand at her stomach.

The colorful fauna and flora filled the view when Ziot landed. The tranquility made her bounce on her toes in excitement. Nerx tightened his arm, crushing her against him.

He mumbled in her ear, "Quit moving, *ensa*."

She twisted to smile at him. "Make me."

"We will discuss this later," he said, as the shuttle's door opened, flooding the compartment with fresh, organic-smelling air. "Remember your vow. Wait here." He drew his blaster and strode out, leaving her alone with Ziot.

With the chain granting her some leeway, she inched closer to the weak sunlight streaming in. Her mouth dropped open. It was the sounds she relished. Screeches came from overhead and lizard-like birds flew above. Rustles and tweets came from the bushes on the outskirts of the clearing. She had to assume those were insects or crawling animals.

The wind filled her ears while the sun warmed her outstretched hand. Four men formed a circle around the shuttle's entrance then took up spots on the outskirts, gazing outward.

Nerx escorted Haiz and her team about seven meters away but close enough to run back if they needed to. They gathered between him and the shuttle, their stances that of exhaustion. They'd been healed, fed, had rested, as far as Britta knew. She winced at her selfishness. For the first time, she realized whatever they'd seen on board their sister battleship might have been traumatic for them.

Nerx took this seriously, as expected of a commander. Pride expanded her chest. She gazed at him, no longer interested in this moon and its landscape. *That's my man.* Three shuttles landing blew dust around her, so she shifted away from the door until the wind died. Out marched about a dozen Etterians per shuttle, bolstering the men guarding the parameter.

The Viqrians shuffled with Haiz stepping between her women and Nerx, using her body as a shield. That alone told Britt what kind of leader the Viqrian was. Nerx had been right. She'd been honorable in her attempts to prevent a war.

This incident was about to be done and dusted. Britt could forgive and forget, especially if it garnered peace.

One man, massive across the shoulders, held himself with such authority as he strode across the circle. He gripped Nerx's arm, a grin splitting his cheeks.

When he mumbled something, she angled her head to hear better.

Nerx laughed. "Prince Citus, this is a surprise."

"*You* are surprised when Xeus tells me you found a new species?" Citus peered into his eyes and beamed. "Congrats on finding your Dar Eth."

Nerx glanced at shuttle, forcing her to duck back. "My thanks."

Citus caught Nerx's braid and ran his thumb across it. "It looks good on you."

Nerx stiffened. "Dishonor?"

"Freedom, my battle-bond. Not a single Etterian warrior would believe you lack honor." Citus withdrew a dagger and sliced his own braid in half. As his hair unraveled, he held up his braid, then tossed it at Nerx's feet.

The men sucked in sharp breaths, then, one by one, did the same.

In horror, Nerx threw out his hands to stop them. "No!"

They ignored him.

Something tickled Britt's cheek. She flicked at it, then blinked at the moisture on her fingertips. She sniffed, trying to stem the tears.

Ziot raced past her to toss his braid on the pile. "Take my honor, Supreme Commander."

"And mine," Sena said, throwing in his hair.

"Enough," Nerx roared.

"This change has been coming for a while. Time to forge a new tradition," Citus said, smiling at the men. "Now, introduce me to these Viqrians."

Nerx hesitated, then stepped aside. "Regent Haiz, commander of the battleship *Kunakar*."

"On behalf of Etteria, as ambassador and prince, I welcome you." Citus focused on her then froze. Pain twisted his features. He swayed, then crumpled to a knee. A shudder swept through him.

Nerx gaped, then lunged between a man and the prince. "Do not touch him." He glanced at Haiz, his eyes widening.

Britt rose on her toes, trying to see what was going on.

A frowning Haiz clasped Citus by the arms, as if she could lift him to his feet. When he groaned, she released him. But he caught her hands and tugged her down. At her gasp, her women charged to her side, no doubt ready to defend her.

She held up her hand. "He is not harming me."

"I would never," Citus croaked, opening his eyes, now an all-too-familiar neon blue.

"Oh, shit," Britt whispered. Haiz's frown didn't say much. Without knowing anything about their culture, Britt had to assume the regent didn't know about the Ethera.

Britt whipped her gaze back to Nerx. *Wait.* Was this how Nerx's eyes changed color? When? Why hadn't she seen it happen?

A shadow fell across them. She inched deeper into the shuttle, shielding her eyes from the sun's glare even as a dark blue ship landed on the outside of the circle and opposite to the Etterian shuttles. Viqrian, she supposed, since it matched the color of their battleships. The door opened to green light and women filing out.

One look at the woman striding ahead of her unit stiffened Britt's shoulders. Ziot stood before her, having not returned to the pilot seat. She bolted toward him, snapping the chain taut. With a growl, she stretched out her hand and grabbed his shoulder, tugging him backward. Glancing at her face, he complied, withdrawing his blaster within the shadows of the shuttle's compartment.

"It's the woman who stole my mom," she whispered.

He peered through the door and repeated what she said. She frowned. Why had he done that? Did he have a private channel with Nerx? And if so... Oh, yup, that's right. She didn't have an O.D.I. yet. *Typical.*

Nerx met her gaze and nodded. With a gesture at his males, they widened their circle to encompass the new arrivals. "Oh, good, you are on time," he said. "We officially hand over your females—"

"You want me to believe you do not recognize me?" Shioll smirked. "Have you been demoted? Or is this a rebellion in the making?" She nudged the pile of discarded braids with her boot.

Movement caught Britt's attention. She narrowed her eyes on Haiz helping Prince Citus to his feet. Then with one swift lunge, she unsheathed Citus's blaster and fired, hitting Shioll between the eyes.

"On behalf of our empress, you are judged." Haiz swung the gun wide as everyone drew theirs.

Britt gasped, torn between hiding and praying a tub of popcorn would materialize. This could turn into a mess or the most epic showdown.

Citus drew a greatsword from down his back, somehow hidden behind a built-in sheath. Because, *dammit,* surely she would've felt something on Nerx during one of those many passionate embraces. Still, it was a freaking visual delight.

Gunfire followed, green and white bolts zigzagging across the clearing. For the most part, the greens bounced off the Etterian armor. The whites hit limbs or shoulders, nothing too lethal. She didn't think the Etterians wanted to kill the Viqrians.

One glance from Nerx had him bolting toward Britt amid shots fired. Her breath hitched, and fear coiled its debilitating numbness through her body. "What the fuck?" she asked when he swept her deeper into the shuttle.

"You vowed," he roared. "Ziot, guard her."

"Don't you dare yell at me, asshole. I'm in the damn shuttle, aren't I?" She grabbed the chain and waved it at him. "With this."

He peered through the doorway, his blaster raised. "You were on the ramp."

I was? She must have inched out in her eagerness to see better. "Oh."

He didn't hear her, already sprinting into the fray.

Harumphing at her mistreatment, she hurried to scan the

If she'd had popcorn, she would've gotten in a few mouthfuls, that's how quick the fight ended. Viqrians and Etterians had Shioll's unit kneeling in the center. A glance showed some men bleeding. A man moved between the wounded, Viqrian and Etterian alike, with the med gun.

Citus took his blaster from Haiz, then tapped the red button. "You just stunned her." He handed it back to her and stepped aside.

"No talking me out of this?" Haiz arched a brow at Citus.

"As a commander, you have procedure to follow." He ran a finger along her jaw. "Duty is a tiresome burden but necessary."

She stared at him, then marched across to Shioll and fired at point blank range. "Anyone else want to question our traditions?"

"The High Council refuses to listen," a kneeling woman spat, blue blood dribbling from her temple. "We want more to this life."

"I lost five sisters to servitude for perceived slights." Another raised her chin in defiance, while nursing her side.

"I am surprised you did not bother to clear the *yarva*, Haiz," a woman tutted, stepping down from the Viqrian shuttle. She strode past Shioll's body without glancing at it. Confidence was in her swagger, her gaze bold, determined, and arrogant.

"Kaara, I expected better of you," Haiz snapped, sweeping out her arm. "This is not how you instigate change."

Kaara shrugged. "You know how I feel about the powers-that-be."

"As you know my stance." Haiz raised the blaster. "On behalf of our empress, you are judged."

"I do not die so easily," Kaara cried out, leaping forward with her dagger drawn.

Citus lunged between her and Haiz, swinging his greatsword in a wide arc.

Shit. Britt gawked at the head bouncing across the ground toward her like a scene out of a movie. *How sharp is that damn thing?*

Citus swiveled, sword held high. He lowered it to place his hand on the gun Haiz aimed at the women. "May I suggest a trade?"

"I am listening." Haiz angled her chin but didn't glance at him.

"Release them to our care, and take me in their stead."

"No," Nerx growled. "Xeus will shave my head—"

Citus held up a hand, silencing the outcry. "As her Eth, I go where she goes. You know this."

"My what?" Haiz faced him.

"I will explain later," Citus said, sheathing his bloodied sword.

She opened her mouth then shut it before spinning on a heel and striding toward Nerx. "Have your pilot comm Tarni and tell her I have my own *yarva*."

"Do it, Ziot," Nerx said, as if the man could hear him from within the shuttle.

Ziot, still at the console, called Tarni, relaying the message. "It is done."

Britt peered into his ears, trying to figure out how they spoke to themselves yet heard each other.

"We will deal with the *Bronvol*, or do you want those females too?" Haiz smirked. "Are you worth that many?"

"We can send them to Fuyra, a mining moon orbiting Etteria," Nerx said, then glanced at Haiz. "Where we put dishonorables to work."

"The operatives you have on board must question each female. Test their participation. Some may have been forced. Those who test poorly will serve in your mines." Citus gazed at Haiz, his fascination revealed by the smile teasing his lips.

What mines? Britt opened her mouth to ask then swallowed the question. Now wasn't the time.

"If Fuyra is secure, then I will accept on behalf of my empress." Haiz touched her temple. "I am certain she will agree it is a fine solution."

In bloodstained uniforms yet healed, the Viqrians marched in single file onto the Viqrian shuttle. Citus joined Haiz, his focus on her when the door shut. When they launched, the five women still kneeling watched but didn't move. They ogled the men around them, some leaning in to whisper to each other.

"Trav, Eriz, Karg, take these females to the *Sasay*. Question them then release them to the *Kushin* with instruction—Fuyra or Etteria." Nerx scowled, his arms folded across his chest, as he waited, watched, not even flinching when all except their shuttle left.

When only his men remained, he relaxed. "You did well, and my report to our king will reflect my high praise." He clasped his braid. "Thank you for your gesture." He tapped the clip. "Retrieve yours; you will need it."

Then he headed to Britt, who squeaked and ducked back inside, lest he yelled at her again. That still grated, and she'd give him a piece of her mind first chance she got.

He unlocked the chain from her belt. "Come, *thamani*. Walk with me."

Blinking at his offered hand, she hesitated, then accepted, letting him usher her onto the grass. Her boots squelched, and the spongy ground added an extra bounce to her steps, as if she walked on a mattress. She shivered but didn't say anything, not when she'd fought hard to come with. The next planet might be nicer, but she wouldn't get to find out if she whined now.

"Did it go like you hoped?" she asked, stepping over what looked like a dead trunk. Odd that when there were no trees nearby.

"No, but I know better than to expect anything to go as I envisioned." He halted on the edge of the clearing, peering into the forest.

She would've guessed pine trees for they looked similar. They smelled like vanilla though. Not saying anything, she took deep breaths, savoring the sweetness of the air. She closed her eyes and tilted her face to the sun. Sunlight, fresh air, greenery were things she hadn't thought she'd miss. Silence reigned, the 'insects' no longer tweeting. She suspected the recent battle had a hand in that.

"I am sorry you had to witness—"

"I don't faint at the sight of blood, Nerx. Now, if you're going to crap me out, you better rethink it." She peeked at him. "I didn't realize I'd stepped onto the ramp." She raised her hand as Citus had done. "I was outside the shuttle but not off it."

"You endangered yourself," he said, his voice low but without anger.

She grimaced, liking his calmness less than the yelling.

"Not willfully." She faced him. "I spent most of the time peeking through that door. And hiding isn't in my nature, Nerx. So either give me some slack or teach me to defend myself."

"This is true," he said, cupping her face. "My prince handing himself over did not evoke as much emotion as seeing you standing in the line of fire. I never want to experience that again, *thamani*."

"That I understand." She looped her arm through his and pressed her cheek to his bicep. "Every day when I got home from work, I'd hope my mom would've come out of her shell. I feared losing another parent. Being afraid's horrible, crippling, and a tricky bastard to get rid of." She smiled at him. "So, you're training me?"

He chuckled. "You are incorrigible."

She nudged her head at the shuttle. "Let's go. I've had enough of Luchur. And when we get back, I'd like an O.D.I. please."

"I agree," he said, lacing his fingers through her hand as he led her to the shuttle.

Against the one wall sat the Viqrian prisoners, the men guarding them while standing in the center again.

"I also want a private channel with you," she said, settling her gaze on Nerx.

He paused mid-buckling her into the chair, this time without the chain. "A what?"

She flicked a gesture between Ziot and Nerx. "You know, being able to talk and you hear it over there." She hitched her thumb behind her, indicating outside.

He laughed. Sena and Ziot joined him.

Folding her arms across her chest, she huffed, tempted to kick Nerx since he still crouched before her.

He stroked her knee, sending a ribbon of heat up her leg to her core, but she was too pissed to savor it. "Britta, we have enhanced hearing."

"Bullshit," she said.

"Whisper something to me," he said, touching his ear.

"Oh, we're reverting to parlor tricks? Okay." She leaned in close, making sure her lips brushed the shell of his ear. "Will we be *talking* later?"

His cheeks darkened. His eyes smoldered. He cleared his throat. "Ziot?"

"'Will we be talking later?'" the pilot said without glancing over his shoulder. He was focused on getting them off the ground and into space.

"Fine," she huffed, "but I still get that O.D.I."

He stood, and in the process kissed her, pushing her back until her head tilted up. With a sweep of his tongue, all her anger fizzled, now replaced with a different fire.

"Seducer," she muttered when he released her.

He gave her a sexy smile and said no more.

Chapter Nineteen

MAKER. NERX WANTED TO shake, kiss, and hug Britta for an eternity. When she'd watched from the ramp, his heart had leaped into his throat. And she fought him, even when she was in the wrong. She drove him crazy. Then her silliness about a private channel. He chuckled.

"I have to comm my king," he said after Ziot docked and opened the *kuta's* door.

"Go," she said, striding past him and into the bay.

"Britta..."

"Nerx..." she called but didn't stop, marching through to the common.

Sena said nothing, Ziot too.

Nerx shook his head and strode to the comm room. She wasn't in the common as he'd hoped. He wanted to find her, to do...what? Duty called.

"Sub-Commander Matir, Pilot Edon," Nerx said in greeting. "Comm the king, please."

Adviser Kanzo appeared on the display vid. "Greetings, Supreme Commander Nerx." His gaze snagged on Nerx's short braid. "A tale for when you arrive?"

"One you will know before that, Adviser," Matir said. "I have submitted my report."

"Excellent." Adviser Kanzo glanced at Nerx. "And the purpose of the comm?"

"Prince Citus has found his Dar Eth." Nerx grinned. "She is Viqrian."

Kanzo blinked, then cleared his throat. "I...do not know what to say. One moment." The vid flicked to black.

Minutes ticked past. They waited, arms clasped behind their backs.

When the comm resumed, King Xeus occupied half of the vid, Kanzo the other. "Repeat your news, Supreme Commander Nerx."

He did.

King Xeus roared his delight.

A radiant Queen Macera joined him, peering at them. "Did I hear right?" she asked. "Another species of Dar Eths?" When King Xeus nodded, she laughed then danced on the spot like Lily would do. She froze and frowned. "But...Citus's alone on an alien battleship? I dunno how I feel about that."

"My brother knows what he is doing, especially when an Eth must follow his Dar Eth." King Xeus faced them. "What manner of female is she?"

"Do we have an image of Regent Haiz?" Nerx asked Edon.

A static sec vid appeared in the corner of the display.

Silence reigned.

"Whoa, pretty with that buzzcut," Queen Macera said.

King Xeus's gaze flicked to Nerx's braid. "I used to believe short hair meant dishonorable, but I have met many who do not lack honor. I will henceforth strip Foot of Honor from our laws."

"I shall send out a royal missive and inform Ava, my king." Adviser Kanzo arched a brow at Nerx. "Regent?"

"Commander of a battleship," Nerx said. "They do have an empress."

"Nice," Queen Macera cheered.

"Prince Citus's O.D.I. is active, my king," Edon said.

"My thanks, Pilot. I shall reach out to him. This is wonderful news."

"Our operatives will need to interview each female on the *Bronvol*. The few we have will not be sufficient for such a task. The Viqrians who instigated the rebellion will be sent to Fuyra. The innocent to Etteria." Nerx pursed his lips before saying, "As negotiated by Prince Citus."

"Then I must agree. Send the females you deem unfit to Fuyra." King Xeus hesitated. "I shall comm your father."

"Please, my king, I will attend to that task. Please accept my resignation as Supreme Commander. Of course, we shall meet en route to port Aldur and Lady Dahlia to you."

"Resignation accepted. Etteria will feel the loss of your service." King Xeus thumped his chest in a gesture of respect.

"I would like to serve on Fuyra, beside my father." Nerx smothered a grimace. "If that pleases you."

"Very well, Ambassador Nerx. Sub-Commander Matir will replace you as supreme commander. Kanzo, document as such." King Xeus ended the comm.

Nerx slumped. "Why is speaking to either of them so draining?" he asked when he'd endured this before in silence.

"Protocol? Not wanting to offend?" Matir gripped Nerx's forearm. "Congratulations, Ambassador."

Nerx snorted. "A title without meaning, especially when Father does not know the word 'diplomacy.'"

"That will change with you at the helm." Matir grinned.

"True." Nerx released Matir's forearm. "King Xeus chose well. I cannot think of a more deserving male, Supreme Commander Matir."

"Should I comm Ambassador Tarx?" Edon asked.

Nerx grimaced. "No... Thank you."

All their O.D.I.s buzzed. Only priority messages notified them all. Nerx tapped it. A vid played of Prince Citus and his males sacrificing their honor for him. His eyes stung in remembrance. The vid followed with a missive regarding the amendment to the Foot of Honor law, that Maloidian bracelets to permanent brands would be issued based on the severity of the crimes. And ended with Nerx and Matir's promotions, along with Nerx's final destination.

Maker. His father would know before Nerx could comm him. Shit, as Britta would say. He opened his mouth to ask Edon to connect him to his father when Lily skipped through the door. Colors were woven through her braids.

"Nerxie?"

"*Minus susa.*" He lifted her into his arms for a cuddle. Lady Olivia had been adamant children needed affection. He'd found he craved it more. "Did you have fun?"

She hummed her answer, her arms around his neck, her head on his shoulder.

"Hungry?" he asked.

"A little," she said, then yawned.

He smothered a smile. A nap was soon, but if he mentioned it, she'd be up and about to prove she wasn't tired.

"Ambassador Tarx." Edon raised his hands. "He commed."

Nerx made to put Lily down, but her little body stiffened even though her breathing had deepened. "Put him through."

"What nonsense is this? Rebelling against centuries of tradition—" His father blinked at Lily, the sight of her, no doubt, silencing him.

"You got the missive." Nerx met his gaze, not cowed like he used to be as a youngin.

"The cancelation of the honor law... Is that a—"

"A human child and my daughter." Nerx raised his chin in defiance. Let his father say one disparaging word about how Lily wasn't an Etterian, and there'd be hell to pay. "If you wish to talk to her, I suggest you load the Earth English Language Protocol."

Father's eagerness to do so twinged Nerx in the chest like a spasmed muscle. While he waited, his father aged—his face hardened and the lines around his eyes and mouth deep trenches. His shoulders slouched. Something like tears glistened in his eyes.

He cleared his throat. "I will have quarters built for you and your blood-bonds."

An unexpected boon Nerx didn't know how to interpret. "My thanks. Berrann Falls will not be denied to my daughter. I want your best engineer carving steps. We mine Fuyra rock. If anyone can master the mineral, it is us. Install a protective railing as it should have been done—" He bit the inside of his cheek to silence his resentment—the sweet taste of his blood calming him a little.

"Nerxie?" Lily pulled back to cup his face. "You angry?"

He lowered her to the floor. "Go find Britta, and bring her to meet...your grandfather."

As Lily gaped at the display vid, she rubbed her eye—a sign of her exhaustion or so he'd learned. "Two Gramps?" Her smile was beautiful, her joy breathtaking. She squealed, bounded up to the console, and peered at his father. "Is he your daddy?"

"Yes." Nerx smiled. "Father, this is Lily."

"Gramps." She clapped her hands together.

Nerx caught her shoulders and steered her to face the door. "Find Britta, *minus susa*."

"Oh," she gasped and bolted.

"The energy of *damu*," Father said, rare humor in his voice. "You used to tear after Kyerx every waking moment. Who is Britta?"

"My Dar Eth," Nerx gritted out. Bringing up Kyerx's name as if he hadn't died? Fury fired along his veins, stiffening his muscles to snapping point.

"We have much to discuss."

"Indeed," Nerx snapped. "I meant to comm you before the news of my promotion reached you. I must complete my mission for King Xeus. Only then will we head to Fuyra. The first order of business is making the falls safe. The second is my wedding."

"Wedding?" Britta asked from the doorway, her cheeks a radiant peach.

"Ours." Nerx caught her hand and pulled her into view of the display vid. "Britta, this is my father, Tarx."

She dragged her wide-eyed gaze from Nerx to the vid. "Hello," she said. "It's a pleasure to meet you."

Nerx sucked in a slow breath, having half-expected her to be her usual spirited self.

"Greetings, daughter." Father's voice had hoarsened. "I am eager to meet you in person." He glanced at Nerx. "I had heard of Earthians triggering the Ethera but thought it nonsense. Until I met Queen Macera. Nerx, my son, that you have been so blessed eases my heart, and I can now seek the void."

Nerx scowled, torn between losing a single male, even his father, to the void and roaring that he should let the void take him. Nerx tried to school his features, take control of his emotions, made harder by the Ethera's interference. He'd known reconciling would be difficult, had expected it to be so...and yet, he struggled to be civil. Discuss things? They'd do it one on one and at Berrann Falls, the location at the center of their unhappiness.

Britta sliding her hand into his bathed him with peace. "You can't," she said. "You've got a granddaughter to think about. She's suffered enough hardship that losing a 'gramps' would devastate her. And also, with the Viqrians coming to Fuyra, your Dar Eth might be among them."

Never had Nerx seen his Father stunned. Nerx smothered a smirk, then released Britta's hand to tuck her body into his side. She splayed her fingers across his chest.

"I have many questions, like who are the Viqrians? And why are they on their way to Fuyra?" Father flicked his focus between Britta and Nerx, not sure who would be answering.

Matir stepped between Nerx and the display vid. "I shall share the official report I submitted to King Xerus. It will answer all your questions and more, Ambassador Tarx."

"My thanks, warrior." Father bowed his head.

"If you will excuse me, Ambassador Nerx, I am in need of a hot chocolate." Matir strode from the comm room, swerving to avoid Lily, who carried a painting she'd done.

"Look, Gramps," she called, trying to hold up her artwork. This one was of herself in pink, standing between Britta and Nerx—in her childlike hand where they had sticks for arms and massive heads.

Nerx scooped her up when she hopped on her toes, trying to show his father.

"What is it, *ensa*?" His father gentled his voice in a way Nerx had always prayed to hear.

"It's a picture of my family." She tapped each figure. "Tomorrow, I will add my two gramps and Granny."

"You did this?" Father gasped. "It is beautiful."

Lily preened, ducking her head while wearing a massive smile.

"You can call your granddaddy tomorrow, kiddo. I don't know about you, but I'm craving pizza." Britta held out her arms to Lily. With a wave to his father, she let Britta carry her away.

His father sniffled, snatching Nerx's gaze. "You did well, my son." He coughed. "I await your arrival."

The comm ended.

"What in Alodon's hell just happened?" Nerx muttered as Matir entered, sipping from his mug even when he handed a hot chocolate to Edon. With a nod at his males, Nerx left the comm room, intent on finding his family.

A plate of kreso and momaberry sauce with a glass of giyua awaited him. Britta and Lily shared a pizza, a pink milkshake for Lily, and a soda for Britta.

"So," she bit into her slice, "wedding? That's news." She chewed, her gaze fixed on him. "I could mention the tension between you and your dad, but I want to know about our wedding more."

He smiled, appreciating her honesty and her selfishness. Discussing his relationship with his father would sour his mood further. "You did say it was a childish hope, and it is one I can grant you."

"But—" She choked on a mouthful and hurried to drink from her soda. "It's a dress, cake, tuxedos, the works and a shit ton of effort for what?"

"For your special day." He popped a forkful of kreso into his mouth and smiled.

Her cheeks flushed, and her eyes glazed over with this incredible softness that made his breath hitched. He drowned in her expression of pure joy. Never would he have thought she could look more beautiful to him.

"It won't be too much trouble?" she asked, her voice a whisper.

He put his utensils down and held her gaze. "Dates, a wedding with your father walking you down the aisle, our first house, and falling pregnant." He savored his juice to buy him time to find the words. "We can date every night for the rest of our lives. I would like that."

She chuckled. "That's just dinner."

He ignored her. "You have two new fathers. Though they can never replace your love for your human father, I have no doubt both would be honored to step in for that day. Our house is being built in preparation for our arrival. I am sorry."

"It's still our first home, Nerx," she said, sipping from her soda.

"As to falling pregnant, I am working on it," he said, running a gaze over her tunic. Images of what lay beneath that fabric hardened him. "Perhaps *we* can work on that soon?"

"Sure," she said, her gaze hooded as she smiled at him. "How did the chat with your king go?"

"Well." He took up his knife and fork and cut into his steak, swirling the piece in the sauce for good measure.

"Is that so, *Ambassador*?" She arched a brow.

"I resigned as supreme commander."

"Oh, and you were going to tell me..." She waited. "When, Nerx?" She pushed her soda aside, clasped her hands on the table and leaned in. "A marriage is all about communication. You share, I share, and nothing momentous is decided on without checking with each other."

He paused, intrigued by this woman before him. "I...*we* cannot raise a daughter on a battleship. It puts you both in harm's way."

"I agree. So where to?"

Stunned at her response, his answer tumbled from his tongue. "Fuyra. I can be of service there, hence the promotion."

"Makes sense."

"Of course it does." He eyed her. *Why is she agreeing with me?*

When Lily drooped, Britta dragged her across her lap, cradling her close. Within seconds, Lily slept.

"Do we get a honeymoon?" Britta asked, her voice breathless. "We'd have to take Lily with, but still."

"Honeymoon?" His breath caught at the imagery his O.D.I. flooded his mind with. He snatched on the first few, that of beaches and barely clad females. Britta in something that looked like lingerie... He cleared his throat. "We do have such a place. The Galaza beaches—one of the few places the carnivorous omeika avoid."

"No flesh-eating omeika sounds amazing." She grinned. "How much will it cost? I don't want to go into debt over this."

He frowned. "For Etterians, Galaza is free, as humans term it. We do not do 'vacations,' though we understand the concept of tourism."

"Can we go there? For a day or two?" This time, her waiting was peppered with eagerness.

"Of course. As to the honeymoon, we are already on it." Lest he ogled her again, he stood, cleared the table, then reached for Lily. "Come, *thamani*, it has been a...long day."

She trailed him, her demeanor too docile for his liking. It had him on tenterhooks, like he was stuck in the eye of a storm. As he tucked Lily into bed, he listened to Britta's movements in his...*their* quarters. Was she readying for bed? To sleep? His malehood twitched, almost with disappointment and resignation.

The day had been long, eventful, with too many emotions and too few things registering, as if his mind reeled. From commander to ambassador, from estranged to talking to his father, forming an alliance with the Viqrians, to realizing what pulsed through his chest when he glanced at Britta.

Now, all he longed to do was hold her. And if that meant while she slept, then so be it.

Chapter Twenty

Britt gargled with shower water she captured in a glass. It sure made dental hygiene easier. She finger combed her hair, then sniffed her pits. She'd already showered after Luchur, but now that she was going to get it on with Nerx, she worried she might smell. With their sensitive everything, she couldn't be too cautious. She wiped her damp palms on her baggy sleepshirt.

When she'd promised to make it worth his while, she hadn't thought she'd be this anxious about it. She could count on one finger how many times she'd 'blown' a man. But that's what she wanted to do. She had no doubts he'd never experienced it. And since she was it for him for life, the poor dude, she might as well see if he liked it.

"What's taking so long?" she whispered, then yelped when he filled the door to his room.

"I need a cleanse," he said, striding into the bathroom. The door shut on his ass.

She huffed and paced, wringing her hands while she ran through scenarios.

But he came out again in nothing but his gaping pants. She swallowed hard, refusing to blink when he marched toward her.

"What's the matter?" she rasped, then hurried to clear her throat.

He took her hand and ushered her into the bathroom. Then he placed her against the wall. "Keep me company," he said.

"Okay," was all she could manage when he peeled off his pants and stepped into the cubicle.

"*Malia pado,*" he muttered after unclipping his hair. She grabbed the clip from him, getting her forearm drenched.

While twisting the heavy metal thing in her hands, she drooled over her man. He'd splayed his hands high on the white wall, dipping his head in and out of the spray. This was the stuff of erotic fantasies for every woman, she was sure. Well, she knew damn well, seeing a man shower had to be the sexiest thing. Especially when his body was this beautiful. Water droplets trailed every muscular dip and ripple.

He watched her ogle him. Her heartbeat froze, then scattered.

Throwing caution to the wind, she whipped off her shirt, dropped it to the floor, and the clip on top of it.

"What are you doing?" he asked. "Did you not cleanse?"

Standing naked before him should've made her self-conscious, but he'd seen her like this before and would again. Besides, he didn't even care that he was buck-ass-naked as well. With a body that damn lickable, he had a right to 'strut his stuff.'

She flattened a palm to his chest and pushed. He didn't budge. *Damn brick shithouse.*

"Your back against the wall," she commanded, clipping her words.

He frowned. "Why—?"

She stroked him from his balls to the tip of his cock, lingering on the ridges running along the length.

His eyelids fluttered, but he did as she asked. She walked through the water, then crouched, using his knees to find her balance.

"Britta?"

"Nerxie?" She met his gaze before using her tongue to follow the path she'd caressed.

His leg muscles flexed. His erection bobbed. She wrapped her fingers around his cock's girth, as best she could, then swirled her tongue over the tip that looked like a garden gnome's hat. He was magnificently bronze there too, except a darker tone closer to the base.

While she licked and sucked, she peeked at him, trying to judge if she was doing a decent-enough job. Her knees throbbed, not used to the permanent crouch position. But damn, if his pre-cum wasn't sweet like apple pie.

She took him into her mouth but couldn't go deep.

He groaned even as he thrust his fingers into her hair. His abs twitched, and his breathing turned ragged. Unable to bear the knee pain any longer, she did one more long lick before standing. She retreated through the spray to the other side and watched him.

His eyes glowed with need for her, and he clenched fists at his sides, as if he hadn't wanted her to stop.

"Good? Bad?" she asked, not daring to blink.

"Amazing. The instructional vids had shown this, but to experience it, *thamani*, is incredible."

"What vids?" She tapped the gray button for the panel to open and grabbed two robes. "It makes sense that you train for war, but for sex?"

"With humans, yes. We want to please our Dar Eths." He left the cubicle.

She offered him a robe. While he slid into it, she donned hers. "That's sweet, but we could teach what brings us pleasure. It's different for each woman."

"Having a foundational knowledge gives us confidence." He cupped her cheek, running his thumb over her freckles.

"True." She clasped his robe closed, activating its body contouring. "Come, I plan to finish."

"Finish?" He trailed her into their bedroom. "I do not want to spend my seed on your face."

She froze in horror, realization dawning on her. "Are these training vids porn movies?"

"Yes, I do believe they are called such."

Laughter bubbled up, and even though she didn't want to offend him, she couldn't stop herself. She clasped her waist and giggled until tears spilled free. "Oh... This is priceless."

He smiled at her, but his puzzlement lay in his knitted brow. "What is?"

"Porn is a form of entertainment. Your males are learning unfair expectations of what women can do in the bedroom."

"Ah," he said. "I disagree. What you did with your mouth—" He squeezed his eyes shut and growled. "*Maker*, will you do it again for me, *thamani*?"

She grinned. "As soon as you get on the bed. Robe on."

He obeyed, clambering in place like a child before Christmas.

Unable to resist, she slithered out of her robe and let it pool on the floor. He lay there like something off the cover of a historical romance novel. And the way his gaze ran over her body sent heat spiraling to her core and lower.

He drew in a deep inhale and moaned. "Your scent drives me wild."

"You didn't just say that." She chuckled, crawling onto the bed between his legs.

With a flick, she parted his robe to expose those incredible legs of his. When she stroked his knees, he jerked. Up she trailed her fingers, gathering the robe in the process until only his pelvis was exposed.

The way desire pulsed through her, she was tempted to impale herself and ride him until she begged him to take over, to pound into her, and grunt her name. But this was her thanking him for taking her along. So any end to this had to come from him.

She dipped and ran her tongue along his inner thigh, tasting warm, spicy man. He widened his legs, giving her a little more room. For that, she lapped the tip of his cock.

He arched off the bed, thrusting his erection at her. She obliged him by sucking him into her mouth.

His breathing came in huffs as she took her time, learning every inch of him with her fingers and her tongue.

His forehead glistened, his pulse flickered at the base of his jaw, and he fisted the blanket beneath him.

"Want me to stop?" she asked, rocking backward to run her nipple along his inner thigh to knee, then forward to do it again. There she stopped, licked the pre-cum off the tip, then repeated the action.

"I want...in you now," he gritted out.

"Permission granted," she said, though her voice sounded wrong, too husky.

He lunged, faster than she'd ever seen anyone move. She was on her back, her legs spread, and his mouth on her throbbing clit. The pleasure was too exquisite for her to mutter anything more than whimpers. She'd gone from aching for him to blinding need until a screaming orgasm swept over her, sending her off the cliff into gravity-defying bliss.

She'd yet to come down from that high, the residual tremors still pulsing through her when he thrust into her. A scream lodged in her throat. She arched, pressing her breasts against his chest which sent another rivulet of pleasure to her core.

He didn't show her mercy, not that she'd ask for any. From the inside out, he owned every inch of her. More so when he caught her chin and urged her to meet his gaze.

When she squeezed her eyes shut, shielding herself from the intensity in his eyes, he tutted. He stilled and waited, until she looked at him again. Like a carrot on a stick, she did whatever he asked just to have him conquer her, to show her a wealth of pleasure, and draw every last ounce of ecstasy from her.

Her heart swelled, filling her until she couldn't breathe.

He huffed with each thrust, then slowed, his face contorting into an agonizing happiness as he pinned his hips in place. Such passion lay deep in the man she'd come to know...

Tears pressed at the backs of her eyes, but she shoved them down.

"Tired?" she asked instead, wiggling to free a hand. She stroked his jawline, pausing to brush her thumb across his uneven mouth that she found so damn sexy.

"Yes." He hoisted her into his arms, clasped her against his chest, then sank onto the bed.

Like a ragdoll, he shifted her limbs until she was snug, tucked into the curve of his body with her cheek on his shoulder and her fingers on his sternum. He stretched to yank the blanket over them, and only when satisfied, he tightened his arm around her upper back to hold her close.

She had this to look forward to until the honeymoon phase was over. Then what? Before Dad died, she'd been selected for an internship—a once-in-a-lifetime opportunity to study xeno-zoology in the far reaches of their known galaxy. Mom's downward spiral had Britt giving up her dream. Her talents were wasted at Stay Alive and any previous short-lived job she'd suffered through. But it meant coming home every night, keeping Mom company, making sure she ate and slept. Especially when she'd blamed herself for almost losing her patient's baby. It had been a difficult birth, with long hours putting strain on all the medical staff.

"Exhaustion is no excuse for negligence. I could've stepped aside and let a fresh doctor help her." After that, Mom closed her practice and allowed herself to grieve.

Making sure she flourished wasn't Britt's responsibility anymore. Instead, she had a husband and a daughter. To travel through space to discover new creatures, to document their amazing biology, would never be on the cards for her.

She hadn't meant to find love or to fall this hard. But never in planning her life had she considered her husband wouldn't love her back.

Damn idiot that she was.

Tears slipped free, though crying without making a noise was harder than apologizing. And it didn't help that her blocked nose dripped. She tried to suck in the emotions, to somehow take control after the horse had bolted. Tomorrow, she'd look like an extinct puffer fish. Nerx would know something was wrong.

And yet, no matter what she tried, there was no stemming the flood.

With his enhanced hearing, he had to know she was this blubbering mess leaking all over him. Giving up on trying to remain silent, she pulled out of his arms and peeled on her discarded robe.

"Britta?" he asked, rising to sit. "What is the matter?"

His concerned gaze shattered her defenses, and she bolted, sobbing as she sprinted to Aldur's quarters. He'd follow, she knew that. And he'd pester her until she revealed how she longed for his love. No. No way would she lose face. She pressed her back against the door once she reached her 'sanctuary.' Thankfully, no one had been in the common when she'd rushed through. Still, being seen in a robe didn't scare her as much as Nerx being hot on her heels.

Short of jettisoning herself into space, there was no escaping this.

Sniffling and with blurry vision, she ordered tissues from the replicator. She was through the third nose blow when Nerx entered. He hesitated in the doorway, looking damn fine in his robe. But the intensity in his eyes snagged her breath.

"Just let me cry without asking why," she said, dabbing at her eyes.

"All right, if I can hold you?"

She flung herself at him, and he caught her. Fresh tears fell as she clung to him, drenching his shoulder. Him tightening his arms around her, the hand he trailed up and down her back, and the kisses he pressed to her head fueled her sorrow. Such care had to mean something. But despite her 'bravery,' she was a coward through and through, unable to ask him outright.

He crossed to the bed, keeping her in place even as he sprawled out. "Sleep. We will talk when you are ready."

She nodded, curled her fingers into his hair, and let his warmth sooth her.

BRITT'S EYES WERE SWOLLEN when she woke up. Nerx lay beside her, his arms cradling her close, but his focus was on her face.

"Morning," she croaked and winced at the pounding headache making itself known, like a mild hangover. "How long have you been awake?"

"A while," he said, brushing a curl off her cheek. "Are you in pain?"

"Yup, but a coffee will help with that." She pushed herself up, knowing she did so only because he let her.

He followed, twisting to meet her gaze. "Much happened yesterday. I offer my apologies for not realizing this sooner."

"What?" She frowned.

"Your mother is safe." He dipped to kiss her, then leaned back when she touched his waist. "You are relieved and are finally able to express how much you did worry."

She smiled. If only that was all her issues. But he'd given her a way to avoid revealing the state of her heart. "You're right. A weight's off my mind."

"Will you be fine with her not staying on Fuyra?"

"If she visits often. I... I also need to find something to do, Nerx. I once planned to become a zoologist." Her regret hit like a sledgehammer to her chest, pressing fresh tears behind her eyes. She sniffed. "I was such an eager student, fully committed to my goals in life. Until the news of Dad's accident reached me." She sucked in a shuddering breath, searching for strength. "His car's fusion pulse failed on the way to work, forcing him to crash land. He died in an instant." She shrugged. "Or so they say."

He raised his arm, showing her the scar. "Kyerx fell, but I was not strong enough to save him. That is why I keep this, just like Lily has a circular scar her bad daddy gave her."

"To remember?" Britt asked, her voice breaking. She swallowed over the lump in her throat. "I knew she'd been through much, but I wasn't sure what."

"My father blames me for my mother's death at my birthing. She died at Berrann Falls, which was forbidden to us." Nerx offered a weak smile. "Kyerx was a little rebellious, so we went there often without Father's knowledge. When... When I commed him that Kyerx was dying, the pain in Father's voice resonated in me. He barely spoke to me afterward, not that his attitude toward me before that was good."

He laced his fingers through hers and pressed a kiss to her knuckles. "Losing Kyerx expanded my void as if a decade of my life had passed. I had to assume a façade to minimize emotion. I refused to let it claim me before Father succumbed." He grinned. "It is why I scowl at my males."

"You used to be grumpy. That's what you said."

"And that you are beautiful," he said, feathering a kiss along her inner wrist. "I meant it."

She shivered, the warmth from his lips seeping into her. But when her stomach gurgled, he leaned back with a chuckle.

"My Dar Eth must be fed," he said, sliding off the bed and dragging her with him.

"I *am* hungry. What will you have this morning?"

"French toast if I get to lick the syrup off your lips."

She laughed. "Ew. Saliva all over my—"

He whipped her against his chest and kissed her, snatching her breath. "Do not ever believe that you cannot share what bothers or pains you, *thamani*. I will always listen."

Her heartbeat skittered. "Do I get to hold a blaster to your chest if you don't listen?"

He laughed, flashing that knee-quaking dimple of his. "Please do. I like your fire."

"So I've learned," she grumbled. "Kind of diminishes its effectiveness when it doesn't shock you."

"I have faith that you will never fail to surprise me." He nudged her at the replicator. "Dress. Aldur is well enough to install your O.D.I."

"Oh?" she gasped, excitement dancing along her nerve endings. Or was this reaction from his hot, sensual kiss? She ordered jeans and a T-shirt, then sat and slipped on her sneakers. All while he donned another set of armor. Her imagination painted him in low-riding jeans, bare feet, and a tight black T-shirt. Her mouth dried, and she blinked at him.

"I'll wear something Etterian, if you put on a pair of jeans for me."

He arched a brow. "Intriguing, but yes, doable."

She hummed her excitement. "I look forward to you putting it on...and taking it off."

Chapter Twenty-One

Dear Diary,

I know, I've been neglectful. My bad. Expect this to be a long one, then nothing for a while. Days have blurred. Happy ones, though. Still, I can't help feeling like I'm just pretending we're the perfect family and that Nerx loves me. If he truly did, I'd be more than this lumpy sack of shit, faking the smiles.

The memory of his dimple had her humming.

Come bedtime, he worships my body, flooding me with hope that he could, at any moment, up and confess that I'm his moon and stars.

She winced. Nothing was stopping her from telling him how she felt.

Not that I'll blab first either. Hell no. I suppose, a one-sided love is better than nothing. Imagine if I still hated his ass. That would suck, for sure.

Mom and Aldur blinked across to the king's ship on day eight with promises to attend my wedding. Yup, you heard right. Somehow I doubt they'll make it, considering they're heading toward the Viqrian battleships and we're heading away. Might have to postpone, which I'm okay with.

Since Aldur is Nerx's medic, we got Lima Coll in exchange. Lima stands for 'teacher,' and is reserved for the oldest of Etterians still fighting the void. Oops, sorry for the lesson. Their culture's fascinating, and no doubt, about to be messed with—us humans can't leave shit alone.

Come to think of it, neither do us women, so the Viqrians might make a bigger impact. Who knows.

Got sidetracked. Oh, yup, my quarters. You guessed it. Coll's arrival got me kicked out and 'moved' into Nerx's, making it official. I should've asked for keys to our apartment, but that would've been an inside joke only I'd get. No point of sniggering to myself. That's just some sad shit right there.

She tapped the side of the tablet, trying to gather her thoughts. What had she wanted to say?

Well, I asked for a honeymoon, and the sweet ass said we were already on it. Can you believe the audacity of trying to wiggle out of a beach trip? I put paid to his sad attempts. So we're going to Galaza.

She chuckled, excitement exploding inside her like fireworks.

I ordered him suitable beach attire. Just for funsies. I can't wait to see those legs of his in swim shorts. Yum! Lily's as enthusiastic about a holiday. I'm trying to keep everything to a beach bag each. No point in carrying tons of buckets, spades, towels, umbrellas... You get the gist.

Every morning, Lily asks Edon to call Granddaddy then Granny and Gramps. She always has something to show them, whether it's her distorted Ollie sweater she finally finished or a beach ball we ordered from the replicator.

Tarx has changed, becoming warmer, more forthcoming with information, and not as stick-up-the-butt as I expected. The real shocker is Nerx softening toward his dad. No doubt due to their almost-daily conversations on the mines, what was needed, the operations, the inspections, what to do with the Viqrians...

Nerx's been busy reading the documents his father sent over.

Oh, and hubs did the most amazing thing. I cried like a freakin' baby. He showed me all their information on alien animals with everything I could possibly want to know about their kingdom, phylum, class, order, family, genus, and species. That's the main reason I've been so absent. Every spare moment not spent with Nerx or Lily goes to studying. And I'm so desperate to see these creatures' worlds.

Of course, Nerx said no, but we'll see. I do have a talented tongue.

She smirked. He did love blow jobs.

Lily's approaching footsteps snapped up Britt's head, and she grinned.

Gotta go.

She tucked the tablet into her beach bag, then bounded off the bench in the common to cross to her daughter. "Ready, squirt?"

"Yup." Lily in her swimsuit, hat, and sandals, spun her beach bag filled with toys and a towel.

The twirling mesmerized Britt. She pressed a hand to her stomach, nausea plaguing her. She blamed her excitement and trepidation. They were about to end a two-week journey and start a new chapter. Space travel wasn't as awesome as she'd thought it would be with weeks wasted in a flying box. She was eager to stand on solid ground, with Luchur but a distant memory.

Nerx strode in wearing shorts, a flowery button-up, short-sleeved shirt, and flip flops. He shoved his hands into his pockets and smiled. Wearing sunglasses had been a hell-no from him, but since he wore everything else, including a sexy pair of jeans without complaint, she let it go.

She wore his kimono-like ceremonial gown over her swimsuit, a hat flopped, obscuring her face, and forced her to lift the brim so she wouldn't trip in her sandals.

He bid his men farewell, clasping their forearms even as they teased him about his clothing, which he handled well.

"Lady Britta, a pleasure." Matir pumped her hand twice.

Ziot smiled, but his cheeks and eyes darkened. "I will miss...hopscotch."

"Me too," Lily said, hugging his leg and accidentally whacking him with her bag.

Sena, Edon, and Lima Coll shook Britt's hand but said nothing.

"Three to port, Pilot Edon." Nerx arched a brow at Edon, who bolted for the communications room.

Nerx chuckled, clasped Lily's hand then drew Britt against his side.

The gray sand and red sea wasn't what she'd expected. Nor the pink sky with two suns. Still, it was beautiful, made more so with the sunlight warming her cheeks. Lily threw down her bag, kicked off her shoes, tossed aside her hat, and waded into the waves. Nerx took after her, grunting when he had to abandon his flip flops too.

Britt laughed, watching them for a few minutes, then spread out the towels. Just sinking her feet into the hot sand made her soul sing. The beach was empty, like it wasn't tourism season. And when she scanned the forests around them, there were no buildings in sight, even when she squinted. Instead, a hush surrounded her with muted chirps and calls she didn't recognize. She need not travel the universe to find fauna and flora to study when a new world was her home. What awaited her on Fuyra? She almost rubbed her palms together with glee.

While laughing at her hubs and daughter frolicking, she sank onto the towel. Again, her stomach lurched. Perhaps it was Etteria's gravity? A fresh breeze swept across her cheeks, so she rose, slipped out of the gown, and strode toward the water's edge. The damp sand cooled her toes, so she ventured deeper, letting the warm waves lap her calves.

"What are you wearing?" Nerx asked with Lily thrown over one shoulder. She wriggled, her feet spraying clumps of wet sand.

"A bikini," Britt grinned. "You like?" she asked while flicking the ties on her bottoms.

"Very much," he rasped.

Day fourteen and their passion had yet to fizzle. She'd swear it was growing stronger with each passing moment. As he ran his hooded gaze over her, what that expression meant sent fire along her veins to settle at her core.

"You had me this morning," she whispered.

"It is never enough with you, *thamani*." He threw her a grin before lowering Lily to the wet sand. Off went his shirt, then he was back in the water with Lily clutching his shoulder as he waded deeper.

She joined them, lowering herself until she bobbed with the waves.

Frequent glances at the suns showed them crossing the sky. Not that she could tell the time from that. Which one should she track? She snorted, her stomach twisting.

"Um, Nerx," she said, striding out of the water. She angled her head to wring water from her hair. "I'm starving." She swept out her arm at the forest-covered hill behind them. "Where are we staying?"

He smiled before stealing a kiss. "We are surrounded by buildings. They are hidden to not impact the beauty of this landscape. Come." He held out his hand which she accepted.

"What about our stuff?" she asked, tugging on his arm to reach her towel.

"We will return after we eat."

"Hot dogs," Lily called, dancing around them.

They marched toward a gap in the forest, and as they neared, Britt spotted a path. Behind the tall trees, deep in their shadows, glass glinted on windowed units.

A lone man waited for them. He wore cream-colored yoga pants, a tunic, and sandals. "Greetings, Ambassador Nerx, miladies. Help yourself to any cabin. Enjoy the duration of your stay." He bowed his head at Nerx. "The *kuta* is on standby as requested. Your personal items are on board."

"My thanks, Lima Tico." Nerx veered left and opened the door to the first unit.

White floors rolled toward windows on three sides overlooking the forest and glimpses of the beach. A massive bed dominated the space, facing the view. On the wall behind the bed was a door, probably leading to a bathroom. Opposite to the door was a short counter with a replicator and rehydrator. Two chairs and a table sat in one glass-walled corner.

"What would you like to eat, *thamani*?" Nerx strode across the room to the rehydrator.

"Hot dogs are fine and a soda for me, please." She strolled to the windows and peered through the tinted glass.

When it slid open, bathing her with salty air, she squeaked. No railing made this dangerous. She couldn't shake the idea they'd designed this place with children not in mind.

When she stepped back, the glass doors shut. "Can you lock it so they don't open?" she asked, accepting the plate of hot dogs.

Nerx tapped the wall beside the door to access a panel. "Done."

"Thank you." The smell of hot dog hit her when she kneeled to offer one to Lily. "Take it," she said, shoving the plate at Nerx, then bolted for the bathroom.

Despite the nausea, she couldn't throw up, so she splashed water on her face then dried it with a toweling robe. In her home, she'd make damn sure they had normal towels.

"Are you not well?" he asked when she emerged.

"Too much sun." She smiled and accepted the soda he offered her. "Probably dehydrated as well." She took a deep pull from her can and hummed when it chilled her throat. "Much better." But she didn't go near the hot dogs, just in case. What would he do if she turned out to be allergic to his homeworld? She snorted at that bit of silliness.

Lily sat on a chair, her mouth full.

"After this meal, we are building a sand castle?" He frowned at Lily.

She nodded, her wide smile revealing a chewed sausage.

"You can stay here and rest, if you like." Nerx caressed Britta's cheek, concern in his pinched brow.

Britta squeezed his arm, tugged, then pressed a kiss to his mouth when he dipped forward. "Thank you. And don't stay out too long. She's as sensitive to the sun as I am." She broke away to flick Lily's braid. "Have fun, kiddo."

Into the shower Britt stepped, eager to wash the sand and salt off her. When she emerged in her previously used toweling robe, the room was empty. She sank onto the edge of the bed, then flopped backward. Strangely tired, she dozed amid the odd silence. No insects or birds filled the forest with their music.

A coil of nausea tightened in her stomach, waking her. She stretched her arms and yawned. Maybe she was coming down with something—

She sat up, tapped her O.D.I., only to stare at the calendar, counting the days twice.

"No, no, no," she sobbed. "It's too soon. I can't do this, not without love."

There'd been so many moments Nerx could've told her he loved her. But he hadn't. And sure, she'd accepted her role as wife and mom. Her life wouldn't be *that* bad. But no matter how many times she tried to convince herself she had enough love for them both, her arguments sounded weak, uncertain.

"What is too soon? What can you not do?"

She jerked at finding Nerx standing in the doorway.

Lily shot past him, disappearing into the bathroom.

"Britta?"

"Nerx?" Britt fluttered her eyelashes as if innocent.

He ventured deeper into the room. "Tell me, *thamani*." He sat on the bed beside her.

She sucked in a shuddering breath. "Can you call, comm...whatever, a medic?"

"You *are* unwell." He leaped to his feet, then whisked her into his arms.

"Nerx," she cried out when he carried her to the door. "Put me down. I just need to confirm whether I'm pregnant."

Her feet hit the floor hard. He gaped at her, his cheeks darkened, and she'd swear those were tears in his eyes.

"Nerx, please, a medic." She nudged him at the door.

He didn't budge, a glower forming. "What can you not do without love? Bear my *damu*?"

"I..." She offered him her back as the tears fell, unable to explain how much she yearned for him to love her.

"Britta, *thamani*, how can you be such an intelligent woman and so stupid at the same time?" He gripped her upper arms and spun her to face him.

"What?" She glared at him, despite the tears. "That's a big insult, and you better have reasons—"

"I have loved you since Luchur, *ensa ra ensa*." He cupped her face, rubbing her damp cheeks with the pads of his thumbs.

She hit him hard with no armor to protect his chest. He laughed, caught her fist, and pressed a kiss to her knuckles.

"Why the hell didn't you tell me? I've been sick with not knowing." She yanked on her hand, but he just tightened his hold. That silly smile she adored teased his lips.

"*Ensa* means 'heart,' *ensa ra ensa* is 'heart of my heart,' and *thamani*..." He stole a sweet kiss. "Is 'beloved.'"

Like an overflowing container, emotions tumbled out, dragging a sob from her. "Hormones," she croaked, despite not knowing whether she *was* pregnant. A full-on crying session started when she realized she might not be. Until that thought, having a son terrified her. Not having one sent her into a deep, spiraling morass of sadness.

Nerx enveloped her in his arms, tucking her face into the curve of his neck. As she cried, he said nothing, just held her. Sniveling, she tried not to wipe her nose on the corner of his tropical button-up shirt. No matter how tempted she was. He'd known since Luchur. No, before, when he'd called her '*thamani*.' She should be furious with him.

"I'm sorry. I hate crying." She huffed as she pulled away. "I love you too, in case you didn't know."

"Good," he said, but his voice had roughened.

"What?" she asked, lunging for a nearby beach towel to dab her face.

"I did not know nor did I realize how hard your confession would hit me." He lifted her and spun her, beaming at her. "I am...happy."

She gripped his shoulders, peering at his upturned face. Gone was the asshole he'd been. Now this charming man remained, and one who handled her sass without flinching.

"So am I," she said, smiling at him.

"My turn," Lily called, skipping out of the bathroom. She raised her arms for a spin.

He lowered Britt, then knelt to scoop Lily up while pulling Britt close for a three-way hug. "My favorite females," he said.

Britt winked at Lily, and together, they pressed a kiss to each of his cheeks.

Britt pulled away first. "Come, squirt, let's see what we can find to drink. How about a mocktail."

"What's that?" Lily asked, wiggled until Nerx let her down, then hurried to the rehydrator.

"You'll see." Britt ordered a non-alcoholic strawberry daiquiri and handed it to Lily. "Medic," she whispered to Nerx.

He typed on his O.D.I., bounded to the door, and swung it wide. "On his way."

A minute later, a man hovered in the door, wearing the same color and style as Tico. "I am Medic Udia. How may I assist?" His gaze swept between Nerx's eyes to Britt, to Lily, then back.

Britt crossed to stand before him, just so she could whisper, "I suspect I'm pregnant."

His eyes widened. A smile twitched his lips. "You seek confirmation." He tapped his wrist, then scanned her. "Indeed, milady. You bear a son."

Ice trickled down her back as her chest exploded with joy. "A boy?"

"Thank you, Medic Udia, for delivering such wonderful news." Nerx pressed his palm to the man's shoulder.

"Will that be all, Ambassador?"

At Nerx's nod, the man left. Britt was frozen in place, tears spilling through her laughter.

"Why are you crying?" Lily asked, then licked her ruby-red lips.

"Because the Maker sent you a brother." Nerx knelt, looped his arms around Britt's ass, and rested his temple on her stomach. "My son."

She sucked in a sharp breath. Mom always advised women to wait sixteen weeks before announcing it. What if something went wrong? She couldn't rely on Etteria's amazing medical tech, like Mom seemed to do. Especially when Mom was the extent of their knowledge on the subject.

But the cat was out of the bag. Britt would just have to be super careful.

"A brother? Where's he?" Lily handed Britt the mocktail to dart around the room.

She smiled. "He's still being made, squirt."

"Oh," Lily said, trudging back to take her cup. "What's his name?" She twirled her finger in the strawberry slush then sucked it.

"Kyerx?" Britt raised both eyebrows at Nerx.

He shook his head. "I want him named after you."

She chuckled. "Britta is not a good boy name."

"In Etterian culture, the last letters of the father's name pass to the son. If the father wishes to honor the mother, then the last letters of her name are used."

Her chest clenched and released at his thoughtfulness.

It made sense, though: Tarx, Kyerx, and Nerx. "So, what did you have in mind?" she asked, letting his unbound hair curl around her fingers.

That he loved her... She couldn't contain the emotions roiling within her, nor control the smiles that formed at random and without her bidding.

"Vitta?" He peered at her, his chin digging into her stomach, but not painfully.

"How about Kyta? Half Kyerx and me?"

He rose, cupped her face, then kissed her long and leisurely. "The Ethera chose well, *thamani*. You are perfect for me.

"Flattery will get you some appreciation." She grinned. "And Kyta it is."

Epilogue

Nerx touched the *Kuta* down on the co-ordinates his father had sent him. In the display vids, their quarters sat, alone, with tundra rolling out to the Gaelsi Mountains. He punched the button to open the door, then bounded out of his seat, eager to unbuckle Britta and Lily.

"It smells good," Britta said, drawing in a deep breath as if to prove it.

"Welcome to your new home," he said, kneeling to free her.

She kissed his head, then passed him to the ramp.

Lily squirmed, kicking her legs as she waited. He lifted her off the chair and set her down. She scampered out the door, sprinting past Britta to squeal, "Granddaddy."

Nerx smiled at how much Lily and his father had bonded. Time spent with both her grandfathers had gone a long way to cement her place in the world. She now loved them and without hesitation or fear.

Nerx held Britta's hand and ushered her toward his father.

His stomach wrenched, but he let it calm. Over the last week, he'd come to see his father in a different light. Easy to do now, when Father held Lily with one arm and pointed at the mountains and the house, even as Lily jabbered questions.

He laughed, then met Nerx's gaze. "Welcome home, son." He glanced at Britta. "And daughter."

She sniffled, hesitated, then hugged him and Lily. "Thank you," she said, stepping back to wipe her cheeks. When she smiled at Nerx, she missed his father's shock.

"They cry when they are happy or sad," Nerx grumbled, too low for Britt to hear.

"I welcome her with open hearts," his father said.

Britta frowned at Nerx. "You okay?" she asked.

He cleared his throat. "I am well." He laced their fingers, settled beside her, and came face to face with the male he'd hated for decades. He raised their clasped hands to kiss her knuckles. "Before we go farther, I need—"

"We're going to explore our house, right, squirt?" Britta took Lily from Father's arms, strode past him, and disappeared into their home.

Father stared after them, then gestured to Nerx to walk with him in the opposite direction. "The day your mother died, my void expanded at an alarming rate. It is no excuse for the way I treated you, but I could not spare the emotion. Kyerx expected affection, your mother's influence. So I suffered, making sure he did not notice a change in me. I could not bear to love you and lose you too. So I pushed you away the only way I knew how." Father paused to gaze at the mountains, his eyes glistening. "When Kyerx died, I feared the worst. I meant it when I said I can seek the void. That I need not live like this anymore." He smiled and twisted to stroll toward the house. "But my daughter is right. Let me meet these Viqrians first. Now that you have brought joy into my life, I find I no longer want to die. Not yet."

Nerx rolled his lips. Years of nurturing his anger disintegrated with one realization—he too had felt the void's expansion and become a hard male because of it.

"News of your accomplishments was met with pride. You far surpassed my expectations. But I had not heard you adopted a daughter or found your Dar Eth. The Maker has truly blessed you."

"And continues to do so," Nerx said, clasping his father's forearm. "Britta bears my son."

With a yank, Nerx found himself in his father's embrace, strong and crushing. He blinked back tears and tightened his arms, returning the hug.

"A son..." Father chanted between chuckles.

"We will name him Kyta."

Father thrust Nerx back to grin at him. "Perfect." He spun to throw an arm around Nerx's shoulder as he led him into the house. "Tell me, how did it feel when Prince Citus honored you so? I was both shocked and impressed."

Nerx chuckled. "You saw. Angry, stunned, close to tears. The Ethera unravels years of control. Now... Now I *feel* everything."

Father paused. "And the void?"

"A bright light."

A single tear slipped down Father's cheek. "I am...pleased."

"Nerxie, come see my room." Lily skipped to him, grabbed his hand, then tried to drag him.

He laughed. "All right, *minus susa*."

"Thank you for this," Britta said, gesturing to the house the moment Father entered. "The size is perfect with three bedrooms and two bath...cleansing rooms. Anything bigger would be a nightmare to clean. The wall-to-wall windows are amazing, the views spectacular. It's like we live on a farm without a soul for miles."

"You do," Father said. "These fields are for kreso grazing. The beasts do not flourish as well as on Etteria, but their numbers are growing."

Nerx smiled at Lily's room, all in pink. "Your favorite color," he said.

"Granddaddy asked me what I wanted. Isn't it awesome?" she squealed, bouncing on her bed.

"It is. Let me see the rest of our home." What he wanted was to return to Britta and bask in his father's love—something he'd always yearned for.

"May I offer you a beverage?" Britta asked his Father. "Something from Earth, perhaps? Nerx's favorite."

"Please," Father said. "What do you think of Fuyra?" He settled in one of five comfys while Britta ordered a hot chocolate from rehydrator built into one wall. Father stared at the brown liquid, sniffed it, took a sip, then grumbled his appreciation.

Nerx watched this all unfold from their bedroom doorway. He'd given the space a token glance, then sat in the comfy beside his wife.

She smiled at him and clasped his hand, bringing it to rest on her thigh. "The silvers and grays appeared monotone at first, but then the pops of red trees and foliage, the orange-brown sky, the bright sun... I love it, to be honest. It's desolate and peaceful. Stark but beautiful. And I'll need to learn how to fly a *kuta* for emergencies." She raised her chin in defiance.

Nerx chuckled. "And you shall."

She beamed and muttered about 'talking' to him later. Heat unfolded in his pelvis, hardening him. One look, smile, whisper, or touch from her had him eager to have her beneath him.

"When are the Viqrians due?" she asked Father.

"Some have arrived, but I have not met them yet. The journey is half-a-day away, but I chose to be here, instead." He leaned back when Lily climbed onto his lap, clutching a sand-coated Ollie to her chest. She curled against him, humming to herself. "I am told their battleships travel toward Etteria, escorted by many of ours. King Xeus is going ahead in his *Celeeri*."

"So a royal visit is imminent," Nerx said. "About Berrann—"

"Made secure. I checked it myself."

"Good."

"Will you be staying for lunch?" Britta asked. "Could I tempt you with a human meal?"

Father looped an arm around Lily to keep her from falling off his lap. He nodded. "Whatever Nerx has tried and deemed worthy." He smiled.

"Oh." Britta jumped to her feet. "Challenge accepted."

What followed would forever remain in Nerx's memory. She'd ordered plate after plate, letting Father sample from French toast, bacon, cheese, and syrup, to Tagliatelle Alfredo, to pizza, and finally steak, French fries, and barbecue sauce. Soda, beer, and mocktails washed the bites down. Laughter filled the room, his father's more precious now that Nerx knew the truth.

"Ambassador Tarx, we have a situation." The voice from Father's O.D.I. silenced them.

He tapped his wrist. "What is it, Commander Cewa?"

"The Viqrians have escaped."

Father lifted a sleeping Lily off his lap and tucked her onto the comfy he vacated. He took a moment to stroke a black curl off Lily's temple. "Thank you for the meal, my daughter." He smiled at Britta then nodded at Nerx. "My son, I expect you in the office tomorrow."

"I will be there," he said, staring after his father as he left.

"Aren't you going with?" Britta asked, gaping at the empty plates on the table.

"If he needs me, he will ask." He caught her hand when she reached for a plate. "Now truth, what do you think of your home?"

"Planet or house?" she teased. "The house could use color and a sink, but other than that, the windows... Love those. And the planet, it's beautiful."

He released a slow sigh of relief. "Wait until you see Berrann Falls. But first, I will organize a pilot to begin your lessons. Lily needs to start her training as soon as we think she is ready. Though, I expect she will be a bad influence on other *damu*." He laughed.

"We go with you tomorrow?" Britta arched her brow.

"If you like. Anything big you want to order must come from the central mining office."

"Rugs, cushions, furniture?" She swept her gaze around the common room devoid of color with the white Fuyra stone walls and floors. The rehydrator and replicator were stark dark shapes and the comfys white as well. "Yup, I'll come with. We need some color." She leaned over the side of the comfy, bringing her lips close to his. "Have I told you today how much I love you?"

He wanted to lie, to deny he'd heard it, in the hopes she'd tell him again and again.

"Well, I suppose I could show you..." She feathered a kiss along his jawline. "Wait for me in our bedroom. Let's christen that bed."

Eagerness drove him to obey, but as he reached the door, he glanced over his shoulder. His heart swelled and the bright light in his chest pulsed when Britta tucked a blanket around Lily.

With anger, resentment, unforgiveness no longer tainting his soul, he accepted that his life, love, and future were perfect.

Glossary

Etterians worship one God, one Maker since the universes have only His fingerprint on all of it, a single golden thread through all of creation.

Tokens: an intergalactic form of currency

Kliks: predetermined length of distance.

Hatimaye – To bring an end (Hutt-ee-my-ee)

Etterian

Alodon (A-low-donn): who accidentally shot his balls off with his own blaster.

Teacher: lima (lee-ma)

Great teacher: lima kuu: (lee-ma koo)

Directions: semit (semm-it)

Lemon: giyua (gee-you-a)

Young one: damu (daa-moo)

Heart: ensa (enn-sa)

Heart of my heart: ensa ra ensa (enn-sa raa enn-sa)

Beloved: thamani (ta-mar-nee)

Little joy: minus susa (mee-nas soo-sa)

Little cat: minus cesu (mee-nas sess-oo)

Large: magnus (mag-nis)

Orgasm: fulfillment/deite asteri (see stars) / released (day-ta ass-tare-ree)

Starfighter: asteri peju (ass-tare-ree pear-joo)

Collection of glass vials: virak (vee-ruck)

Scum of the galaxies: xemi (ze-mee)

Hair up: malia pa (Mar-lee-a par)

Hair down: malia pado (Mar-lee-a par-dow)

Lysaran

Visitor: kashi (Kaa-shee)

God: Kaiha (Kigh-haa)

King: Kuna (Koo-na)

Orange fleshy fruit: Lemte (Lem-ta)

White flowers: Myameru (My-a-me-roo)

Precious: Delica (Dell-ee-ka)

Sweetheart: Sali (Saa-lee)

Arum Lily-type flower: D'nastu (D-nass-too)

Love Blossom: aroa loulu (A-row-a low-loo)

Maloidian

Title of respect: lommia (Lomm-ee-a)

Stubborn, lethal tree: tewaa (Tee-wah)

Tokauri/Kulai

Blade – Sulac (soo-lack)

Bone – Ukog (you-cog) - bone from some dumb animal, probably an ukog.

Braided – Gisul (gee-sool)

Father – Danno (dan-no)

Heart – Kassu (cass-soo)

Maker – Mugbu (Mug-boo)

Mother – Manno (man-no)

Sapphires – Buha (boo-ha)

Shit – Saho (sa-ho)

Star - stuon (stoo-on)

Stupid – Ungog (oon-gog)

Vessel/ship - sakay (sa-kay)

Viqrian

Haiz – Haze

Kaara – Karr-rah

Shioll – She-oll

Tagana – tar-garn-ah

Tarni – Tarr-nee

Viqrian – Vick-ree-in

Pronunciations

Names

Aaro - Ah-row

Adda – Ay-dah

Aldur - Al-durr

Alllero - A-le-row

Balllio – Bah-leee-oh

Bos - Boss

Bry-dar - Brigh-darr

Brynr - Brin-ner

Cales - Cale-es

Cento - Sen-tow

Cewa – Cue-wah

Citus - Sigh-tuss

Coldar - Coal-daar

Cria - Kree-ah

Eriz - Sigh-low

Danic - Dan-eek

Deeezo – Dee-zoh

Der - Durr

Diso - Dee-sow

Diyo - Die-oh

Eira - Eye-raa

Enyl - E-neel

Eriz - E-rizz

Garix - Ga-ricks

Gayn - Gain

Iddan - Ee-dann

Idon - Eye-donn

Illan - Ee-lann

Jarg – Jar-g

Jokta - Jock-tar

Kanzo - Can-zow

Keelu – Key-loo

Keryr – Kerr-eer

Ksal - Ka-sell

Lazu – Lah-zoo

Lurz - Lurr-z

Malo - Mail-oh

Matir - Mat-teer

Myan - My-ann

Myn-ras - Min-russ

Naio – Nay-oh

Nerx - Nurcks

Nuos - New-oss

Oyaz - Oh-yaz

Prex - Precks

Ronin - Row-nin

Saan - Sarn

Sena - See-na

Siio – See-ooo

Sy'mar - Sigh-marr

Syna - Sigh-na

Tamra – Tum-rah

Taro - Tah-row

Tenu - Ten-oo

Trav - Trahv

Tinh - Tin

Vytus - Vie-tuss

Vodin - Vo-din

Ulriq - Yule-rick

Vorn - Vawn

Vyar - Vie-arr

Xan - Zan

Xeus – Zeus

Zaro - Zah-row

Ziot - Zye-ott

Places

Aberdus – A-burr-diss

Argaxx – Are-jax

Berrann – Burr-anne – A waterfall near Nerx's childhood home on the mining moon Fuyra.

Crustiiu – Criss-tee-oo

Dyuqa - Dee-you-ka

Etteria – E-tare-rea

Gaelsi – Gale-zee

Galaza – Gah-lar-zah

Gikaet – Gee-ka-ett

Iphara = Ee-far-ra

Kulai – koo-ligh

Lysara – Liss-saa-ra

Luchur – Loo-churr

Mascroba – Mus-crow-ba

Sarvis – Sarr-viss

Sosu – Sow-soo

Tokauri – Too-cow-ree

Yithia – Yith-ee-a

Battleships

Bronvol – Bronn-vole – Viqrian battle cruiser.

Chikara – Chee-kar-a - Force

Gladio – Glad-ee-oh – Sword

Kunakar – Koo-narr-karr - Viqrian battle cruiser.

Kushin – Cush-shin - To Pierce

Surata – Soo-ra-tah – Beginning

Usaha – Oo-saa-hah - Endeavor

Shuttles

/Smaller ships

Celeeri – See-lee-ree - swift

Denessi – Denn-ess-ee - sodge

Eshima – Ee-shee-ma - respect

Kevol – Kev-oll - agony

Kuta – Koo-tah - modular shuttle.

Liri-ny – Lee-ree-nye – freedom

Misaia – Miss-aye-a - memory

Sasay – Sass-ay - whispers

Yakin – Yuck-kin - belief

Yarva – Yarr-vuh – Viqrian name for a shuttle/kuta.

Creatures

Asnu – Ass-Noo – buffalo/donkey

Eiltur – Ale-turr

Gracc – Grrr-ack

Ilag – Ee-Lug– leggy slugs that feast on sol.

Kreso – Kreh-soo

Omeika – Oh-may-ka

Pagsu – Pug-Soo - cocksuckers

Reshy – Resh-Ee - huge, like the size of a kuta shuttle, with massive jaws and rows of sharp teeth.

Sogair – Sow-gare

Wilanegy – Will-anna-jee

Znorg – Zuh-norg

About the Author

Sevannah Storm is a fiction writer who immerses herself in fantastical worlds both magical and science fiction. She has a flair for the creative having studied art and interior architecture and spends her time drawing, oil painting, and writing. An avid reader from an early age, Sevannah finds her inspiration from various sources: games, novels, music, and the land of make-believe. The unique versus the practical has brought on numerous debates.

In her spare time, she does Krav Maga, CrossFit, and rereads novels that snatch her breath away. Having embraced the social media world, you can find her on most platforms.

Her home is a land south of Wakanda, where animals roam free. Born in Zimbabwe, she grew up in South Africa. The crisp blue skies with cotton-candy sunsets expand her heart and soul, encapsulating a sense of freedom.

Words she lives by: "Know your pothole and dodge it. Don't work in a pencil factory if you're a vampire."

Sevannah loves to hear from her readers. You can find and connect with her at the links below.

Website/Newsletter:

https://www.sevannahstorm.com/

Facebook:

https://www.facebook.com/sevannah.storm

Instagram:

https://www.instagram.com/sevannah.storm/

Twitter:

https://twitter.com/sevannah_storm

Thank you for taking the time to read Lust Forged. If you enjoyed the story, please tell your friends and leave a review. Reviews support authors and ensure they continue to bring readers books to love and enjoy.

SOUL FORGED

FATE FORGED

The Gifting Series #2

Jacqueline (Jack) Dunois struggles to find a man not intimidated by her career as a law enforcement instructor, especially in the small town she calls home. She would sacrifice a kidney to find someone who would make her ovaries clap and didn't live with his mother. Then she meets a supreme commander from another world who thinks the stars in the galaxies shine in her eyes... What's not to love about that?

Supreme Commander Ulriq doesn't believe in love, an archaic term for a volatile and untrustworthy emotion that Etterians were no longer subjected to. Until he meets Jack who triggers the Ethera, the soulmate force that irrevocably changes a male when he finds his ideal female. At that moment, his world, his focus, his very loyalty shifts. But when she is taken from him, it is too much to bear. Under the influence of the Ethera, he launches a rescue. He'll start a war and kill anyone who dares stop him, just to have her back in his arms.

Read it here:

https://books2read.com/u/bMY09v

SUN FORGED

Meeting a drop-dead gorgeous man, who falls onto a knee the first time they meet, sounded too good to be true for Ava. Of course, with her luck, he had to be an alien. Thrust into an unknown alien world, meeting weird and scary creatures, and fearing for her life, Ava tries to survive as best as a hairstylist can.

Kanzo never expected to find a life mate, a Dar Eth. Since he was young, he was taught that pairings were rare with fewer females born. The statistics on finding his Dar Eth would be slim to none. Instead of dreaming and longing for companionship, he focused on being the best male possible, to end his life on a battlefield with honor. But when he experiences the Ethera—the life mate force, and is blessed with his female, he isn't prepared for the level of pain, pleasure, and need she invokes within him.

Unable to save her as she's teleported from him, the dark consuming pain in his chest drives him into a blinding rage. With no idea who stole her or where to begin the search, he will scour the known universe to find her, to hold the female he never wanted.

Read it here:

https://books2read.com/u/3n5vaB

WAR FORGED

THE GIFTING SERIES #4

Being kidnapped by aliens does not sit well with Quinlan. Not only would her seven guardians give her hell if she doesn't attempt some sort of escape, but she refuses to be at anybody's mercy. With her practiced military skills, the help of an underground lounge singer and a personal assistant, she takes over the alien slave ship. Not knowing how to fly the damn thing, she sends a distress signal. ...The rescue comes swiftly in the form of a bronzed man with exquisite ice-blue eyes. Leaving her to ask the true question: has she just given up her newfound freedom for a gorgeous man who seems determined to have her for eternity?

As Elite Supreme Commander of the Etterian Forces, Xan answers a distress call in Earth English. That is all he did. The female who captured the slave ship shows remarkable skill, making her a warrior in her own right. Said skills should be respected and honored. Except she is his Dar Eth, calling forth the Ethera—the soulmate bond. How can he protect his female when she can do so herself? What can she possibly need from him? What can he offer a female, not Etterian but human? Not that he can think clearly in her presence when she scents so good and makes him want to kiss all of her.

Maker help him.

Read it here:

https://books2read.com/u/bz1QGD

STAR FORGED

The Gifting Series #5

Macy is feeling a little left out, as usual. Who would have thought moving from one planet to another wouldn't change that loneliness? She is never alone these days since Etterians guard human women with an urgency she understands. But the lack of companionship is like a dark aching abyss inside her chest. On some days, it threatens to implode, and Macy Mitchell would cease to exist. Looming is her impending meeting with King Xeus of Etteria. How is she supposed to keep her shit together when presented to royalty? Not after she ran from the last king she met.

For Xeus, the void expands daily. Duty, honor, concern for his dying people, and endless loneliness fill his life. Having decided to search for pairings among other worlds, he is pleased his son found his soulmate among human women. It doesn't mean that Xeus's loneliness and longing haven't ended until he stumbles upon a crying female. Meaning only to soothe, he is spellbound when her presence brings him peace. Unable to resist, he forms an attachment to a female he can never have

Read it here:

https://books2read.com/u/3nXgp5

SHADOW FORGED

Forty-year-old Caroline is too old to start dating and too bored with her vibrator, but what other choices does she have. On the day she burns her shirt and breaks a fingernail, she meets Etterian warriors. As part of her job at E.S.A. (Earth Space Association,) she must 'entertain' the hot-as-apple-pie Chief Engineer she suspects isn't who he claims to be.

Operations Commander Malo, Head of Espionage, must act as an engineer and ambassador, hoping to invite human females to visit Etteria and save his dying race. From Princess Oriana, he has strict instructions to distrust humans. What he finds he cannot trust are his emotions and his body whenever in the presence of the human ambassador, Caroline. She does not believe in soulmates or in a forever with him. Convincing her to choose him is the greatest task ever set before him, one he cannot afford to fail.

Until she is stolen from him. He calls in favors, utilizes all his resources to find her. And *when* he does, he is never letting her off his battleship...or his bed.

Read it here:

https://books2read.com/u/bPNd8j

EARTH FORGED

The Gifting Series #7

Guilt hounds Izzy, who caused her sister's injury and subsequent blindness. But no matter how she cares for Simone or what she sacrifices, it doesn't ease the ache in her chest. With Simone and naive Caro, her best friend, Izzy's role as protector is fully realized. The cost? Hiding behind quirkiness, pseudo-joy, and giving up her hopes and dreams. What she needs is a knight in any armor. After all, beggars can't be fussy. She has no idea that armor, in her case, means black military and that a knight could come in any color, specifically bronze.

Oyaz wants to find his life force, his soulmate, and he'd like her to be human. Earth's females are soft, amusing, passionate, and their scents rival a garden of hahyt blossoms. His task is to guard their planet that promises so many salvations for his males. It's a duty he's pleased to perform, one he would die for. When Operations Commander Malo orders Oyaz to retrieve a human female, he's eager to oblige. That it would lead to his salvation is something he couldn't anticipate. What he hadn't planned for is an ambush that costs him more than his memory, the loss of his soulmate.

Now what? Nothing in their training prepared him for this.

And yet, despite not remembering kneeling for Izzy, he longs to claim her with every inch of his soul.

Read it here:

https://books2read.com/u/31V82D

LUST FORGED

THE GIFTING SERIES #8

Ex-socialite Leona wants nothing more than to enhance the mechanics within sex-cybs, not to mention improve their performances with their 'lovers.' It's a job where she's safe in an all-woman factory on Callisto, and far from her matchmaking mama. When the chief engineer is incapacitated, Leona's required to gift—her term would be pimp—sex-cyborgs to prospective clients. On an Etterian battleship, surrounded by gorgeous males, she tries not to think of sex when it's her work, especially with the Sub-Commander Aaro whose neon-blue eyes are the stuff of her erotic dreams.

As a diplomatic favor, Aaro must abandon his task to guard Earth, and perhaps find his Dar Eth or soulmate, all to protect cargo en route to many worlds, including the dangerous and unpredictable Yithia. Princess Oriana is most concerned for the two human female engineers determined to ensure the deliveries are successful. A simple enough mission until one human enters Aaro's cargo bay, dropping him to his knees.

But revealing to independent Leona that she's now trapped in a marriage isn't something Aaro can bring himself to do. He violates all he stands for, every ounce of honor by not telling her the truth. All in the hopes that she will choose to love him.

Read it here:

https://books2read.com/u/3LdA1w